HUNTERS

A MORNINGSTAR STRAIN NOVEL
(Z.A. RECHT'S MORNINGSTAR STRAIN)

DAWN PEERS

PERMUTED
PRESS

A PERMUTED PRESS BOOK

ISBN: 978-1-68261-231-6
ISBN (eBook): 978-1-68261-232-3

Hunters
A Morningstar Strain Novel
(Z.A. Recht's Morningstar Strain)
© 2018 by Dawn Peers
All Rights Reserved

PERMUTED
PRESS

Permuted Press, LLC
New York • Nashville
permutedpress.com

Published in the United States of America

DEDICATION

To the memory of ZA Recht. Your imagination changed my world.

CHAPTER 1

NEW ENDINGS

"*WELCOME TO FORT HOOD, Home of America's Armored Corps.* At least that's what it *used* to say." Brewster grinned sardonically and held out his goggles. "The place looks like it's gone to shit. Just as well it's us paying them a visit, and not General Sherman."

Krueger rolled his eyes, accustomed by now to the darker side of Brewster's humor. He glanced down the comfortable and familiar NVGs, scanning across the entrance to Fort Hood, Texas; the world's largest military base bar none, and the last bastion of the sinking ship of the RSA. Krueger whistled lightly under his breath.

"It's *President* Sherman, dumbass, though you're not wrong. I was expecting more from these guys, to be honest, after everything they've put us through."

The RSA had been a thorn in their side seemingly since the start of the Morningstar outbreak. Craving power for themselves, they'd harried and harassed all efforts to reassemble the traditional power structure of the United States, choosing to try and enforce their own military-based rule.

"Why? We've got them on the run, man. This is it—their last stand."

"Exactly," Krueger responded grimly. "We've seen their outposts before. Shit, without you, we'd never have penetrated Mount Weather in time. That place was a fortress." Krueger carried on quickly before Brewster took the opportunity to add more fuel to the fire of his ever-burning ego. "What I'm saying is, this isn't like them. They're an *organization*. They have structure. This," Krueger dashed a gloved hand in the direction of Fort Hood. "Isn't them. Something's off."

"I don't know, man. Maybe our hard work has paid off. The RSA command was decimated at Mount Weather. They can't have any real leadership left. Our luck could finally be turning."

"It's the end of the world. You know what Sherriff Keaton always says."

"Yeah, I know. *Nothing is ever easy*. So, what do you think is happening in there?"

"You tell me. This is your rodeo. You got experience with your recon of Mount Weather. What's your feeling here?"

"I had weeks checking out those guys. Holed up in that fortress, they had a slick operation. It was only towards the end when morale dropped, and they started in-fighting that I really made any headway. They weren't exactly sloppy. Down there just looks half-cocked, as if they're running on autopilot, you know? We haven't seen any scouts posted, and there's no guard rotation. I can't see any defined groups or command. They know the motions they're meant to go through; there's just no one there to give 'em any direction."

"Is that what your gut is telling you or is that what you see down there?" Krueger grunted.

Sighing, Brewster snatched the goggles back and took another slower, more scrutinizing look at the men and women milling between the uniform brick buildings and concrete courtyards. Half a dozen seemed to be out in the open at any one time, their focus on a couple of curtained transports parked with the driver cab facing out toward the watching soldiers. They all still wore the anonymous black BDUs synonymous with RSA personnel. There were no insignias to speak of to distinguish one rank from another.

Fort Hood was massive. Brewster had forgotten, in his years away from the sprawling complex, just how over-awing the scope of the base was. Unparalleled worldwide in its size, he and Krueger had left their men behind on the far east of Killeen while they scoped out the base from various vantage points around the town. Their last spot was on the eastern side where they could check the edge of the airbase as well as any potential transports. Despite the terrifying wealth of firepower Fort Hood should have had available to it, they were both underwhelmed by what they saw so far.

The abandoned buildings and the disarray across the compound should have had them both pumping their fists. Sherman had sent them here tentatively to scout before launching a potential attack. A victory here would be easy, even with the relatively small detachment they had with them. Krueger felt unsettled. This was far too easy; something was off.

"Krueger, do you see what I see?"

Shaking his head, Krueger held his hands out again for the goggles. "What am I looking for, Brewster?"

"Two o'clock, by the residential blocks. Got it?"

Krueger focused his attention as directed, swearing under his breath at what he saw. "Is that...?"

"It's not as if they've never used them before. Are you actually surprised?"

Five men had moved out of the side door from one of the red-bricked housing blocks Brewster had indicated. Each wielded a long pole with a leash on the end, not unlike those used by impounders. The creature at the end of each pole had Krueger breaking out in a cold sweat. Snarling jaws snapped as the infected twisted in their restraints, trying to turn and reach the hot living flesh walking just behind them. One, a shambler by the look of his face, missing its lower jaw and left ear, buckled at the knees. The soldier trying to steer it dropped too. His colleagues spared him a disparaging glance before moving forward, leaving him to try and push the infected back as he staggered to his knees.

"Where have they found that many infected way out here?"

"Killeen is a ghost town, so my guess is they've been here since the start. I wonder how many deadasses just ended up drifting down here?"

"There's five closed transports in the main square, Krueger, plus the one they're loading now. We have to assume if the other five aren't already full, they soon will be. They're not transporting bananas. You know what? I've got an idea."

Krueger dropped the goggles. Propped up on his elbows, he glared at Brewster. "Care to share it with me?"

Brewster threw Krueger a grin. "Not yet. We just need to wait a bit longer. I don't want them to leave our transports half-empty."

★★★★★

Krueger was a patient man. His years of training, and his discipline as a sniper had molded a certain iron will that never wavered. Still, there was something about Brewster's casual humor in the face of adversity that rubbed him the wrong way. With the remnants of the RSA about to head out of the gates of Fort Hood with truckloads of shamblers, their target unknown, Brewster remained incredibly cagey about sharing details. He even sounded amused, both by what he was concocting and by Krueger's frustration at being unable to extract any more details.

Interestingly, Brewster had pointed out that the RSA troops didn't appear to be in a hurry to leave. As Krueger had eyed the C&C area, Brewster described blow-by-blow what he thought the soldiers were up to. Krueger had to hand it to him. He'd been right, on every count, and hadn't even been looking. At that point, they'd called in to the rest of the command unit, letting them know they were on their way back to the rest of the Hunters.

Hunters. This was their test run—not that this assignment in Fort Hood was public knowledge. The Hunters were President Sherman's idea—both the unit and the objective for their beta mission. The rest of the fledgling US government wasn't so keen on either the founding of the Hunters or Sherman's vision for them. Unlike the self-serving, career-chasing politicians surrounding him, however, Krueger and Brewster, along with the hand-picked specialists on their team, had been knee-deep in the shitstorm caused by the Morningstar strain since the very beginning. Sherman knew that to stand a chance of reunifying the United States, he needed to start establishing power centers under his command. The Hunters were the first step towards achieving this goal. His vision was an elite and trusted core unit of soldiers, bloodied and tested at every stage of the Morningstar pandemic.

And, unbelievably, Ewan Brewster, former Private First Class, was their Commander.

"You think this…this *plan* is actually going to work? Back when television *was* a thing, someone would be calling this nonsense a hare-brained scheme. He's going to get everyone killed!" Major Bentley had been opposed to both the Hunters and Sherman's vision for them from the outset.

Sherman paced the floor, annoyed already with the constant bickering between the men and women that were supposed to form the backbone of his support. Sherman had seen Brewster in action from the earliest days of the conflict. Even back in Cairo as a cocky private, he'd shown flashes of brilliance that had helped keep hope alive even during the darkest moments of the outbreak. It was the soldier's creative spark, something borne out of a desire to live, rather than the desire to follow the rules, which appeared to drive every other soldier. That appealed to Sherman the most.

In his days as a general, Sherman wouldn't have put Brewster in charge of a coffee pot, let alone the deuces he drove through the desert. Since then, Sherman had seen Ewan Brewster save the free world—more than once—and he was willing to put his faith in that man to lead the team of Hunters. Sherman didn't care what others said about his soldiers when they thought he wasn't listening. Career military like Bentley and Spivey might struggle to understand, but they, most of all, should know that brilliance can often be borne out of ignorance.

"Right now, Major, and since this all began, my soldiers have been the ones staring this threat in the face. I trust them to make the right decisions in pressured situations, and I would stake my life on it. If they execute Fort Hood as they've suggested, with the worst of our opposition finally suppressed, we can get to the matter in hand that we all *really* care about—ridding the world of this infection and rebuilding our country."

A tense silence settled in the room. Bentley seemed to shiver as if shaking off an unwanted thought. "Of course, Mr. President. You've led us this far. It would be wrong to question you now."

Francis almost winced. He abhorred his new title, and the last thing he wanted now was to be surrounded by supplicants. All he asked was for them to have a little faith in him and his men, in the here and now.

By God, Brewster, they're right. Your plan is insane, but I trust you; you'd better not screw this up.

★★★★★

Brewster stood at the center of a small circle of unimpressed colleagues. He'd started explaining his strategy to them. Already he thought it could be a hard sell.

"They're not going anywhere for a reason. It's dead around here—almost literally. There are no shamblers in Killeen. No survivors either, unless they're really good at hide and seek. You know what that means?"

Castillo folded her arms across her chest, her head cocked. Brewster had the cynical veteran intrigued, at least. "Go on."

"Well, it could mean two things. That they've cleared the place out for us, and there's no threat. That includes picking all the homes and stores dry—which we know they've only partially done because of the recon so far. We've gotten supplies from a sporting goods store *and* a pharmacy, and I'd expect those to be clean. Everywhere we've checked has had zero infected."

"What else could it be?"

"Simple. The place is clear of infected because they're inside that compound. The RSA aren't moving out because they know they have the threat contained. They're preparing—getting ready to attack us…" Brewster rolled his eyes. "Again."

"So, why have they stopped?"

Brewster grinned. "Because they've spotted us. Now, they're waiting for *us* to attack."

"How the fuck is that a good thing? First, you're telling us they have weapons *and* infected, and now you think they're expecting us?"

"No. They're expecting an army." Brewster gesticulated at their little circle. "They're not expecting us."

The five soldiers gaped, but only for a moment. Krueger; Garibaldi, beaten and battered, but alive after his experiences at Mount Weather; Castillo, formerly Garibaldi's squad leader; Kiley, a trusted soldier from the hospital squad in Omaha; and Brent, newly transferred from McChord and introduced to the Hunters as one of the toughest melee soldiers still alive.

Between them, they knew they shared a wealth of RSA- and infected-fighting expertise. But...*alone?* "We've got dozens of soldiers waiting to move with us, Brewster. Isn't this suicide?" Castillo, used to taking the lead, didn't hesitate to question his angles.

"There are less of us, so it's going to be harder for them to locate the threat once we've set a few tactical charges. I'm guessing there can't be that many of those RSA fuckers left, from what we've seen, and right now they've been caught red-handed loading their infected goods into a convoy. They'll think we have them outnumbered, so they're going to figure they can use the territory to their advantage. I'm willing to bet high stakes that not one of them knows that complex as well as we should.

"I'm going to call in a strike deliberately at the far end of the compound, closer to the landing strip. They'll be scared, sure, but they'll have no idea where we're coming from."

"And once they're looking the other way..." Krueger realized where Brewster was leading with this.

"We hit them quick and hard."

"Still...just the six of us?" Brent asked, mystified.

Brewster smiled. It was a thin line; not a pleasant expression. "No, not just us. We need to get to those shamblers."

★★★★★

Nestled in the west of Killeen, the former military base of Fort Hood *sprawled.* Moving from the civilian area to the military base, you'd first encounter accommodation for families; entertainment; stores. All the trappings of domestic life. As Brewster crept past these buildings, sorely aware of just how desolately empty they all seemed, he was struck by how hard the pandemic had hit America.

Even here, in a base with more than enough military personnel off deployment to cope with any normal assault in peacetime, and with a fierce arsenal at their disposal, they had been utterly overrun. Lawns that had once been finely manicured were overgrown into a miniature forest, a sprawling mass of gnarled knots of debris and weeds. Peeling window frames held shards of shattered glass. Desiccated corpses were strewn around, now nothing more than a backdrop to a world gone mad.

At least with the RSA finally gone, the free men and women of Sherman's America might stand a chance of reclaiming and cleaning up places like this; even easier if they had been picked to the bone. Shit, ghost towns like this were a damn sight easier than trying to clear out city centers. He knew at face value his plan was simple. Brewster liked to avoid *complicated*. More steps just left more scope for error. He had learned the hard way, losing too many friends to overcomplicated, to hesitation, and to mercy.

Brewster reached position. He was on the edge of the civvy accommodation and took up a spot in an end house with a clear enough view to the C&C where the shamblers were loaded. Krueger would take up his traditional sharpshooting position to Brewster's southwest, with the remaining Hunters flanked out surrounding the C&C and armed to the teeth.

Personnel from McChord were already on their way. Now, they just had to wait.

The post-Morningstar U.S. had no commercial aircraft. The lack of constant vehicle noise had taken some getting used to initially. As a result, when planes did approach, ears accustomed to the silence seemed to hear them much sooner. It wasn't long, therefore, before the RSA followers stopped loading shamblers and looked to the sky.

Brewster had asked for something ostentatiously loud. He didn't believe what remained of the RSA had the experience or hierarchy to understand what kind of hardware Sherman's men could throw at them now. Moreover, Fort Hood was a huge asset, and if they could take it without damaging too much of the base, all the better. Brewster had asked them to drop just south of Cowhouse Creek. It was close enough to look threatening and cause panic, but far enough away from the base and, critically in Brewster's mind, the airfield, that the majority should remain fully intact.

As expected, you could hear the whining approach of the aircraft long before you could see them. Brewster was stunned to see a trio of Bones break the skyline, screaming towards their position. They took a low trajectory and dropped their payload. All of the Hunters settled in around the loading bay of infected, covered their ears. None closed their eyes. They had to make sure that the decoy worked. Their targets needed to scatter.

It worked perfectly. Brewster grinned as the RSA skittered away from the trucks and into hiding, like rats heading for the gutters. They wouldn't need another pass.

He palmed the radio. "McChord, this is Hunter One. Mission accomplished—go home. Hunter Team, we are go."

Krueger had to bite his lip and bide his time when Brewster's signal came over the radio. His own orders were clear, and unfortunately, they made sense: hold fire. The squad was to make it look like Sherman was attacking with a huge force. With how disorganized their enemy seemed, it wouldn't take much effort to make the Hunters look like real predators. With pressing fire coming from all sides, the aim was to push them back to those hot trucks. Once there, Krueger, with his sharp eye and steady hand, would unleash on the unsuspecting enemy the hell they'd been preparing to inevitably steer towards Omaha.

"Come on, guys," Krueger whispered as he shifted, taking up a position comfortable enough to keep his eyes down the scope. *Give me something to do.*

Castillo had to admit her blood was pumping. It seemed like a foolish idea, but with twilight and dusk descending into night, it was begrudgingly evident that Brewster's stunt had some merit. Minimal casualties; minimal exposure; minimal expenditure. Sure, it was a huge risk for those involved, and they all knew, after the efforts to recover Omaha, that small tacops didn't always work. That was in the past. They'd all learned lessons since then.

For example, here, they'd keep away from the fucking infected.

As the bombers scythed through the sky, she prepped her M4 carbine. Once their payload dropped, Castillo threw a couple of grenades into the edge of the yard. She was so far from the transports that it didn't even particularly matter how good her aim was. Step one of Brewster's plan was chaos. For payback at the obliteration of her squad on Mount Weather, Castillo was ready to deliver.

Garibaldi knew he should feel nervous. He'd been in worse spots, even before Morningstar. This mission, though, felt different. He knew that he was a part of something big. With Dr. Demillio's efforts to finally create a vaccine for Morningstar, Garibaldi knew he was on the right edge of the side about to turn the tide. For the first time since the plague began, he was beginning to believe they could win. Only their long-term enemy, the RSA, stood in the way of progress now.

The planes approached. Garibaldi set his game face. Time to clear the board.

Kiley and Brent were within eyeshot of each other, not that the RSA had spotted them yet. The closest Hunters to the shambler threat, the pair of them represented the fake face of the assault from the direction of Fort Hood's airbase. One would hammer out suppressing shots, while the other laid waste with fire. The devastation at New Abraham at the hands of the RSA showed Sherman's men just how devastating flames could be. It wasn't a pretty tactic, but they weren't aiming for pretty. They were aiming for victory.

Brent took off his safety, palming his vest for the magazines he already knew were there, ready to reload. Kiley put on his goggles, mentally psyching himself in anticipation of the destruction he was about to lay down. It was going to be hard mentally, not physically. Burning; that was a hard way for any man to go.

Brent shook his head, clearing his mind. He knew what sort of crimes the RSA had committed in the name of freedom since zombies took over the world. These weren't men. They were animals, and they were what stood in the way of a Morningstar-free United States.

Fort Hood burned.

Hot orange flames and plumes of choking black smoke poured into the twilight sky as the six Hunters unleashed their carefully-selected and expertly-targeted arsenal into the bodies of the fleeing RSA.

Krueger watched it all through his scope. It was a massacre. The best men and women of the RSA were already long dead. The remnants and stragglers panicked and left at the first explosion. They didn't stand a chance of resisting whatever Sherman's best chose to throw at them.

Krueger pulled his head back when Kiley stepped forward: he didn't fancy burned corneas as a flamethrower lit up the point of his scope. Little licks of flame ignited the edge of night as the RSA tried to retaliate. Then Brent, Castillo, and Brewster stepped up for their part, cutting through the haphazard enemy like a hot knife through soft butter.

Krueger sighed. It looked like he wouldn't be needed until the grand finale. Still, small though his contribution would be, he'd make sure the show they were putting on for the political brass went off with a real bang.

Brewster hung back, his immediate job done. He already knew that he'd prefer to be in the thick of things, but Sherman had told him in no uncertain terms that to lead the Hunters was to be aware of your team and their safety, not just your own orders. It may be his first command, but Brewster knew the skills of the small team Sherman assembled for him, and the former PFC would be no use to anyone swinging his gun around. From his vantage point, he saw near two-dozen RSA scatter, pouring out of the command building and bunkers and heading straight for the perimeter fences of the compound. They'd be the cowards; the ones that had joined up just for safety in numbers. It was anarchy down at the C&C and to the casual observer, it looked like the Hunters had won the day with ease.

Brewster knew, though, that this was far from over. *Nothing was ever easy.*

Even as he thought this, a unit peeled out from a warehouse door, keeping in some semblance of a formation and firing in Brent's direction. Brewster grabbed his radio, knowing he was going into an earpiece worn by each member of the squad. "Castillo, I need some of those grenades over towards the C&C."

She wouldn't be able to respond verbally, but ten seconds later the air thumped faintly as three blooms of fire sent two of the soldiers to the ground, with the remaining eight turning, now uncertain about where the threat was coming from. Brewster grinned, though the feeling of success didn't last long as another two dozen soldiers sprinted out of another warehouse. They weren't as disciplined as the first unit, most of them running in completely different directions. Crucially though, they all headed towards transports loaded with infected.

"Krueger, you're up. Pop the two trucks closest to Castillo's position."

Expecting nothing but brilliance from probably the best sniper left alive in the country, Krueger shot off the simple locks keeping the wagon doors shut. Loaded to the brim with infected, the shamblers spilled out onto the tarmac. Panic set in with this new threat, and the RSA turned their fire to the corpses now struggling to their feet in search of a new meal.

"They're distracted. Brent, Kiley, finish this."

Brewster put down his binoculars as the screams started. He didn't want to see how this ended. His stomach twisted at the stench of scorching flesh. He walked back towards Killeen with the feeling of bitter satisfaction at a job well done.

CHAPTER 2

PARADE

"CAN YOU BELIEVE HOW far we've come, Mark?"

Mark Stiles' heart burst with pride at what he'd seen and heard this week. To hear Rebecca, his beloved wife, so vibrant and full of hope made it leap another beat to full. To see near a thousand survivors and citizens of Omaha gathered to witness the opening of their first fully-functional post-outbreak hospital was nothing short of unbelievable. Angela Castillo, one of the victors in what they hoped was the last assault against the RSA, stood on the makeshift podium alongside Rebecca and Mark. More than anyone else, she knew what heartaches and losses lay behind those walls.

They all keenly remembered the cost of the first attempt to claim one of Omaha's overrun hospitals for the residents of their growing city. Now, though, that same hospital wasn't just secure, it stood empty of infected, had been cleaned down, and contained enough rudimentary medicine, power, and services, to serve as an almost completely operational facility. While it would be a long time yet until they were capable of advanced surgical procedures, and they had no life support facilities, there were other, more pressing matters at hand. Mark glanced down and grinned at seeing Rebecca's palms resting on her growing belly. At best guess, she was six months along. Rebecca was stubbornly sure that there wouldn't be any problems with the delivery; still, it made Mark feel infinitely more comfortable that her first labor would be attended by professionals in a sterile and safe environment.

It would be hard for her to manage the medical care of the entire community with a baby to look after, but Mark knew that, like with everything else she did, Rebecca would excel at her new and infinitely-deserved role.

"It's amazing, isn't it?" Mark grabbed Rebecca's free hand and squeezed, just as Danny and Jimmy, part of the original squad to attempt to take the hospital, approached the stage steps. Old habits dying hard, both men threw smart salutes as they approached both the savior of the new free world and their old squad leader. Neither Danny nor Jimmy were military men now, so Mark waved them down, instead clasping each of their arms in a warm and friendly greeting. Angela pushed him to one side, embracing them both in a long and sincere hug—Danny and Jimmy had been on her squad to try and take the hospital the first time around.

Jimmy was a farmhand now, helping with the ever-critical task of growing crops for Omaha, and he still did perimeter duty, like most men able to bear arms. Danny was looking forward to volunteering in the medical corps.

"It's good to see you both," Mark said. "You deserve to be up here as much as anyone."

"Thank you, sir, that means a lot," Danny said.

Jimmy nodded in agreement, his face stern. "We've all lost a lot getting to this point. I can't believe we actually have a working hospital. It doesn't seem real."

"Oh, it's real alright," Rebecca said. "And a good job too. I'm not sure how much bigger Omaha could have grown without a hospital to serve everyone. It's not as if it's all roses and light out there these days."

Mark reached out to hold Rebecca's hand. Those darker days she mentioned were further apart now, but the young medic was right. Their security and safety seemed to come at a continuous cost. While the assault on Fort Hood had gone almost without error, they were still far from safe and self-sufficient. Supply runs were still a necessity, and skirmishes were a daily occurrence; that didn't take into account the basic daily needs of a human community. Wanting to keep the tone light, though, he couldn't help but say, "I'm not sure how much bigger Omaha could get, either. Are we ready to get this show on the road?"

The group of friends and colleagues turned to the crowd, buzzing with anticipation, Mark reached into his pocket to grab an agonizingly-written and extensively-rehearsed speech. He cleared his throat and approached the podium—a small microphone intending to broadcast his message—when a tumult at the back caught everyone's attention. It started out as a few exclamations, turning quickly into screams as a path opened in the crowd towards the stage, like Moses parting the deep waves of the Red Sea.

"Get back, Becky," Mark said, calling her by her nickname in his haste. "Jimmy, get her out of here." Mark had no idea what was happening yet, but with people scattering as they were, there was no way it was going to be good.

"I got her. Becky, come on," Angela's voice cut through the mayhem threatening to break out, tugging at Becky and imploring her to retreat to safety. Mark made a mental note to thank the woman later.

Sane thoughts melted away though when the cause of the chaos finally emerged no more than a hundred yards from the stage. An absolute giant of a man strode confidently towards them. He must have been nearing seven feet tall, with mountainous shoulders and a barrel of a stomach. Thick black hair was highlighted with a shock of gray running from the center of the forehead, graying stubble scattered over a jaw set with purpose. This man radiated strength; he'd need it for what he brought through the crowd. Held at the end of a sturdy animal trap was a fully alive, snarling, hungry sprinter.

Sprinters. A rare breed, these days. The people of Omaha were *guaranteed* safety from infection. The majority of infected out in the wilderness might have been sprinters once, but most had died of their wounds or starved long ago. The rotting shamblers that managed to get to the edge of the Omaha safe zone's border fence, even on the sides still facing the populated city, were easily taken out by the patrols of five that regularly policed the perimeter.

Mark shuddered at the sight of the vicious, snarling reminder of what Morningstar represented—what they had all somehow survived. The hulking man came forward, no one seemingly brave or alert enough to stop him. Finally, as if shaken from a waking dream, a group of men and women from Omaha's evolving police force rushed to the edge of the stage and brought their sidearms to bear.

"Freeze," one of them yelled. "Stop where you are!"

As soon as the crowd realized they weren't in immediate danger, they held their ground. It was *meant* to be the opening of their hospital. But no. Something significant—something *disruptive* was taking place. Like slowing down to watch a car wreck, no one could take their eyes off the scene.

Mark's eyes were practically out on stalks at the grasping, scowling creature that had been brought within these safe walls and to within mere meters of his wife—and his child.

One of the friendliest men in Omaha snapped. "Who the fuck are you," Mark raised his voice over the hubbub. "And what do you want?"

Mark felt a thousand feet tall, but this man guiding a sprinter with casual ease simply laughed. It was a laugh so forceful the man's ribcage almost rattled. It wasn't a sane sound.

The giant man's laughter ceased, and he replaced his maniacal smile with a snarl. "Who am I? You should know, you jumped-up excuse for a soldier." He pointed a large finger at the stage. "So should that bitch standing behind you."

"Who do you think you're talking to, you—"

"No, not your *wife*. The other one." The man spat on the floor. "Castillo."

Angela stepped forward, Becky lingering at the back of the stage behind Jimmy and Danny. None of them, it seemed, were in any immediate danger. If this deranged fool of a man had wanted to hurt people, he'd have simply released that sprinter at the back of the crowd. It wouldn't infect anyone, but by God, it would have been a sore reminder of just how fragile they could still be. No. Whoever he was, he wanted a show.

Angela's brow squinted in a fragment of recognition. "You look like…McCartney?"

The man bowed. "One and the same. David said you were a good squad leader, that you paid attention to your men. Never really believed him, to be honest. I'm a little bit inclined to change my mind."

"But you're not going to." Castillo's voice was stone, her body angled with her hand resting on the M-9 holstered at her side.

"No. I'm Michael, by the way. Did it feel good, building that little hospital on my brother's corpse? Washing his blood from the floor so you could tie a bow on the front door?"

Michael nodded behind the group and the stage, then hawked on the floor again. Almost on reflex, most people turned briefly to look at the building where, what seemed like so long ago, Castillo and her squad had tried the first ill-fated recovery. David McCartney had lost his life in the attempt. His death still cut Castillo deeply, along with every other soldier she'd served alongside who had lost their lives in service to their country.

"Your brother—and for some reason, as you need reminding, millions of others—have died trying to make this country a safer place for the people that have survived Morningstar."

"Oh, so because he's one of many, he's not special? Didn't he *mean* anything? Is that what you're trying to tell me?" Michael's voice hit a fever pitch as he thrust the infected toward the makeshift stage. The crowd ebbed and retreated around him as the barely-restrained sprinter thrashed on its leash. McCartney's forearms bulged as the infected man, who must have been north of two hundred and fifty pounds in life, hissed at the people around him. Bloody stubs of fingers sought out flesh.

McCartney yelled, yanking at the rod and bringing the sprinter to its knees. Those closest simply wanted out of there, though a couple of men pushed their way to the front, hands reaching for their weapons. New Omaha might have the honor of first city in post-Morningstar America to be vaccinated against the virus, but that didn't quell the peoples' fear of getting bit.

"That's not what I'm saying," Castillo responded angrily.

Protective by instinct, Mark stepped forward, his arm against Angela's body. "That's not what anyone is saying, Michael. We are trying to work together to build a new, safe community. We're trying to reclaim a whole damn city, and to do that, there are sacrifices. We've all lost family and friends."

"You've built that hospital on my brother's corpse! None of you standing up there care what happens to us in this city. We work and build, and we guard that perimeter every day. People are dying still, but we're expected to just keep *understanding*? You're murderers, all of you. You don't *deserve* to rule. No one has asked you to do this. We didn't vote for you, or your regime."

Mark shook his head in disbelief. This man was clearly delusional. When they'd come to Omaha, the city had been in ruins. Sherman had dragged their world out of the ashes! And Michael McCartney had the gall to stand in front of them and...

"I'm not alone, Stiles. We're sick of *President* Sherman and his pathetic little government. We're going to take Omaha back and make it our own. You see this?" Michael pushed the sprinter forward again. "You think you've beaten Morningstar? You're wrong. Not everyone wants this vaccine of yours. We don't even believe it works, not all of us. Morningstar happened for a reason, and it was to make sure people like *you* don't have power over people like us anymore. The infected were meant to cleanse the earth of pestilence like you, and we're going to make sure it happens!"

During his rant, the big man's tunnel vision didn't spot Castillo's rapid hand gestures. From the edge of the bystanders, two pairs of men closed in on McCartney. Wary of the sprinter, not wanting that loose in the crowd, one soldier took and landed a clean headshot on the infected before two others leaped at McCartney, flooring him before he could react. At the report of the gunshot, the crowd screamed and dispersed.

Mark considered taking to the microphone again, but it was too late. People fled in every direction, but McCartney was down, and the sprinter eliminated. There wasn't a threat anymore. Still, McCartney's calculated words sent a cold shiver up Mark Stiles' spine.

"Mark?" Rebecca, her brow creased with concern, one hand resting on her barely swollen belly where their child grew, came and held his hand. "Mark, I'm worried."

He nodded, squeezing. "Don't worry. The vaccine is mandatory. There won't be another infection, Becky. We'll be okay."

"No, that's not what I mean. Don't you realize what he said?" Rebecca dropped his hand and faced him, looking him in the eyes. "He said *we*. McCartney's not alone. Omaha's in trouble. I think you need to call Frank."

CHAPTER 3

BUNTING

SHERIFF KEATON TOOK A deep breath, basking in the brief quiet of the breaking dawn. Most days it was difficult to believe, after everything that had happened, his little town was somehow not just standing, but growing. It had been almost destroyed by RSA agents as they sought to take power. With the help of Sherman and the men and women of Omaha, his township was rebuilt and reborn. Even this early in the day people walked past with a quick greeting for him as they headed to work.

Bartering was still their main form of currency, and Keaton had no reason to believe that would change soon. If you wanted to trade, you needed to bring something to the table and, to do that, you needed to work. It was archaic compared to the world before, but it had worked from the start for the people of Abraham, and they weren't inclined to upgrade the system anytime soon.

Familiar footsteps approached from behind. A hand rested on his shoulder, squeezing gently. Keaton would allow only one person in

Abraham to sneak up on him like that. He turned, smiling, and Janine placed a ghost of a kiss on his rough lips. Soft, gentle; she didn't need to use words.

"You didn't come to bed last night?"

Keaton shook his head. "No. I'm worried. Not all of the scouts returned yesterday."

Janine rolled a shoulder. She was sore; yesterday had been spent attending patients from sunrise to sunset. It had been a long time since she'd plied her pre-Morningstar craft for an extended period, and she certainly hadn't missed dealing with extractions and cavities. "The scouts are often late; they're usually fine when they stay in their units. Why the worry?"

"It's Marie's unit."

Janine understood his concern. Everyone was fond of Marie. Since her rescue in the early days of the outbreak, she'd become a hugely efficient scout and a friend to most everyone in the close-knit community. Marie headed up her own unit of four others, and they were widely reputed to be the best unit New Abraham had to offer.

If their team was late back from assignment, there was a chance something wasn't right. Still, Janine tried to put her lover's worries to rest. "I'm sure it's nothing. Perhaps they've found more intel and decided to stay out in the field while they've got the opportunity?"

"They always take enough rations for their set recon. The longer they remain out there, the likelier it is something's gone wrong. If she was okay…I'd expect her to have said something…try to make contact in some way."

The radio at Keaton's hip crackled, startling them both. "North Gate to Sheriff Keaton, over."

Keaton unclipped it, turning from casual chatter to stern business. "Keaton here, what's the matter? Over."

"We've got a wounded scout at the gate. Medics are on the way but she's asking for you."

Keaton's gut dropped. She. *Marie?*

He and Janine wasted no time. They both sprinted to the gate—it wasn't far and running would be quicker than grabbing a vehicle. As they approached, Keaton's heart went from rapid to worse, and it wasn't from the sudden burst of exercise. A couple of medics were tending to someone on the ground, but where was the rest of the squad? Just one of them?

"Marie!" Keaton rushed to her side, sliding to his knees and cradling her head. "Marie, are you alright?"

One of the medics put a hand on his shoulder. "Sheriff, please be careful. We need to keep her stable."

Keaton cursed, stiffening and holding her head steady. "Of course. I wasn't thinking."

And he wasn't. The sight of Marie had taken him aback. She was a mess. The young woman was covered in blood. A horrendous gash split the left side her face from skull to jaw, muscle and sinew exposed to the cool dawn air. Her left ear was missing, and her clothes were charred. Her mouth moved; he was astonished that she'd be able to speak at all.

"Don't, Marie. Don't talk. You're not well. They need to work on you."

"Please. Important." Her voice cracked, sounding tiny in the open space by the gates amongst the clamor of the medics.

"Bring some water!" one of the medics called out, gesturing toward a water barrel. "Quick!"

A guard rushed to them with a bucket, handing it over. Keaton held Marie carefully as a medic gently dabbed some water over the scout's parched lips. Marie groaned; wanting more than they were giving her, but with how dehydrated she was they couldn't risk making her any worse. She just needed enough to be able to talk—and Marie seemed desperate to get those words out.

"Sheriff, I'm sorry…" She blinked a wet eye, a single tear coursed down her ruined cheek. "They're all gone. The rest of them."

"What happened to you, Marie?"

"So many Sherriff. Herman. It was meant to be simple. Just following them. Just a little group. We were wrong. So wrong."

Keaton didn't want to rush her, but her utterances made little sense. If she couldn't convey things clearly, she needed to rest, so she could tell him the whole of her story. If she survived.

"It's a group, sheriff. Call…call themselves the Nomads."

Nomads—a new group. That didn't sound promising.

"They're not like us, sheriff. They're like…they're using steam to move…people around. They're taking…*everything* when they go. And when they leave…." More tears trickled from Marie's eyes. "They… they raze it. Flames. Everywhere. They just leave ashes."

"What firepower do they have? What are we up against?"

Marie sobbed. "Didn't see guns. Knives. Axes. Torches…fire… firebombs. They hack…destroy. Doesn't matter if you're…you're human or infected. Nomads just…want to kill…."

She gripped his hand in her own blood-soaked one and squeezed with surprising strength. "They…they're coming here next. They want Abraham."

CHAPTER 4

RED TAPE

Francis Sherman—no, President Sherman, now, didn't think he'd ever get used to the airs and graces surrounding his new role. He felt isolated amongst the bureaucrats, though with his time spent in the military he was finally finding his stride to match the pace and angle of boardroom tactics. It wasn't so far removed from the battlefield, he was starting to find.

He was far from what he now considered home, the expanding borders of Omaha. Still, with rudimentary computer networks and communications back in place, partial telecoms and the ever-constant radio, his friends were never far away. Which, these days, was no bad thing.

"Mr. President? Shall I send him in?"

Snapping out of his daydream and back to the present, Sherman nodded wearily. The last thing he wanted was another meeting, but this one was critical. And his efficient assistant assured him it was the final one in a day that felt like it had lasted forever.

Ewan Brewster walked through the door. Back stiff and chin up, Sherman mused that the man before him now was a shadow of the cocky deuce driver that had somehow scraped his way through the devastation of Africa. Then, after the door closed behind them, a grin crept across the young man's face, and Sherman was reminded that under the formalities, the old Brewster still shone.

"Mr. President, it's a pleasure to see you."

"The pleasure is mine, Brewster. Take a seat." The office was not oval, and his huge desk was an assortment of paperwork to check and process, not some grandiose statement of power. The room was only big enough for one small couch, but Ewan perched himself on the edge of it, arranging his hands on his knees in an attempt to remain formal. This was, after all, supposed to be an official debriefing. "Let's cut to the chase. Do you think Fort Hood was the last of them?"

"Of the RSA? I think so, sir—sorry, Mr. President."

Sherman waved a hand in a silent plea for Brewster to drop the formalities. If he couldn't stand down from protocol with one of the few men he'd stood with since the beginning, then he'd never be able to relax again. "They weren't at all organized, much like we'd suspected, and the survivors there confirm there weren't any comings and goings of other personnel. It seems like that was their last stand. Approximately two dozen are alive still, I think, but they ran as soon as the shooting started. I don't believe they'll pose a future threat."

"Remind me about these survivors. Your initial recon advised Killeen was empty?"

"Yes, sir. We found people in the C&C when we swept the base after the RSA fled. They were all residents of Killeen, bar a couple of refugees they'd managed to pick up. That's where they got their infected from, sir. They were gradually turning people to use as weapons."

"Sick bastards." Sherman sat back, clapping the desk with the flat of his hands. "Better for the whole world that their faction is destroyed. I can't believe it. That faction has been a thorn in our sides since almost the very beginning. I was starting to think we'd never see the end of them. I still can't. Part of me is just waiting for another nest to spring out of nowhere."

Brewster shook his head. "I really doubt that, sir. They weren't posting proper scouts on their perimeter. We were practically on top of them before they realized something was wrong. They didn't have much by way of a food or weapons cache. This place was nothing like the fortress they'd created at Mount Weather. There was no real defensive plan in place in case of attack. We took them down with minimal minor casualties. I didn't think zero losses was a possibility these days, but it happened. And now we have complete control of Fort Hood."

"Thank you, Brewster. You were under the spotlight, and the mission couldn't have gone any better if we'd had years to plan it. Now, I can take this to the rest of the cabinet and convince them that the work I have planned for you and your team is in trustworthy hands."

Brewster chuckled. "I never thought I'd hear you call me trustworthy, sir."

Sherman grinned—a rare treat these days. "I meant *my* hands, Brewster."

The door knocked again and Jessica Wren, Sherman's new assistant and nearly ever-present aide in helping him navigate his unwanted political life, stepped into the office. She looked apologetic—a look that usually meant another meeting.

"I'm sorry, Mr. President; the Vice President would like to see you."

The taste of the victory in Fort Hood wasn't given long to linger on Sherman's palette; Spivey was a politician who played games far too much for Sherman's liking, and he remained the top opponent to Sherman's plans for Brewster and his Hunters.

"Send him in."

"Not to overstep the mark, sir, but you look tired. You should try to get some rest."

Sherman rounded the desk, holding his hand out to Brewster. They shared a firm handshake and a familiar smile. "They don't give you the chance around here. Sharks, the lot of them. Take me back to the battlefield where I belong."

"We've got that covered. I'd much rather see you fighting our corner here."

Sherman sighed. "That's the answer I was afraid of, son."

As Brewster left, Spivey strode through without waiting to be announced. While Sherman didn't particularly want to stand to protocol, for some in the new White House, he was willing to make an exception. The ex-Navy man had been forced into this post after the disaster which had killed the president and his general staff. Spirited out of a dead and dying Washington and to the hallways of McCoy, Spivey found himself ill-prepared for the role thrust at him, but eager to take the promotion with both hands. It was a role-reversal for the pair. They did, after all, have a history.

"Mr. President, thank you for seeing me."

Sherman gave the man a bland smile. Spivey was skinny, tall, and seemed to have a constant sheen of sweat coating his pale skin. Sherman shook the proffered hand. It was like palming a flatfish. "Actually, I'm glad you came. Now is as good a time as any to report on the mission we sent our Hunters on."

Spivey's smile looked forced, Sherman thought; still, the enthusiasm was there. Full of piss and vinegar he might be, but the man's intentions were honest. "We're still calling them that, Mr. President?"

"They aren't just an assortment of soldiers, I assure you. I served alongside some of them before this all began; others are leaders in their own right, and we've seen what they can do at Mount Weather. They are a force to be contended with, and I see no reason to obstruct their formation any longer."

"Mr. President, we all applaud your enthusiasm for this project, and your military knowledge is not for me to question, but...."

Sherman raised his hand. "I'm sorry but this is not up for discussion. Five days ago, the Hunters took out the RSA base at Fort Hood. Our intel shows this was their last sophisticated stronghold, and even calling it that is generous. They are eliminated, Spivey. The Hunters were given their test, and they passed…" Sherman leaned forward, his voice dropping to emphasize his point. "…without human losses."

Spivey's mouth worked, trying to formulate a response. "You insisted it was a full military operation!"

"It *was*. Reinforcements were in place should it have been required. Ultimately, it was, but only to safely secure and evacuate the hundred-or-so civilians the team rescued. They've shown their worth, Spivey. The Hunters are now active under my command, and fully operational."

"Surely this should be brought before the general staff. Major Bentley—"

"I've listened to Bentley's concerns already," Sherman cut in. "And I've acknowledged them the same way I have yours. The Hunters are active…and I have a spectacular first 'official' assignment for them."

CHAPTER 5

FIRECRACKER

"COME ON, MCCARTNEY. YOU think you didn't already expose enough about your group during your little rant in the square? You said 'us.' Let me know who you're working with, and perhaps we can make things a little more comfortable for you."

The huge man snorted, spitting blood and bile in Stiles' direction. "You think you can smack me a couple of times and I'll start spouting like a leaky faucet? I'm not telling you shit."

McCartney was cuffed into a chair, hands behind his back—his broad shoulders forced them to use a pair of cuffs linked together. His large legs had been left free, and they tensed as Mark cracked another hook across McCartney's prominent jaw. He then walked behind the big man and shook his damaged hand, flexed his fingers and looked at his swollen knuckles, split and bloody—yet still nothing compared to the state of McCartney's face. Omaha might be a haven for civilization, but when men like this came to threaten their safety, Mark saw no benefit anymore to playing by the rules.

"You might as well come clean early on, McCartney. The longer you keep quiet the worse this is going to get."

"Worse?" McCartney, despite his split lips, managed to laugh. "You shouldn't even be holding me here. I didn't do anything wrong."

Mark came around to face the man, a perplexed look on his face. "You're joking, right? You brought an infected—*a sprinter*—to a public gathering. You put hundreds of lives at risk. You caused widespread panic, and you think you didn't do anything wrong?"

"No, I *know* I didn't. And, if you ask around, it's obvious why. People have the vaccine, don't they? There might be rules about dealing with the zombies at the perimeter, but there's nothing that says I can't bring one in on a leash."

Mark was stunned. Without even needing to check, Mark had a feeling McCartney was right. The rules they lived by now—their laws—they were all unwritten. Everyone would know and say that McCartney had done something reckless and foolish, but he hadn't broken any laws. He'd caused alarm, yes, but ultimately no one was hurt, despite his reckless actions. That would have to change and fast.

"What's wrong, Stiles? Something I said?"

Through sheer frustration, Mark went to backhand McCartney, catching himself before he could strike the bound man again. Losing his temper was the worst thing he could do, especially when he was going to have to let the man go free.

"I just brought into the open what no one else is brave enough to say," McCartney said with a grin, showing bloody teeth. "We're not the only people left in this country—in this world. What gives Francis Sherman the right to be *my* president? I didn't choose him, I don't want him, and I know a whole lot of people who feel the same."

"It's call the Right of Succession, dumbass. When the president was assassinated, Sherman was nominated. He *is* our legal president."

"Well, not for long." McCartney said. "Now, when do I walk?"

Mark couldn't stand it anymore. He left the small, bare interrogation room as McCartney laughed. "See you soon, Stiles," the big man said just before the door shut.

Outside, Rebecca waited for him, leaning back in a chair. She looked worried and exhausted. Mark couldn't let her put herself under too much strain with her pregnancy and this escalating situation. He knew his wife, though. She wouldn't sit back and watch him deal with this alone.

"What's wrong?" Rebecca was staring straight into his eyes; she knew the situation was heading south.

"We can't hold him," Mark replied, trying to keep the bitter bite out of his answer.

"The hell we can't! He brought a sprinter into town, Mark. He could have hurt a lot of people."

"He knows that. He's not as dumb as he looks, Becky. He's also aware that we're trying to do everything here by the letter of the law, and we…he hasn't broken any laws. He's a dangerous idiot and a complete fool, but there's nothing I can keep him imprisoned for."

"What about the panic he caused? And those things he said about Frank? There must be something…."

Mark shook his head. "Nothing I can think of. Christ, I wish more attorneys had survived this thing."

"I don't think many people would agree with you there," Becky muttered. "So, what do we do now?"

"Hold him for as long as we can. Then do the only thing I can do—let him go."

"So he can just start more riots? Bring more of those things into town? If Anna hadn't already completed the vaccination program—"

"But she did, and no matter what that fool did out there, we were always safe. I need to find out where he got a sprinter from and right now that's probably the only thing I can keep him locked up for without causing more trouble than we need."

"Let's go back to the town hall. We need to speak to Francis about this. He has to know what's happening here."

"I wouldn't be surprised if someone has already let him know. News spreads around this town like wildfire. But you're right. Come on. There are enough people here to make sure McCartney can't get up to more trouble."

"It's trouble getting to him that I'm worried about."

A silence settled between them as they considered the weight of those words. Into that silence crept a low humming. It sounded like…chanting? Renner, a young man just promoted into the Omaha policing force, skidded sideways into the corridor. His eyes were wide with panic.

"Sir? I think you need to come and see this."

Mark and Rebecca shared a glance. "Stay here," Mark instructed.

Rebecca ignored the order and followed him to the front of their new station. A group was outside—it wasn't small, and it wasn't projecting the family-friendly atmosphere they'd seen outside the hospital.

"Oh shit."

★★★★★

"Mark, we need to call for backup." Rebecca's voice was urgent, reminding him of the stress she'd be under right now.

"Go back inside, Becky. Please. It's not safe out here."

They both glanced at the crowd, while behind them Renner hopped ever-so-slightly from foot to foot. *Far too green for a situation like this*, Mark thought as he scanned the recruit for signs of a firearm. Thankfully, he wasn't carrying anything which might set the fragile situation alight.

Mark didn't see weapons among the crowd. They weren't rioting, though with the size of the crowd they could easily start taking chunks out of the simple storefronts springing up around the city.

Mark tried to think logically. Was this just McCartney's second way of attacking them? First, bringing a sprinter into the center of town, then demonstrating how many people he had following his cause?

Curious spectators collected on the periphery of the group, adding to the swelling numbers. Mark took a couple steps forward, holding his hands out to Becky and Renner to indicate he'd be okay. "I don't think it's what it looks like," he told them. He would wait for the group to reach the station before speaking.

There was so much chatter it was difficult to pick out specific words, though in all the noise he heard specific names, his and Sherman's included, invariably coupled with curses and unhappiness. He guessed there were perhaps a hundred people in the group, though it was hard to tell how many of them now were just standing around waiting and listening, wanting to see what would happen. Mark recognized this moment for what it was. Not just for Omaha, but for Sherman and his authority over the larger townships of the United States. If dissension like this could happen in what most people locally considered to be the first city to be secured after the Morningstar epidemic, then all they were working towards could collapse. If McCartney had the momentum to already have the ear of this much of the population, it might not even take that long.

"Citizens!" It seemed like the most neutral way to address them all. He waited. A few people stilled, swinging their attention his way. "Friends! Please."

The hubbub continued until a man and a woman, apparently the spokespeople-elect for the mob, peeled away from the crowd to confront him. They stepped forward, and a silence fell. Mark noticed it was mostly young men and women clustered there. Very few elders.

"You can't keep him in there, you know." The female spokesperson said, pointing at the station. It was clear who she meant.

McCartney might not be their leader, Mark realized, but he was the catalyst. This had all been staged. "I cannot discuss police matters with the public. That was true before Morningstar, and it's true now."

"Police matters? You were a soldier," said the male spokesperson. "You don't hold public office, so you have no authority in there."

"You're as bad as Sherman," the woman added. "No one asked for you to run this city for us!"

Dumbfounded, Mark struggled for a response. He had always been a quiet, reserved man. He didn't seek praise or plaudits. He only wanted to do the best he could in the most discrete way possible. He wasn't doing a very good job of that right now. And public office? How long had they practiced this speech? He most certainly hadn't asked for that, or any of what was happening now.

Then it dawned on him. *Asking.* Of course! That's all they wanted. Mark shook his head; the answer to dispel this latest little threat was so simple. How hadn't he thought of it sooner?

"Folks, listen. There's going to be an election," he announced.

The crowd stilled. The couple in front of him, probably ready with a scripted spiel they'd been perfecting for weeks, stood slack-jawed. *That caught you by surprise, didn't it?* Mark thought.

"Election?" said the man, then he looked at the woman, who raised her brows and shrugged as if to say, *that* is *a surprise.*

Mark glanced back at Becky. Her face painted enough of a picture—and a very different one from the spokeswoman's. Clearly, his announcement had caught everyone off-guard, including Rebecca.

Mark took advantage of the silence to drive his point home with unrelenting force. "You're all absolutely right. There are officials here that haven't been elected, and the population of Omaha is big enough now you should have a say on who spearheads the recovery. We've done a good job so far as a community, but it's becoming painfully clear that proof of progress is not enough for some. You want it official; let's make it official. In one month, there will be an election for mayor. I will be running...

"...and so will Michael McCartney."

The crowd erupted into a cloud of whoops and hollers.

Becky yanked on Mark's shoulder. "Are you insane?" she hissed. "This is the most ridiculous idea I've heard in my life."

Mark smiled, though it was wobbly, more nerves and relief than joy. "Yep. This may be the stupidest thing I've ever done, and trust me, I've done some incredibly stupid things."

Slowly but surely, the crowd dispersed. Some ambled away, clapping each other on the back. Others hustled off, no doubt to spread the word about what Mark had announced. A few even stepped up and shook his hand, telling him that's all they ever wanted—a democracy.

"What are you going to tell Francis?" Becky asked in the sudden silence after everyone had gone.

Mark's forehead beaded with sweat as he pictured the bawling he was about to get from the man. "Oh yeah," he said.

"You mean 'oh shit,'" the recruit Renner added.

"Yeah." *Maybe not as green as I thought.* "Oh shit indeed."

CHAPTER 6

FUSE

BURIED IN THE SAFETY of her lab underneath the city's surface, Dr. Anna Demilio frowned as she watched a fuzzy CCTV stream. It had started so positively; the crowd assembled to finally open a hospital where they could start making a real and positive difference to the people of Omaha, then, through the throng, she thought she could make out what he…no, *it* was. Some stranger had brought an infected into the city, held at the end of an impounder's leash.

"Thank goodness we got that vaccine out. What a fool." Anna breathed a sigh of relief when a group of soldiers brought the man down and neutralized the infected with calm efficiency.

She carried on filing notes, one eye on the screen as it flicked from camera to camera. It didn't take long, sadly, before another group was striding through the city as if they owned the place. Anna knew Frank—President Sherman, that is—could access this feed himself from his offices, rudimentary though their networks still were. They'd been steadily bringing the CCTV networks back online so he'd be getting a patchy feed on his computer of the streets of Omaha. Anna also knew he wasn't going to be happy.

The doctor pursed her lips as she looked at the mob. "What are they doing up there?" she said out loud, despite being alone. Anna shook her head, frustrated, but just as much at allowing herself to get distracted by the screens as she was at the events themselves. It was time to get to work.

Anna ran through the math as she subconsciously made her way through the hallways of her second home. They were still stockpiling the vaccine to start shipping it to the wider townships—those that had made themselves known to Omaha, at least, and accepted the conditions of friendship, mainly having their population inoculated. Rumors circulated about places declaring independence, locking their doors to outsiders and creating their own laws, but that was for another day and a situation Francis would deal with. The wider world had to accept the vaccine sooner or later, unless they wanted to die horribly like every other victim of the strain.

"Robbie, how many eggs have we got left in storage?"

Robbie Chastain poked his head up from where he'd been hunkered packing labeled vials into cases and marking them. His usually clean-shaven face was dark with stubble, as were the circles around his tired eyes. Robbie had come to Omaha during the recovery, yet had just recently let them know his love for biomedical science, in which he also had a degree. Anna instantly recruited him into the lab when she found out, along with the recently-joined Phyllis; between the three of them, they were trying to create enough vaccine to make sure the remaining population of their devastated country remained safe from the savagery of Morningstar. It was a slow-going process. As Robbie checked, Phyllis had been shifting stocks into line for their next run of production.

"We've got enough for another ten thousand units, doctor."

Anna sketched a rough calculation in her head. Those units would cover the rest of Nebraska state, for the settlements they could reach by car. Every day they received contact from new clusters of survivors, reaching out to try and get in line for their allocation of the vaccine. All it needed was one shot, and Anna was desperate to make sure everyone who needed it would get it.

So far, only Omaha, McCoy, and New Abraham were documented as being one-hundred percent vaccinated. New arrivals would be quarantined for a day—the stronger strains of Morningstar manifested in less than twenty-four hours, even from an innocuous bite. Once they'd cleared the Nebraska state area, along with Sherman's plans for the Hunters and the zone they had to secure, they'd concentrate on the larger secured population centers, no matter how far away they were located.

"Phyllis, do we know when the next delivery of produce is coming from New Abraham?"

"Last contact said four days, which should hopefully give us enough time to process through the majority of the stock we have left."

They needed more hands. Just three of them to produce was not enough, even though they'd gotten the process of vaccine production down to a fine art. Anna hoped as they kept coming across more survivors they'd find more doctors or scientists. The more the world's living populace "grew," the more likelihood knowledgeable people would crop up—those who had kept folk alive during the worst of the outbreak. And *when* she found them—not *if*—Anna would be recruiting them hard into the world's largest vaccination drive in history.

"I need to head to my office to write up some of these notes. We need to make sure we don't lose track of where these units are heading. Are you both okay to keep going here?"

They both smiled at her through exhausted eyes. Usually, they worked in rotation so there was always someone on the line, but occasionally they scheduled a shift so they were all in the lab at the same time. This gave them the opportunity to directly share notes, observations, and ideas on their process.

"We'll be fine," Phyllis answered.

Anna left, nagged again by the feeling that she knew Phyllis from somewhere. In her long and now-distinguished career, Anna had met hundreds of people, and it wasn't unlikely they'd shared a brief chat at a conference or met in a lecture somewhere. Still, Anna didn't feel brave enough to drill her new assistants too much; something inside gave her the sinking feeling she might not want to know the answer.

Anna went mechanically through disinfection, pulling on her office attire in the shivering cold of the antechamber. Heading out to the elevator, she waited until the door closed before punching the buttons for level one and for the basement at the same time. They didn't use the basement level much; it was primarily for storage and Robbie or Phyllis normally took the thankless task of drudging around down there taking stock. Anna wasn't interested in the basement, however. She wanted to pay a visit to the level below.

The lift opened into a new disinfection chamber. Far smaller than the one upstairs, which had seating and hooks for half a dozen assistants to suit up and go through. This chamber had but one hook and suit. Anna went through the mechanical process of stripping down, folding her clothes, and climbing into a hazmat. She had to keep up the façade for Robbie and Phyllis, who hadn't been given access to this level yet. The lower lab was only for privileged guests.

The notes she'd been making from her last visit were where she'd left them, on a long steel workbench. She'd made real progress, but the need to ramp up vaccine production had stalled her, and Anna was beginning to feel the strain of being pulled between so many projects. Still, even aside from what she'd achieved so far, this one could *really* change the world.

She picked up her notes and tapped down with her pen at the last sentence she'd written: *The subject appears to be suffering from a localized tissue breakdown in affected sites. There is no evidence of distribution through the nervous system.*

Anna glanced up and through the window of her lab into the isolation chamber. Her test subject was strapped to a gurney, though these days he was so old and decayed that Anna didn't think he needed restraining at all. Honestly, she felt a connection with him, so much so that keeping him strapped down felt like locking up a puppy—even if that puppy could kill someone with a single drop of his blood. If they were unvaccinated, of course.

"Hello, old friend."

Dr. Klaus Mayer, the former volunteer mortician, twisted on the gurney, totally oblivious to the contribution he was still making to the medical world.

CHAPTER 7

CONFLICT

PRESIDENT SHERMAN MOTIONED FOR Jessica to come into the room as he continued putting up with the vice president's deliberation. "I know what you think of this plan, Spivey. All I'm asking is for you to look at it from my perspective," he said to the man. "We are all in agreement to consolidate power and ensure the country can look to a centralized government again. We must attempt this recovery."

Jessica set some papers on Sherman's desk, and he gestured for her to stay. She nodded and stepped back, folding her arms.

Spivey seemed not to notice her. "And who exactly is this *we?*" he persisted. "I had no part in these discussions and, to be quite frank with you, Francis, I'm concerned you'd leave me out of making such a critical decision."

"Neither of us are in the military now. The Hunters operation is different to anything we've been exposed to before, and your experience gives you very little grounding to understand what I'm planning. This isn't going to be a huge ground operation. This is a targeted drop with specialists and a specific brief."

Spivey shook his head. "You're going to be sending them into a literal hell, sir. Everyone knows there are no human survivors in—"

"Can I interrupt?" Jessica had now clasped her hands lightly in front of her. She didn't look at all flustered by the debate raging between the leader and deputy of their country. She seemed nonplussed about interrupting them. It impressed Sherman and reminded him more than a little of the maturity and temerity a certain Rebecca Hall had shown in Cairo all that time ago.

Spivey opened his mouth, probably to shut her down. Sherman spoke first. "Go ahead, Jessica." He ignored the spiteful look Spivey threw at him from the other side of the desk.

"I can see this both ways. We all heard the rumors of the large undead groups clustered in the city, but that's the same everywhere. I believe President Sherman is right—that we have to try, at the very least, to reclaim the most important blocks, and we stand the best chance doing that with a small squad, so they don't draw too much attention. We can achieve more with six than we would with six hundred. The fewer resources we use, the less lives we risk, and we have the opportunity to build a command center to then fan out and reclaim the city zone-by-zone."

Sherman nodded, impressed at her succinct summary of his intentions despite her lack of military background. "Just like we did in Omaha," he said.

"And what if they're all killed in the process, your best squad? What then?" Spivey rattled in response, his voice high-pitched and agitated. He swung out of the chair to pace the room, impatient and irritated.

Taking a deep breath, Sherman responded calmly. Losing the entire team wasn't a prospect he wanted to consider, but it was one that he'd contemplated. "If it comes to that, then obviously we'll have to rethink our strategy. The plan would remain the same. We must take that city back. We have to show people who we are, and what we can do for them, no matter the odds."

"It's crazy," Spivey said, glaring at him and then at Jessica. "You're all crazy. You do realize what slim percentage of support you have in the White House with this?"

"But still a majority. Are you really going to stand against me?"

Spivey sighed, the fight coming out of him as that long breath left his lungs. "No, sir. I stand by whatever you think is right for us to beat this thing."

Sherman nodded. "Thank you. I appreciate that. Jessica, could you send Brewster in please?"

Spivey left, acknowledging the silent dismissal. After a few moments of brief peace, Brewster stepped back into the office. He saluted sharply and stood to attention, given others were present. "Sir?"

"At ease soldier. Jessica, if I could have the room?"

The young woman nodded and left.

Brewster relaxed slightly, raising an eyebrow. "I didn't think I'd be back here so soon."

"I've got your first mission. Take a seat. You're going to need it."

"Are you going to make me Veep?"

Sherman chuckled. "Not this term. Maybe in the future. No. I need you to go back to Omaha and assemble the Hunters. Your first official mission is incredibly simple. You're going to drop into DC to create a beachhead for the recovery of the Capitol."

Brewster blinked, looking on the verge of laughing outright at this ostentatious statement. The smile left his face upon realizing Sherman was dead serious. "Incredibly simple, Mr. President. All right. But, if I may make a casual observation?"

"Go ahead."

"Are you trying to fucking kill us?"

Francis Sherman barked a genuine laugh. "I can see how it looks, and I didn't say it would be straightforward: I said it would be simple. You'll get additional training on the drop, and we'll be sending in a care package for you to make sure you don't run low on resources."

"What about air support? Won't we get anything from McChord?"

"No. We can't stand the risk of attracting too many infected to your location. You stand the best chance of success if you avoid the obvious epicenters of infected."

"Epicenters?" Brewster sounded incredulous.

Sherman didn't blame him. He knew this plan didn't just carry risks; it was almost insane. Which was why he needed someone like Brewster to lead the assault. "Everyone knows the rumors surrounding the collapse of Washington. The infection hit us hard early on, and the infrastructure in DC caved in almost overnight. We've not heard of a single survivor coming out of there, and no one has tried going back in since the early days of Morningstar. With the size of the general population, we have to assume there's still a huge volume of infected and that they're likely to be concentrated around the more obvious tourist areas. Given the lapse of time, however, they're most likely to be shamblers. I can't imagine there's a single sprinter left in that place."

"And that's meant to be reassuring?"

"We're going to do a brief recon first to make sure we're not sending you in to die straight away, but yes. We think there should be a clear area and some reasonable high-rises close enough to Capitol Hill that we can get you in there safely. From that point, you're on your own, except for radio comms, until you have a secured location and perimeter."

"Well, fuck me. This is going to be one hell of an adventure to tell the grandkids."

Sherman grinned again, feeling almost weak with the pressure of this decision. He felt for the squad, but he couldn't trust anyone else with this task. "That's the spirit, soldier."

CHAPTER 8

ENEMY AT THE GATE

STEAM BILLOWED OUT OF the adapted hood of the mustard yellow GT Mustang. If he was going to drive around the rural US scouting towns to loot and destroy, he was going to do it in style. Jonathan Sturm, former yard laborer turned renegade leader, stood on the light-curved roof checking out the walls of the latest community ripe for the taking.

Road signs declared it as Abraham. People they'd caught and questioned gave it the moniker *New* Abraham, though at a glance it wasn't obvious why. Strong gossip had it this place was nothing more than a pet project for the people claiming to be in charge these days. Jonathan—he preferred "Johnny" these days—didn't really care what people thought in terms of authority. He'd already rejected the advances of one organization wanting to ally with him against the government. Ultimately, Johnny knew all they wanted were his people and his firepower. He had a strong, loyal following, so he'd told those fuckers where to stick their alliance—he'd be back for them later.

Now, he'd been told the center of the free world was Omaha, of all places, and New Abraham had a trade agreement with them. Well if that was the case, then behind those walls were riches waiting to be scooped into the Nomad's trailers and convoy. Johnny practically slathered at the prospect of hundreds of homes and livelihoods he could destroy as soon as he broke through those defenses. New Abraham thought it had big friends in high places? They could think again. No one was safe from the Nomads, and he was about to make their presence felt on the world stage.

He jumped down to the dirt. Dying grass and dust crumbled under his leather steel-toe-capped boots. The weather wasn't kind, and the land around New Abraham was parched. Before long, his people would make sure these peons learned the true meaning of the word *scorched*. "Come on boys! Let's take down these milking, hiding, old world fuckers."

★★★★★

Sheriff Keaton carefully watched what little he could of the Nomads' approach, and what he'd seen so far made him nervous. With Marie's warning, they'd been able to muster a defense he'd been certain could stand any attack the Nomads chose to throw at them. Watching the fleet of cars approach, Keaton wasn't entirely sure his judgment was correct. If his estimations were near accurate, the Nomads were approaching with over forty vehicles and perhaps three hundred people. Keaton didn't even know how much of their main group this insane convoy constituted, but after Marie's harrowing report he was willing to bet it was a mere tip of the iceberg.

Sherman in the New Whitehouse and Stiles back in Omaha were aware of the danger brewing on the borders of New Abraham. Keaton just hoped they understood from his recon how serious it looked. The entire town was on lockdown, with those unable to fight hiding in secure bunkers. If what Marie said was true, Keaton had a gnawing doubt that leaving them underground may be a death sentence in and of itself. Still, if the Nomads got past their walls and into Abraham proper, they were all doomed.

Jose had worked through the night working on some new tertiary weapons to make sure those vehicles couldn't approach the walls. Abraham's scouts hadn't been able to identify just what ballistics sat inside the mutated vehicle's shells but having spied at least a couple of pieces of adapted military hardware, he was glad they'd made the effort now. Marie had said they didn't use guns: Keaton couldn't let himself believe that.

"Keaton to Evans, over."

"Evans here, sheriff. What's the sitrep? Over."

Following the death of Wes, which still stung Keaton when he allowed himself to think about it, young Micky Evans had stepped into the role of deputy; he'd been making himself indispensable of late, and Keaton was relieved to have an enthusiastic soul filling those deep boots.

"See that Mustang? If I was looking to make people understand just who was in charge, that's what I'd be choosing to drive. Targeted shots around there, over."

"Targeting what, sir? We don't have a clear view of any passengers."

"Target the vehicles. Let's see just how many of those engines are steam-driven. If they can't approach us, their attack is crippled. Over and out."

Keaton dropped his radio and lifted his binoculars to check how well his strategy would work. All he needed from the Nomads was a light advance, and his people could show these upstarts how wrong they'd gone by driving up to his town.

The first suppressed shot *thumped*. Keaton didn't bother hiding his grin as he was rewarded with the sight of men ducking into vehicles and leaping for cover. It was hard to tell at this distance if anyone took serious injuries, but the steam which had already been pouring out of exhausts and modified hoods now billowed out in huge clouds, rising like an artificial mist.

A few brave souls darted around with extinguishers trying to limit the damage, but Keaton could see the unexpected volley had caught them by surprise. The Mustang lurched forward. Wheels spun, other vehicles moving to follow, signaling some sort of advance. This was the moment. Now, it was just a matter of waiting for the perfect time to catch as many of them in the net as possible.

"Evans? Prepare the shot, over."

"Acknowledged, sheriff! Over and out."

From guesswork based on Marie's implication that the Nomads left nothing standing, they attackers were all meant to head in one direction: straight for the walls and fences of Abraham. Aghast, Keaton checked the flanks to see four cars, all as ostentatiously adorned as the Mustang he'd picked out, spearheading assaults to circle around and pincer their defenses.

The sheriff had no idea what firepower they'd be using. He'd prepared for this, but they had to act quick. "Evans, fire at will! I repeat, fire at will with everything we have. McChord, are you getting this, over?"

After a heart-stopping wait when Keaton thought they might have lost contact with their only hope of support, McChord base responded. "We hear you, Sheriff Keaton. What do you need? Over."

"Full cover, over."

"On the way. Over and out."

Keaton dropped the radio to hear four reports, none of them suppressed. With the Nomad's attack already this far gone, the time for subtlety was long past.

Half a mile outside the walls of New Abraham, hell erupted. Gouts of choking black smoke and orange flame billowed into the sky as the targeted shots from the township's defenses ignited the oil-soaked terrain. Moving confidently in a deadly arc more than a hundred feet wide, the Nomads' vehicles drove straight into a cauldron designed to do one thing: destroy.

Keaton held his breath as he waited to see what would emerge from that concentrated zone of death. The cars had just been edging the perimeter of the oil field, and the slower Nomadic hardware hadn't accelerated much to gain momentum. Sherman didn't expect the armored vehicles to be troubled by the flames, but their confidence and arrogance was his primary hope.

The first explosion *thumped* through the air, impacting Keaton only a second after he saw the fireball billow into the sky. New Abraham didn't have many mines. Most of their arsenal lay in that field of death, just waiting for someone to drive over it. This should be adding to the confusion, giving them the chance to start picking at the Nomads if they managed to emerge from the smoke and flames.

The Mustang, seemingly not even scratched, accelerated fiercely from the smoke and towards their walls. Not far behind it, more cars came. Not as many as before, Keaton knew beyond doubt, but not as many as he'd wanted. Focusing his sights on the driver of the Mustang, Keaton got his first look at the leader. Through a dirty windshield, all he could make out was a young-looking face split into a wide, maniacal grin.

Keaton shuddered as he gave the order. "Fire at will."

As cars emerged from the flames, the sharpshooters spread across the tall walls of the town resumed their potshots, aiming for tires and engines. With the enemy now mobile these were less likely to hit their targets, but the attackers were still out of effective range of the M16s many of the defenders carried. Holding the advantage of terrain with their walls and still not knowing what the Nomads would come at them with, Keaton wasn't taking the risk of moving his men anywhere. Those that couldn't fight were bunkered down in shelters, hidden from any superficial attacks.

They could repel this. They had to.

"Plucky fuckers, aren't they!"

Johnny opened his windows to let out the choking smoke that had filled the cabin of his car. In his rearview mirror, he could see bonnets catapulted, vehicles flipping back onto their roofs as they drove over mines hidden in the madness of the oil field. *Sneaky.*

Some of the bigger townships had tried holding his people off. They'd been spirited, though most shitty defenses never kept them out for long. So, the people of Abraham had some tricks up their sleeves, did they? The way Johnny saw it, the more they struggled to keep him out, the more they had to hide, and the greater his reward. Sure, there'd be some losses, but it would be worth it for the sheer havoc they'd cause, and the new hardware he'd gain for his crews.

Johnny signaled down a Dodge Charger, its V6 engine idling as the driver leaned out the window. Eric, a grizzly ex-con Johnny had worked with and recruited as his second-in-command, leaned out. "Need a ride, boss?"

"Nah, my rider says it'll keep going; just superficial. I need your CB."

"Oh? What are we calling in?"

"We're going to drive straight at 'em. Call in the boys."

"All of 'em, boss?"

"You got it. We're gonna tease 'em. I reckon they're hiding something. Not sure what. I want to make sure they know what they're dealing with."

"You got it, boss."

Johnny climbed back into the driver seat as Eric spun off, already calling in the rest of their vehicle support. Those farmers probably thought they were a bunch of kids in cars. Oh, how wrong they were.

Jonny turned to his rider; all the command had one. A trained mechanic, one of the rare trades Johnny would keep someone living for, to look after the car while others could focus on what the Nomads did best: destruction.

"We good to go?"

"Nothing leaking, boss. It'll do the rest of the assault if we miss any direct shots."

"That'll do."

Gunning the engine, Johnny set off again. He steered to the left, keeping away from the walls. If they had more long-range weaponry he'd have expected to see it already in the panic of the assault. That had just been the welcoming party—they hadn't seen nothing yet.

If this place really had the ear of whatever was left of the military and the government, he had to keep some cards close to his chest. Abraham was under protection. Johnny Sturm wasn't going to show the world the worst he could do unless he absolutely had to.

As he peeled away from continuing a direct attack, the other cars followed suit. They weren't all able to keep out of harm's way, but their circling would be enough to keep the defenders wary while Eric's call went through. He might have kept the majority of the Nomads back; after seeing just how desperate these people were to repel the assault, there was every chance that, in a blind panic, they might just show Johnny the kind of support they could call in. He was counting on it.

"Why have they stopped attacking?"

Micky sounded even younger than his twenty years with the concern edging his voice. Keaton clicked his tongue, watching the circling cars with dread. On the horizon, it looked like a storm was kicking up.

The sky was blue. The choking black smoke from the oil field drifted straight up, no wind to push it away.

There was no way it could be a storm.

"I think, Micky, we have more company. Head to the college. Make sure that bunker is sealed tight. If they get through the gates, I don't want them touching our people."

They'd adapted the basement and storage long ago to be short-term housing in case of disaster. It wouldn't do long term—it was just enough to keep people alive while, say, a group of renegades drove through town setting fire to whatever they saw.

It was enough to keep people alive.

Micky had already dropped down from the guard tower, hopping onto a 50cc to get across town as quickly as he could. Keaton only took his eyes off the horizon for a moment. When he turned back, he was glad he'd already called in McChord.

"Forrest, this is Sheriff Keaton, do you copy?"

"Forrest here. You need me to call off support? Over."

"Negative. How far out were your pilots waiting? Over."

The crackle of flames and the growl of engines filled in the silence. Keaton couldn't take his eyes off the Mustang, circling like a vulture, waiting for its prey to fall. "ETA five minutes."

"Oh, good."

They weren't ones for picking up stragglers, though it was amazing what vehicles people would leave behind when they weren't paying attention.

Johnny really wanted a tank. He was sure his mechanics would be able to do some *amazing* things with a Bradley. Beggars couldn't be choosers, though he did like to think of himself as picky. The defenders had stopped with their potshots now. They were in a standoff. He could see the rest of his attack support approaching now.

Those people must be shitting in their pants.

"Boss, looks like something coming in from the east."

"What you got for me, driver?"

His mechanic, Johnny thought he was called Bobby, but couldn't recall, pointed out across to Abraham. A couple of pinpoints in the sky could have been mistaken for a couple of birds, though with the chaos going on, you'd assume they'd avoid flying in this direction.

"My my, they *do* have good friends here."

"I need you out of the town, Janine. They're not covering the east. Get out into the forest and take a detachment of scouts with you."

"I'm not leaving you to face them on your own, Keaton Wallis."

Janine looked furious and he didn't blame her, and though he felt mildly ashamed, he couldn't help but notice how damned attractive she looked when she was angry. "I need someone out there, just in case we lose the town. Someone I trust. If we lose the walls I'll go into cover, I promise. Support is on its way. Please. Go now."

She hesitated, her jaw set. For a terrifying moment, he thought she'd refuse. His request was honest. Leaving a group outside the walls for recon, or even to just carry back what happened at Abraham if it all went wrong, was sensible. He just wanted to make sure she was out of range of the Nomads' flames.

Keaton would risk his own life in a heartbeat for her. Because he knew she'd do the same for him, he wanted her as far away from him as possible.

She kissed him, not a peck this time. She lingered, holding his gaze. "Don't you fucking die on me. Asshole."

Keaton watched her go as the Apaches approached.

★★★★★

"Oh ho, here we go fellas!"

Johnny watched gleefully as the air support approached. Three choppers. He couldn't tell what they were, though he didn't really care. He slapped the roof of his Mustang and held up three fingers. The car behind took up the signal, its driver picking up her CB and chattering away.

Half a mile down the road two APCs, their bodywork now painted black and covered with dents from previous assaults, peeled away from the main body of the attack.

Abraham had air support? Good. Let them come. Johnny had ground control.

"Go on," Keaton muttered under his breath, willing the pilots from McChord onwards as they flew overhead, wind stirring around him as they dropped in altitude. A rocket screamed from the lead Apache, landing in the middle of the oncoming new wave.

"No, no, no, the closer ones!" Keaton yelled.

The first 70mm Hydra did damage enough, though it wasn't much to dent the sheer volume of vehicles the Nomads came with. Keaton saw, too, part of the main cluster of cars had moved out of their rough group formation, now covering the effective no-mans-land between their main troops and the vulture cars with the Mustang. These three breakaway vehicles looked like adapted military hardware.

As he watched, Keaton saw the roof of an adapter APC open. A man shouldering an RPG took aim at one of the Apaches, hovering with its 30mm canons thumping round after round into the enemy. He closed his eyes as the shot fired, though the noise of the explosion was unmistakable.

They'd taken heavy losses in the short time McChord's support was in the air. Seven missiles and countless rounds from their chain guns. In short-range combat, though, the Nomads' RPGs were impossible to avoid. The first Apache to be struck took an impact to its undercarriage that Keaton felt thump in his gut. It seemed to stop in midair, tilting agonizingly slowly before spinning into the open fields, rotors churning up grass and soil as thick black smoke billowed from the stricken craft. The attacking Nomads didn't seem to care much for their own kind as they aimed for the second helicopter, on the edge of the main formation. It, too, was dispatched with alarming ease, though when its descent became clear, Keaton was certain the pilot took one last act of revenge. It wasn't a natural flight path; the Sherriff could imagine the grim serviceman or woman, fighting the controls to bring them crashing into the side of the Nomadic offense. Three cars at least were obliterated by the impact. Still, it wouldn't be enough. Their support was taken out without flourish, the enemy's lead vehicles still intact.

Keaton watched with dread as those vehicles now started their inevitable pursuit towards Abraham.

It was happening again. He couldn't afford to let people die needlessly. Not this time.

"This is Sheriff Keaton Wallis. If you are already in bunkers, secure yourselves. If you are not..." He took a huge breath, hands shaking. "...evacuate the town through the eastern gate."

CHAPTER 9

DOMINOS

"ARE YOU SEEING WHAT I'm seeing, Frank?" Anna Demilio's voice might have been quietened by technology and distance, but there was no disguising her fear.

The footage Mark had sent him from Omaha was worrying, and Francis had studied it in a loop for hours. It wasn't just that there were people out there who didn't want him in charge—resistance was inevitable—but what concerned him more was someone had brought a sprinter into a city that was supposed to be vaccinated. And this McCartney had brought the damned thing all the way into the heart of the community. A huge crowd had been gathered outside that hospital. How many guards had this McCartney passed before he'd confronted Stiles and the others? It was obvious the man had to have more than a few allies on the inside of Omaha's domestic and police forces. They had a lot of questions to ask a lot of people, and the way things looked from the outside, they might not have a lot of time to work with.

"I'm seeing it, Anna. And I don't like it one bit. What are your thoughts?"

"On which bit? It seems Mark dealt with things fine, but…"

Frank grunted. "But now there's an election he has to oversee to beat an enemy we have no intel on when we're still fighting wars on other fronts."

Anna chuckled. "Not quite the way I was going to put it, but that's pretty much the state of things."

"I need to be there, Anna. Things are spiraling in Omaha, and I don't like being so far away."

"Frank, you know I'd be the first person to want to see you when you land, but do you really think that's a good idea?"

"If we're running the risk of losing everything we've gained in Omaha because a few dissenters are unhappy with the status quo, then those people need reminding just how we got where we are in the first place. Mark needs backup. And you know I'm the right person to give it to him."

"What about McCoy? Things aren't stable anywhere, Frank. You're the president now, and you need to be visible."

"You're right, and part of my life now is being in the right place when it matters. You know I hate politics, but we're looking at losing control of Omaha. Can you imagine what happens if someone we don't trust gains power? What happens to the vaccines? You've said this McCartney doesn't 'believe' in what we're doing? We can't run the risk of someone like that getting anywhere near having authority."

Anna had to grudgingly admit he was right. If McCartney got the keys to the city, everything they'd achieved would be for nothing, especially if this man and his followers were trying to stop the vaccination program. She relented with a tight sigh. "It'll be good for others to see you, I'm sure. I know I'll be glad. When are you going to leave?"

"I'm getting a transport now. I'll be there today, but I'll have to come back. You're still right, in a way—I can't leave the kids alone to play here for too long. I've got my own enemies. We've had that conversation."

"I'm not going to get to see you then, am I?" Anna tried to sound playfully scolding, but loneliness and sorrow tinged her words.

"If I thought I wouldn't distract you from what you're doing right now—which is more critical to us than anything else happening in the world—I'd see you in a heartbeat. We'll get some time soon. I promise."

Anna allowed a brief smile, before remembering what happened to the last president that had commissioned a helicopter ride into Omaha. "Stay safe, Frank."

"And you, Anna." He cut the call.

Anna placed both of her shaking hands palms down on her desk, taking some deep breaths to steady her sudden nerves. A brief knock at her door made her jump slightly. It opened before she could acknowledge it, and Robbie stepped through with a bland smile that disappeared when he saw her face.

"Uh, everything okay, doctor?"

Anna shook her head to clear the fog from talking to Frank, and from knowing he was going to be so close to her and yet so far away. She wanted to see him. She wanted to help…but knew she was already in the best place to help their government.

"I'm…I'm fine, Robbie." Irritation rose to take over as she realized he'd let himself into her office without her authority. "Can I help you?" She snapped at him, and she'd meant to.

He looked slightly hurt, even taken aback. "I just…I heard raised voices. I was concerned."

Anna knew that she hadn't raised her voice. Not one bit. What exactly was this man doing around her office for long enough to hear her talking anyway? "You must be mistaken. I was just speaking to a friend. Thank you for your worry, though. Is there anything else you want?"

Robbie seemed to hesitate for a second before reaching into his pocket.

She was in her office, Robbie knew. And of course, she'd be alone. He wasn't sure he could go through with this, but ever since he'd found out the extent to which Anna's research might spread, he'd been almost pressganged into finding out more.

Robbie respected Dr. Demilio and the work she was doing. He valued his life more. He knocked on the simple wooden door, not waiting to be let in. His plan was to look congenial, lull her into a false sense of security, but as soon as he saw the ashen look on her already-fatigued face, he stumbled.

She frowned at him, clearly annoyed at the interruption. *Shit. What now?*

"Uh…everything okay, doctor?" he asked awkwardly. He swore inwardly.

She snapped back at him, obviously on guard. "I'm…I'm fine, Robbie. Can I help you?"

Robbie fumbled for the right words. This wasn't going at all as he'd planned. "I just…I heard raised voices. I was concerned."

"You must be mistaken. I was just speaking to a friend. Thank you for your worry, though. Is there anything else you want?"

Robbie struggled to think if there was any way at this point that he could recover this conversation, but it seemed utterly lost. Plan B was his only option. He hadn't wanted it to come to this, but Michael had made it abundantly clear to him what the consequences were if he screwed this up. He pulled the sidearm from his pocket, flicking the safety to make sure it was off. Lifting it, perfectly aware of how much his hand was shaking, he tried to sound calm, confident, and in control.

"I'm going to need you to tell me all about your research, Dr. Demilio."

★★★★★

She was appalled by the absurdity of what was happening. Was Robbie really pointing a gun at her face? Not even that, the boy was shaking so much he was liable to shoot her by accident more than intent. "Robbie, you've been working with me for months. You already know all about my research. What is this?"

He shook his head. Anna could see he looked terrified. Whoever Robbie was doing this for, he wasn't doing it of his own free will. "Not that. The *other* research. We know about your other lab, doctor. My friends want to know what's happening in there."

Despite how much his voice shook, how stuttering his agonizing sentences were, Anna was dumbfounded. She'd taken every precaution in hiding her work, so how on earth had anyone found out about the lower basement?

Even worse—what did they want with her research?

She lifted her hands, palms forward, trying to look both placatory and peaceful. "Robbie, I'm not sure what you think is going on here, but I think we just need to sit down and have a talk."

Robbie shook his head again, twisting it almost so violently from side to side that Anna thought he might free it from his shoulders. If only Phyllis were on shift with them now—someone—anyone else, to catch him unaware.

Still, it might not stop that gun from going off.

"I'm not going to talk about this, doctor. We know that there's other research. We've seen the encrypted correspondence but couldn't break it. If it's the research we already know about, why hide it from your colleagues? We just need to get to your original notes, so we know what you're up to."

"What's really going on, Robbie, as you already know, is that we're trying to save the world. Have you not been listening to anything we've been saying these past months? How many of those vaccines have you prepped and shipped yourself? What else do you think we could be doing? Creating a *different* Morningstar?"

"We won't know what you're doing until you tell us. Now, unless you want me to start shooting—and honestly, doctor, I really do respect you, and I'd rather not hurt you—take me to where you complete your special research."

Anna sighed, not seeing an immediate way out of the situation. Her office was sorely sparse of weaponry, seeing as she'd never anticipated needing personal arms down here with so few people in the lab. She wanted Robbie in as closed a space as possible to try and minimize the chance that he might accidentally let off a shot and injure her.

"Fine. Follow me. We'll need another Chem suit."

They walked the levels in nervous silence, the echoing halls never feeling emptier or more desolate. Anna couldn't help but wonder if this was related to the riots she'd seen in the square, and the man that had approached the hospital brandishing an infected at the crowds. It couldn't be a coincidence. *Michael.* She needed a surname to complete the picture.

As they entered the elevator, Anna reached for the button for her office level. Robbie batted her arm down.

"We've been there," he said. "There's no lab on that level. What are you doing?"

Anna tried hard to keep her cool. "Just watch."

She pressed the buttons for the administrative level and the basement simultaneously to reach the lower basement. Robbie squinted, holding the gun stiffly, his knuckles white. Sweat shone on his forehead, and his arm shook slightly.

Who's gotten to you? she thought. *You're not the young man I hired all those months ago.*

The elevator opened into a small antechamber, containing nothing more than a bench and changing hooks, one suit—all that she'd ever needed—hanging limply in the empty space. Anna felt nervous as Robbie watched her strip down, never more self-conscious in her life than before that moment, his callous stare not leaving her naked body while she climbed into her Chemturion suit.

"You're going to have to go through as well, Robbie."

"You first, doctor."

Clever enough move. If he went through decontamination first, she could leave the lab. With her trapped on the other side, and Robbie with the gun, if she tried anything then he could fire a shot that might potentially trap her down here, without a chance of escape.

As he came through, she saw Robbie had elected to wear thin rubber gloves fastened under the suit's sleeves. That meant he could still control the gun and stay basically protected against any airborne contaminants. He wouldn't be safe working procedurally on a project, but basic impurities couldn't reach his system.

"This is it?"

Robbie was probably shocked at the sparsity of the lab and its compact nature. Anna wasn't sure what he'd been expecting. Perhaps dozens of hidden scientists, all hellbent on creating the next viral strain to destroy the rest of the already-decimated world?

"What more do I need? I'm not trying to rule the universe down here." She started to walk away from him.

"What are you doing?"

She paused, hesitant. Her only companion down here was an old friend. In a strange way, introducing this traitor to him felt like she'd be tainting their legacy. "Come here, Robbie."

She stepped back a few paces, indicating for him to look through the thin observation window to where the shambler lay strapped to the gurney. Robbie obliged, looking slightly horrified when he saw what lay beyond the sterile lab.

"Is that…?"

Anna shrugged, trying to sound complacent. "It's just another shambler. I'm using him to test adaptations of the vaccine on the slower infected."

Robbie sounded awestruck. "You're…you're trying to find a cure."

"At this point, with the state many of the secondary infected are in, I'd call it more of an eradication than a cure, but the end result is going to be fundamentally the same. But yes, I want to wipe Morningstar off the face of this planet. And that's what this shambler, and this research, is about."

Robbie whispered. Anna couldn't catch it all, but the ending sounded like …*was right.*

"What did you say?"

Robbie was still wide-eyed. "He was right. About everything. Everyone here. You're all monsters, and you have to be stopped."

Not for the first time that day Anna was left nearly speechless, though her anger rose to respond to her assistant's coldhearted words. "*We're* monsters? Have you seen what's lying through there? What is trying to get through our defenses still day after day? *Those* are the monsters, Robbie, and that's exactly what we're trying to stop—or have you forgotten the part you've played in creating all of those vaccines?"

Robbie gulped. "A necessary part to play in the bigger picture."

"What bigger picture?"

Robbie grinned, seemingly happy that she was here to indulge him and his views. He effectively held her prisoner; it wasn't as if she had a choice. "Not everyone believes in your picture of the new free world, doctor. We don't all think that President Sherman is our savior. So many of us don't even want him to be president. He wasn't our choice. We didn't vote for him."

"No. You didn't need to. That's what the line of succession was for when the previous president was murdered."

Robbie waved this off dismissively. "Still, why keep clinging to these old ways of life? This old structure of governing. It wasn't working for us—for anyone. Morningstar was given to the world as a cleansing gift, and you're trying to destroy it. This is natural selection, doctor, and you should be ashamed that you're trying to stop it carrying out its work."

"Natural selection? There's nothing natural about what the Morningstar strain has done to the world."

"That's where you're wrong, I'm afraid, and we all know it. The strain came out of the forests of Mombasa. It wasn't man-made, didn't need to be manufactured, or distributed, like your vaccine. It was nature's way of tipping the balance and eradicating the weak and the unworthy." He was ranting now, encapsulated in and driven by the lies of the unnamed leader spinning this group into a frenzy. Frank needed to know about this—them—all of it. Anna had to get out of this lab and tell everyone what sort of deranged threat they faced.

Michael McCartney, Robbie Chastain, the other followers of whoever drove this new movement—they were worse than whatever the RSA had been. The RSA was led by a power-hungry autocrat. This? This was more like a cult, and all they wanted was to see the world burn.

"Only those who are truly deserving of life should have survived the apocalypse," he continued ranting. "But no. You and your people chose to oppose it, and now we still have the weak, and the infirm, and the absurdly young, up at the surface and living their lives as if nothing happened. Did you know there's someone living in Omaha who's blind? There are others, who have never even killed an infected! How can they deserve to live after all the rest of us have suffered to get here?"

"Robbie, listen. I'm not sure who you've been speaking to, but that's not the way the world should work. We've only gotten as far as we have—peace, civilization, technology—by cooperating and helping each other, not destroying everything we have. If you let what you want to happen, we will lose everything. And I mean, everything. The human race will become extinct."

"Well, perhaps that's exactly what the strain was meant to do. And if that's God's will, then so be it."

Anna knew the layout of this small workspace like the back of her hand. She was deliberate in everything she did, and no matter what she worked with, be it pen or needle, it was always put back in the exact same space.

She hadn't needed to look as she'd palmed a shelf behind her, her hand seeking a tiny vial. Spouting his tirade, Robbie didn't notice her slight movements. He'd been so wrapped up in his speech he hadn't seen her other arm slowly disappear to grab a needle, the plastic tip falling to the floor lost under the volume of his words. Anna knew she didn't need much, not on a human being. Robbie had a fully-functional nervous and circulatory system. What only vaguely affected Meyer…well, Anna hadn't been intrigued in knowing what it would do to a live host.

Until now.

"Robbie, I'm trying to understand what you're saying," she began, stepping slowly to close the distance between them and reduce his chances of getting that gun up in the air. "And I think I know what I can do to help."

His eyes, bright with belief and vigor, swung to her, snapping out of his reverie. They went wide with shock as he saw the needle arcing from behind her back and dilated as the needle penetrated his thin gloves and stabbed into his vulnerable hand.

Anna injected Robbie with the experimental vaccine she had been using on Dr. Meyer. The latest iteration: tissue degeneration.

She wasn't close enough, though, and Robbie reacted quicker than she'd expected. She kept the momentum of the needle press going, but it was in Robbie's left hand, and the gun was in his right. Anna pushed him back and away, but in what felt like slow motion he brought the gun up, firing one shot into her stomach at close range.

They both fell to the floor, Anna's head only a couple of feet from Robbie's. His eyes were already going black. The serum spread quickly throughout his system. Borne from countless generations of other failed attempts from a working vaccine, Anna knew its potency. Robbie Chastain would leave this world making one final contribution to eradicate Morningstar, whether he wanted to or not.

Robbie wheezed, trying to get up, but Anna knew his muscle mass was already in accelerated entropy. He wouldn't stand again. He'd be dead within minutes. His eyes turned black, his skin collapsing. Anna turned away. No matter what her professional curiosity, she didn't want to watch this in real-time. Robbie began to scream. It was guttural—a noise of complete and utter agony.

Anna pondered if this was what hell sounded like, and for a disgustingly fleeting moment, wondered what the world would be like if she released this instead of Morningstar. It was a failed sample, just the one vial. It would never leave this lab, and neither would Robbie.

The screaming stopped. Anna risked a glance out of the corner of her eye and saw, contained within the suit, a broiling mess of blood and tissue. She couldn't believe how quickly it worked. Something more dangerous than Morningstar indeed, and she'd created it. If Robbie's people really wanted the world to burn, perhaps she'd provided them with the perfect counter to the vaccinated.

I have to destroy it. That vial can never leave this room.

First, she needed to stay alive. Anna knew that if she stood a chance of surviving, she'd have to move, and soon. At the very least she had to stay conscious. He'd given her a gut shot, but if he'd managed to miss the major arteries…if she could suture her wound and get to a doctor, she stood a decent chance of surviving.

But she was down in her labs. Alone.

If.

CHAPTER 10

DEJA VU

"You listen to me, Jessica, and carefully. You are the only person here I trust. Yes, you should be coming to Omaha, but I need you to stay here and be my eyes and ears."

"But Mr. President, you're only going for twenty-four hours."

"What's the saying? *That's a long time in politics*? No, I don't feel safe leaving without having an ally at my back. Trust me on this. With me gone, you might be able to find out more than you could with people whispering just outside my office door.

"Oh, and please, call me Francis."

"Yes, Mr. President."

Frank rolled his eyes as he clambered into the waiting helicopter. He hated these things and held little trust for his safety climbing into one. A sabotaged chopper had been the end of his predecessor, and Sherman never fancied his chances whenever he got near one.

Still, his pilot—a capable woman named Rachel Campbell—had completed the preflight checks under the watchful eye of his Secret Service detail. Adams, Fletcher, and Simons (and one day Sherman knew he'd coax their first names from them, whether they liked it or not) had scrutinized both the woman and her work. Sherman had no idea what their qualifications were versus her thousands of hours of flight experience, but he wasn't about to interrupt them.

Despite their care, it hadn't been a mechanical failure before that had brought the craft down, and so Sherman also always feared a remote hack. All their techs now, since the last incident, were closely vetted, though that never particularly made him trust them. He didn't know the men doing the vetting. *Who guarded the guards?*

The steady thump of the rotors was enough for him to believe they'd be staying in the air. They flew at a middling altitude of around twelve thousand feet. It wasn't so low that the infected below them as they passed population centers would start following their path. It wasn't so high that the rotors would simply cease working in the thinner air of the upper atmosphere.

Around twenty miles out of McChord, not at all far into their usual three-hour journey to the center of Omaha, they passed over a town which Sherman had taken an interest in observing. It housed a horde, composed mostly, they thought, of shamblers. There was no physical way the volume of infected all compressed together had all lived there before the outbreak, so they must have eventually congregated there. Sherman's own routes over that town were getting fewer and far between, but he did ask for periodic reports on their movement patterns. The group was largely static and therefore, he assumed, eventually decaying. He wanted to know if, without nourishment, the shambler form of zombies would just waste away to nothing. If they did, with Anna's vaccine for sprinters, it was just a waiting game until they won this war. No more science required.

Sherman thought absently that the swarm seemed to have moved from one end of the town to the other before a sharp rapid beeping from the cockpit brought him out of his reverie. He swung the mouthpiece on his headset to talk to the pilot.

"Campbell? What's going on?"

"Mayday. Marine One to McCoy, I've lost control. We're going down. I repeat we're going down. Location…."

Sherman didn't hear the rest as they assumed safety positions—as far as you could get in this tube of death.

It's happening again.

Helicopters. As they descended to earth, controlled, but fast, Sherman swore he'd retire them as a presidential form of transport if he survived. If he didn't…well, who'd ever want to travel in one of these things again?

★★★★★

His ears rang. He must have impacted his head, hard. Vision swimming, he tried to focus on the craft's cabin. They were intact—his detail groaning, but alive. Adams was the first to react and was already unstrapping from his seat. He headed, unsteadily, straight for his Commander-in-Chief.

"Mr. President…" The man sounded drunk. "Are you okay?"

Sherman nodded, not trusting his voice at this point.

"Good. We need to get you out of here, sir."

"What…the others?" Whole sentences were hard.

"The men are fine, sir."

As Adams hauled him out of his seat to the edge of the chopper, his senses came back. Fletcher and Simons were already moving. There was no movement up front, though.

"What about Rachel?"

Adams' brow furrowed slightly, his gaze flicking to the cockpit. "She's dead, sir."

Sherman glanced over to see a tree branch stuck through the screen, jutting out of the poor woman's midsection. At least she'd likely died immediately. And there was no way, in this situation, she hadn't saved their lives.

"Goddammit…"

"There's no time for dwelling on this, sir. If there are infected nearby they'll have heard us come down. We have to get away from this crash site and get you to safety as our number one priority."

Sherman already knew that. He'd experienced the infected world enough to know anything with the virus within sight or earshot, perhaps up to a mile even in built-up areas, would be headed straight to their position. Which direction would be safe?

"We're not far out of Fort McCoy. I suggest we double back to the nearest highway, find a vehicle, and make our way to base." Adams maintained control while the other men came to their senses. The agent propped Sherman against the side of the aircraft, its rotors now still, and they formed a defensive triangle around their asset while they gained their bearings.

In the distance, Sherman heard the first telltale snarl of the undead closing on their position. Part of him wished his hearing wasn't coming back.

"That didn't sound far," he said. "I suppose we need to be moving, gentlemen. Which direction?"

Sherman's words seemed to spur them on, and Adams pointed at ten o'clock. "This way. Let's go."

There was a chance they could still run into some infected on their route back, especially given how close they'd skirted the horde township. Sherman prayed that the noise hadn't stirred that particular nest and that they weren't about to bring a moving hell onto the new Administration's doorstep.

His detail surrounded him in a diamond formation as they hustled back to McCoy. They'd need to pass under I-90 and avoid any clots of infected still in and around their vehicles. Trusting most people stayed strapped in while the world turned, it would be safe enough. They just had to make it back before dark. Sherman didn't fancy their prospects spending a night in the wilderness with undead all over their asses.

CHAPTER 11

UNDERSTOOD

"IF COMMAND JUST WANTS me to kill myself I can jump off the building we drop on. I'd rather that than be chow for DC's undead, know what I'm saying?"

Castillo's former righthand and now her Hunters squad mate, Garibaldi, obviously wasn't keen on the plans to airdrop into the center of Washington. They'd had more than enough training to feel confident about what they were doing, but he remained unable to appreciate the objective of the mission and had been vocal about it. The rest of the squad, fearful though they were, used Garibaldi's doubts to deflect their own fears.

Brewster felt the pressure in these moments too, sure. When Sherman told him he was the first choice to lead an elite squad of soldiers, he thought it was a joke. Then Sherman explained his reasoning: the trust he had for Ewan. His recon and last-minute rescue at Mount Weather had gone a long way to securing his spot as the lead of the Hunters. Ewan Brewster hadn't argued against a man whom he respected more than his own father, and with so much experience in the field.

"I think the idea is for us to survive the drop, Garibaldi, and perhaps actually clear some of the Capitol *before* we become chow for the infected," he said in his own dark humor. "Killing yourself right after the drop sort of defeats the purpose, don't you think?"

Garibaldi shook his head and cursed, while Castillo snorted. "And do we really think this is likely?" she said.

"If it was impossible, President Sherman wouldn't even be considering it. I think he'd rather keep us alive for as long as possible. We're meant to be like—I don't know, the SEALs or Army Rangers now. Not an expendable troop."

"Well, you could have fooled me," came Garibaldi.

Kiley chimed in. "I wanna be the new Delta Force."

This banter within the group was not uncommon, and Brewster was still one of the first to contribute. He felt responsible for them as a leader, but deep down he felt strange, and almost out of his depth. Most of their training so far had been in isolation, in a huge disused warehouse on the outskirts of the city. The inside of the building had long been gutted since the recovery efforts, and it was primarily used to house training hardware. Every day they'd gather here as a group. Even with the jump ahead of them, Kiley was sure he wouldn't miss the smell of damp and brick dust for long.

"I know what we're doing sounds insane…" He took a deep breath, trying to think of what Sherman would say. He hadn't exactly been trained to be a leader, but sometimes it came naturally, so it's best to take your pointers from a good example. "We all know that if this wasn't critical, or if it was pointless, we wouldn't be doing it, right? They think we have a chance of securing a route back into a huge city. Imagine what securing DC would do for the country. Yeah, we're only a small squad, but that's the point. They're not expecting us to take out the whole fucking city, guys. They just need us to carve a path. I know we can do it."

An odd feeling settled over the group as they weighed Brewster's words. Not one of them didn't feel honored to be a part of this team. Through numerous missions and conflicts, they'd all earned the place with the Hunters. This first real mission for them seemed beyond daunting. But they knew Brewster was right. Sherman wasn't the kind of leader to send people to die for no reason.

Krueger stood up, frowning. "I don't say this often, but Brewster makes sense. And if Sherman…the president…is putting his trust in us, who are we to let him down?"

It wasn't a rousing speech to end all doubt, but between the two pep talks, it was enough. The whole group nodded, if not understanding what was needed from them, at least believing in it a little more.

"*Hooah*," Castillo grunted, slapping Garibaldi on the shoulder.

"You mean *oorah*," Brent said with a big toothy grin, flexing the 'USMC Devil Dog' tattoo on his left arm.

"Yeah, yeah, all right," Garibaldi said with a little deflation in his tone. "Hooah. Oorah. All the fucking *ahs*."

"I'll check in with command," Brewster said. "We're scheduled to head out in twelve hours, and we know we're ready. We just need to make sure there aren't any more surprises heading our way."

Brewster strode over to his kit, taking out the two-way radio they'd all become accustomed to carrying. Flicking it on and changing to the channel for general chatter, he paused to make sure there was silence on the airwaves. "This is Hunter One. Final preparation is complete. We are reading for the drop. Any further intel? Over."

"Hunter One, this is command. Standby, over."

Brewster frowned, leaving the channel open. The others looked just as confused, but he supposed that if they wanted him to stay online then it could only be for a good reason, especially at a time as critical as this.

Finally, a voice broke the static. "Hunter One, hey, this is Mark Stiles. What's your sitrep? Over."

Brewster grimaced. If they'd brought Mark Stiles to the comms room, then this couldn't be good. "Stiles, confirm we have completed our last training mission and have been cleared to proceed. Please confirm the Hunters are still going ahead with a zero-hundred departure from Omaha, over."

Static. Brewster could imagine his old friend arguing with someone else, no doubt with intel from Sherman or Abraham, something they needed to know before departing; debating whether to broadcast it on a general channel.

"Switch to secure channel, over."

Brewster smirked. He could get used to being right.

"Everything okay up there, do you think?" Castillo echoed the thoughts of the whole squad.

Relaxed though he was, something just didn't seem quite right to Brewster. "I'm not sure. I guess we're about to find out." Secure was a generous word, but Brewster changed to the frequency they'd agreed that week for comms between the officers and leaders of the new government. "Stiles, this is Hunter One. Do you copy? Over."

Brewster paused again, this time his heart racing a little faster. Something was going down in Omaha, and part of him wished that their mission would be canceled, so he could hang around to see it.

It took a long minute for Stiles' clipped words to respond. "Reading you, Hunter One. Sorry for the cryptic behavior, but you need to hear this, and we don't want everyone up in arms more than they are already."

"Is this about McCartney? Where do you need us?"

In his eagerness, Brewster lapsed on protocol and received a sharp admonition from his superior for it. "You know how to sign off on radio calls, Hunter One. I'm not done with your intel. Do I make myself clear? Over."

Brewster tried to ignore the half-hearted smirks thrown his way by Krueger and Brent. Mark Stiles wasn't a man quick to lose his temper. Brewster was becoming more concerned by the minute. "I hear you. Standing by, over."

"The Omaha situation is under control. I repeat—we have a plan of action. We have problems elsewhere. Marine One was en route to Omaha and has been confirmed as downed. We're not sure if it's mechanical or otherwise. Last location twenty miles outside of McCoy. Confirm this message as received and understood, over."

Brewster's voice stuck in his throat for a sickening heartbeat. Marine One was the presidential aircraft. *Could Frank Sherman be dead?* "Understood and standing by for orders, over."

"There is a force of bandits around the New Abraham area. They have attacked once already. The enemy was initially repelled with air support from McChord, but we have reason to believe they are continuing their assault. New Abraham is at risk. Confirm this message as received and understood, over."

Brewster's pulse raced. Stiles might be running the show, but he was speaking now as if he was communicating to some newly-enlisted PFC, not a veteran of the campaign against the virus. Biting down every sarcastic response the old Brewster wanted to spew, he responded almost numbly. If Stiles wanted them either searching for President Sherman, or supporting Omaha, they'd have already received the orders to stand down, and it wouldn't have been over the radio. "Message received and understood. Confirmed ready to deploy as instructed. Standing by for new orders."

He opened himself up for a glimmer of hope that Stiles had just been outlining the situation in as plain and brutal a fashion he could before telling the Hunters they were needed to save the president's life. Even going up against some unknowns at New Abraham sounded better than dropping into DC and doing battle against who-the-fuck-knows how many undead. But, the longer the silence between their chatter lasted, the more Brewster knew he wouldn't like what he was about to hear.

"Your orders remain the same, Hunter One. You will deploy at zero-hundred as agreed. You will still be able to transmit radio updates, but we will not update you on either of these situations unless it is absolutely necessary. Your primary focus remains the task at hand. Do I make myself abundantly clear? Over."

"Clear as day. Hunter One confirmed. We'll prep and be at the extraction point as advised. Over and out."

Brewster threw the radio limply down onto his pack, almost defeated before he'd begun. No more communications? Why bother telling them then, if all they had to do now was worry about what was happening back home while trying to defeat an entire city of infected? If Stiles' aim had been to throw them all off their game, he'd sure as hell succeeded.

"What the fuck was that all about?" Garibaldi snapped.

Castillo's cheeks were flushed; she looked about as happy as Brewster felt. "That's bullshit, man," she said. "Sprinters being brought into Omaha; New Abraham under attack. And now we've lost Sherman? And they want to chute us into hell? I know where they can stick their orders."

"We're still going," Brewster responded woodenly.

"What?" The rest of the Hunters almost exclaimed as one. For the first time since being given his new posting, Brewster understood what it must feel like to lead; to make the unpopular decision, and stand alone with it, knowing you are in the right despite how wrong it feels.

"Because it's what Sherman wanted. We don't know why his transport has gone down, and we certainly have no idea what's happening in New Abraham. If Stiles says he has it under control, it's not our place to argue. Sherman wants DC tamed. We're still his team to do that. Go get some rest. It won't be long until we fly out."

They all hesitated.

"Go on," he told them, waving his hand.

As the team walked reluctantly away, Brewster fumbled with his radio, bouncing it in his palm. He considered radioing Stiles back and telling him just how he felt. He wanted to radio Sherman, just to hear the man's voice. That he might never again wasn't something worth considering.

Frank Sherman was a tough SOB. He would pull through.

And no matter what, Brewster would lead the Hunters in and out of DC, the way Sherman believed he could.

CHAPTER 12

WARM BEER

THE BURNING TANG OF embers and melting asphalt blended in the air. It was a nauseating combination that he'd hoped to never smell again; Abraham had already burned once before. He'd promised his people he'd keep them safe. He felt like a failure, despite how many of them remained alive. Keaton knew this wasn't the end of it. Marie had already told them what to expect: the Nomads left nothing standing when they were done with you.

"What have we got left?"

Keaton limped through the center of town. The RSA had done enough to them in the past, and rebuilding had been a slow process, bringing them all together as a community. Would this be one assault too far?

"I thought we'd have a lot less than this," Evans echoed in the somber silence.

Their cars had breached the gates, but it seemed like the Nomads had simply made a statement. Some houses were charred; a couple of roads buckled. Beyond that, the core infrastructure of New Abraham remained stubbornly intact. As they trod the familiar path to Eileen's, he expected a sucker punch, certain the bar was another casualty, but there its welcoming walls stood like on any other day. Pushing open the door though, and feeling the heavy atmosphere of those sitting around, the thickness in the air was a pall of dismay and sorrow.

Keaton walked slowly and took a seat at the bar, making sure to nod at everyone who met his eye. They needed to see his face and know he wasn't hiding. The people of Abraham weren't defeated, not yet, and Keaton Wallace wasn't giving up.

Eileen slid a mug across the bar. She didn't ask for payment, and Keaton suspected no one would be asked to pay for their beer today. It didn't matter what the time was. Everyone needed to take the edge off before they took stock of the whole situation. Keaton had to let Sherman know what was happening. The Nomads were a real threat to the stability their alliance had worked so hard to build, and he knew that the new president would want to put out the Nomads' fire before it had a chance to spread much further.

"What's the news?"

Eileen shook her head. "Not many are missing, but that doesn't mean we haven't lost. Look at the faces around you. This is hard, sheriff. Do we...does Francis know?"

Keaton gave her a short swift shake of the head. Everyone in Abraham knew that they would get all the support they needed from the military in and available to their friends in Omaha. It was thanks to their egg production that they'd been able to produce as much of the vaccine as they had. Was it already too late, though? Even without high losses, the entire town was in disarray. By the time word got through and troops were on their way, the Nomads could already have regrouped and attacked again.

"What are we going to do, sheriff? What can I do to help?"

Keaton, briefly, was lost for words. He wished Janine was with him. He still didn't regret sending her away. The longer it took her to return home, though, the more nervous he got. He had no doubts she could handle herself; still, if she had gotten through the attack unscathed, why wasn't she home already? He looked over his shoulder, scanning the room again. The chatter had died down. He knew that whatever he said now could make or break whatever little morale these people had left.

"I'm gathering together all the intel we can after last night. We'll let Omaha know, and they'll send us all the support we need." It was a lie. Sometimes a lie in the right place didn't feel so wrong. Eileen understood this and smiled at him thinly.

Keaton sipped his warm beer, trying to work out just what they could do to rally. He needed a headcount of survivors—most of the town, he hoped—and their skills. As if psychic, one of the men he needed walked through the bar door. It gladdened Keaton to see Jose Arctura's beaming grin as he strode confidently across the room. The man looked positively elated, a complete juxtaposition to every other denizen in the place. Keaton cocked his eyebrow: the mechanic clearly had some news. A few heartbeats behind, Brenda burst through the closing door. She looked just as animated as Jose. Between the two they must have concocted some sort of plan. If people had been trying to listen subtly before, they were being blatant about it now.

"Sheriff, we need to speak to you. About the attack."

"What have you got for me, friend?"

Keaton couldn't help but break into a smile himself when he saw the shit-eating grins creep across their faces. Something they were cooking had them excited, and their positivity was thankfully infectious.

"I think it'd be easier if you come with us to the workshop. Honestly, sheriff, you're going to love this." Jose glanced at Brenda. "I think the honor should be yours."

Brenda leaned forward as if taking the sheriff into her confidence. She wasn't quiet when she spoke, though. Her voice was loud and clear, and everything they needed to hear. "Well, sheriff, it's about some weapons...."

CHAPTER 13

REGROUP

"You should be resting, Anna."

Anna Demilio sat up in bed, wincing as she shifted in her pillows. Her midriff was bandaged heavily to limit movement, and the scarce medication they had for pain relief was only taking the edge off the burning pain lancing across her stomach. Still feeling pain was important. It meant she was still alive. She hadn't been unconscious for long.

Rebecca had been seeking the doctor for a checkup on her unborn child. She arrived at the labs to find them empty. Rebecca had said something just didn't feel right to her and being trusted by all in Omaha, she was one of few who about Anna's research on their old friend Klaus Meyer, meaning she had access to the sub-basement lab and to Anna's extended research on the vaccine.

She had found Anna unconscious and bleeding on the sub-basement floor. Thinking on her feet, Rebecca sutured the wound right away, then called Mark for help. Together, they carried Anna to a hospital bed and hooked up to a saline transfusion, all in less than an hour. Any longer and Anna's survival would have been in serious doubt.

"I hate to be the cliché," Anna said, "but we can't rest at a time like this."

A slight frown creased Rebecca's forehead, clearly worried for her friend's health. "You need rest. That bullet might have passed clean through and God knows you're lucky to just be getting away with tissue damage, but I've seen lesser wounds put soldiers on their assess for long enough."

"Has anyone heard from Frank?" Anna asked, subtly ignoring Rebecca's advice. "Does he know about everything else happening with McCartney?"

An awkward silence fell amongst the group, which the observant doctor couldn't fail to miss. "What is it? What aren't you telling me?"

"Anna," Mark placed his hands on the bed, leaning down in an attempt to seem reassuring. "You've got to concentrate on your recovery. We don't want you worrying about something that hasn't happened yet."

"Bullshit Mark, if something's happened to Frank I want to know."

Mark met her gaze and knew there was no way she'd back down, not after everything they'd been through together as a group. He took a deep breath, steeling himself. "There's been an accident. Frank's transport lost altitude not far out of base. They managed to put out a distress call, but that's it. Radio silence since, though they're scrambling to the coordinates to see if there are any survivors."

Anna clenched her jaw, swallowing the lump that rose in her throat. Frank was a resourceful man. She blinked back tears, although one still managed to stubbornly trace a path down her hot cheek. She sniffed. If anyone was going to make it back alive, it would be Francis Sherman. He hadn't gotten this far to be taken out in a damned accident. "Do we know what caused it?" Anna asked stiffly, her voice cracking but staying firm. "Is it sabotage again?"

In the stiff silence that followed this, Rebecca was sure they were all forced to remember Mbutu Ngasy, their gentle friend who had needlessly died in a helicopter crash—no—assassination—that had killed their previous president.

"It can't be a coincidence," Anna muttered.

"It can—we know that the chairman is dead, and so are his allies. It's got to be this new threat. McCartney, whoever he works for, and his friends."

Rebecca was glad he'd stayed by her side, yet couldn't help but wince at the edge in Mark's voice when he mentioned the man who had brazenly strode into the center of town with a sprinter on a leash. There was no doubt that he was a threat, but he seemed too much of a loose cannon to be part of a wider organization. McCartney was no RSA.

Anna plowed through the awkward silence. "I saw the footage before…before the attack. The riots. We know there have been whispers for a while. Have we all just been ignoring them?"

Mark looked away, not willing to meet Anna's gaze at first when he answered. "Omaha isn't going to be perfect, and the bigger we get, we can't expect to please everybody. None of us could have predicted it would blow up like this."

"But there's pleasing people," Anna retorted, "and there's keeping the peace. Have we been so focused on curing the country that we've lost control of our own town? I'm no soldier, but that's what it looks like to me."

"Look now, you don't know what it's like up top, doc."

"Mark, please." Rebecca put a calming hand on his arm. "You don't know what Anna's been through to get us to this point. I'm not trying to—"

"Can you all stop arguing?" Phyllis strode into the room, shocking them all into stunned silence. "The doctor is ill and you're all gathered here working her up into a frenzy, you should be ashamed of yourselves. I know there's problems upstairs but that doesn't mean you need to involve the doctor in every little decision you have to make. You should all make your pleasantries and leave, thank you very much." She folded her arms, her face stern, looking every inch the matriarch. Anna hid a wry smile.

Mark shook his head, looking embarrassed. "I'm sorry Phyllis. There's just so much going on that I think it's good for Anna to be informed at all stages. I don't want her getting a shock finding all this out at once. The rebels are happy there's going to be an election, sure, but they think we've gone dark and aren't going to honor our side of the bargain."

"People are already saying it's going to be a fix, and Mark is going to win," Rebecca stated bluntly, her arms folded over her chest. "Which is, of course, a load of bullshit."

Mark rubbed his face, too tired to be surprised by his wife's outburst. "Of course, it's a load of crap. I'm not exactly doing much to convince them differently. We need to think carefully about our next steps, otherwise up top is going to turn into a shitstorm before we can blink. Here's what we do know. We're still waiting on McChord to get us intel on Sherman's downed chopper, and until we hear that he's dead we're assuming he's alive. We all know he's been through worse, and I think it's safe to say we know that, no matter what he's going through, he can survive it."

Everyone nodded firmly to this. Rebecca saw tears well in Anna's eyes. The doctor quickly dashed them away.

Rebecca tried to follow as Anna and Mark debated the situation, despite Phyllis' best efforts to get them away from her newly-appointed patient. Anna seemed to think it would be easy enough to import unvaccinated people from outside the Omaha safe zone and infect them, which in principal, Rebecca agreed with. It made sense as a tactic. While it was unsettling to think they'd target people like that, Rebecca supposed that this McCartney seemed more than unhinged enough to go to those lengths.

Mark thought McCartney, like the RSA, was possibly holding sprinters away from prying eyes, waiting for an advantageous time to use them as weapons. It was, therefore, possible that the infected man paraded in the street was from before the vaccinations were rolled out. This seemed plausible, too, based on their encounters with weaponized infected in the past.

Once Mark finally ran out of steam floating his ideas, eyeing Rebecca for support he never got, Anna spoke into the silence. "All of this aside, with everything that's happened to me directly, I have a much simpler answer for you. You're not going to like it."

Rebecca already had an idea of what Anna was going to say. She'd seen Robbie Chastain's corpse. She'd only known it was him because of the limited security access and staff rotation in the labs. It wasn't a pleasant sight.

"One of my lab hands, Robbie, attacked me," Anna's eyes flicked briefly to Phyllis, who looked pale and placed a hand over her chest at the mention of Robbie's name. "You know that part already. Becky saved my life. What I haven't been able to tell you is what Robbie wanted. He was trying to find and sabotage my research."

This was met by cursing from everyone there, barring Rebecca. The former medic's blood was boiling. Robbie had seemed like a nice, helpful guy. Anna had been delighted to have an educated and enthusiastic understudy. She'd been played. They all had.

"Robbie helped distribute the vaccines. It's possible that some of the people he had contact with, were not actually administering the vaccine. What I'm trying to say," Anna sounded tired, and Rebecca wanted to stop her. She knew the doctor wouldn't rest until she was happy their situation had improved. "...is that I think this McCartney, whatever his people are, their corruption runs further and deeper than we'd anticipated, and it's been there for a while. I don't think all of Omaha is safe. In fact, I want to re-administer the vaccine. To everyone."

"But that will cause chaos," Rebecca responded. "It'll play right into McCartney's hands!"

"Which," Mark replied somberly. "Is probably what he wanted all along. If the doc is right, and she usually is, then McCartney never cared about whether Robbie got to the research or not. Now, we don't trust his work, and there are sprinters out there proving just why we have reservations. Our vaccination plan is in doubt and..."

"Our credibility as leaders," Anna said, finishing his thought.

They all shared a look. "They wanted to hear a fair statement from their current administration?" Mark sighed. "We have to be honest. And this isn't going to be pretty."

"Mark, don't be hasty," Rebecca said. "We don't want to make this worse than it already is."

As if on cue, the captain of the local police, Alex Denny, burst through the doors, panting and struggling for breath. "Sorry to interrupt, but you really need to see this. It's chaos out there!"

Rebecca and Mark shared a glance. "McCartney?" Rebecca suggested.

Stiles nodded. "Who else?"

CHAPTER 14

HOUSE OF CARDS

Frank couldn't remember feeling anger quite like the way it coursed through his veins on seeing nothing but blank or stunned faces as he made his way back through the corridors of McChord. Had *anyone* expected him to return alive? Just how many people were in on the conspiracy to kill him?

"I want all the department heads in my office, and I want them there in ten minutes!"

Jessica hurtled out of a side corridor, eyes wide. "President Sherman! I heard the news. I can't believe it!"

"Neither can anyone else, apparently," Sherman muttered, relieved to see at least one person happy to see his head safely on his shoulders. "Get everyone together. I need to...work some things out with the rest of the administration."

True to his demands, eight minutes later Sherman paced his office as Major Trevor Bentley, Adan Forrest, and the Vice President Morris Spivey all filed in behind Jessica and waited for him to speak.

Spivey was sharp as usual, his brow creased in a frown. Adan looked fidgety as usual, wanting to be anywhere but an office. Bentley's face was wooden, almost unreadable. That wasn't like the Major at all, and Francis noted the man wouldn't even look him directly in the eye.

"Gentlemen," Sherman addressed them—he wasn't sure how to approach this. *Which one of you exactly wants me dead?* "I think it's safe to say that I'm lacking in allies in the New White House. Would any of you care to explain how my transport was brought down despite monitored preflight checks? Because I've lost an incredibly competent pilot today, and there was nothing wrong with that chopper when we left McChord."

They looked anywhere but at him while fumbling for words. Adan spoke first, but it was the last thing Sherman had expected to hear. "Mr. President, we're in shock about what happened, and we're glad you're alive, but, sir, there's more…"

"More?" Sherman stopped in stride, his sharp eyes locking on his vice president, then Major Bentley.

Adan squirmed, stretching his collar and casting his gaze at the others, like he was searching for allies. "Mr. President, there's been an attack on New Abraham."

"Attack? By who? We've demolished the RSA. They're done."

Major Bentley stepped forward. "It's not the RSA, Mr. President. It's a new group. We hadn't heard of them before—hadn't even caught news of them on the wind. I can only guess we were too distracted by the threat caused by the RSA to consider other groups out there might be banding together."

"What is this group? What's the situation in Abraham? Is Keaton Wallis okay?"

"Mr. President…" Bentley put up his hands, pleading for Sherman to remain calm. "That's not all. There are issues in Omaha."

"I've been gone a day and things have already gone this far south? What's happened there?"

"There's been some protests against leadership. A man by the name of McCartney brought an infected into the center of town, during the opening ceremony for the hospital." Sherman was about to say he knew this already, but the next words from Bentley made him go cold. "Dr. Demilio was attacked, but she's alive."

Sherman's heart had sunk into the pit of his stomach. "Attacked? How? By who? McCartney?"

"We don't know how, and we're going to bring Keaton and Brewster in on conference. They can brief us more effectively."

Sherman heaved a sigh of relief. So, Keaton was alive, and Brewster had made the return trip to Omaha without issue. "Well, what are we waiting for? Let's get them on the line."

More than hearing what was happening in the cities, Sherman needed to know beyond doubt that Anna was okay. It would only take seconds and would serve to set his mind at ease, so he could focus on the bigger issues at hand.

The RSA had just been one in a seemingly endless stream of enemies. Even with the threat of the Morningstar infection seemingly abated, it appeared mankind was still hell-bent on destroying itself some way or another.

"Hello?" Keaton's voice came first over the loudspeaker. The man sounded weary and defeated. Sherman imagined him slumped over a desk, his head in his hands, not the straight-backed and pragmatic leader he was used to dealing with.

"I hear you, Keaton. We're waiting for Stiles to join us."

"Things are bad everywhere?"

Sherman smiled grimly. "You don't know the first of it."

"I'll have to wait in suspense from the sounds of things."

"Stiles here, over."

"You don't need to sound off, Stiles, It's a phone conversation. You're the last to join. You're speaking to Adan, Bentley, Spivey, and Sheriff Keaton Wallis in Abraham."

"Good morning, gentlemen."

"Okay…" Sherman wanted this to be all business and over quickly. He'd heard enough words. It was time for action. "It's safe to say a shitstorm has been brewing, and it's caught us all by surprise. Here's what I know. Abraham has been attacked; Keaton is alive…"

Keaton chimed in. "Yep, still kicking."

Sherman continued: "Casualties unknown. Sitrep unknown. Omaha has a revolt on their hands. I don't know if the two incidents are related. On my way to Omaha, my transport was downed. I made it back by vehicle and foot. I suspect someone has tried to assassinate me, and I believe they are either resident in McChord or part of a militant group with allies inside the Administration. Is that an accurate reflection so far?"

They all acknowledged his summary without disputing it. Sherman thought Spivey had begun to look a little pale, though of course, that may have just been the lighting.

"Frank, er, Mr. President," Keaton said, "if I may enlighten you on the situation here in Abraham?"

"I think that's a good place to start. Go ahead, sheriff."

"The first hint we had of trouble was when one of our scouting parties was delayed back from a mission. One person made it back, and she's a sore sight. Her intel told us about a group called the Nomads, who have been marauding townships on their way across the country. Abraham was next in their path."

"What do they want?"

"From what I can tell, nothing. Mayhem. They take a few things, but they don't settle or stop for more than a few minutes. According to Marie, the survivor—and I have no reason to distrust her intel— they raze towns once they've taken all they want."

"How did you hold them off?"

"That's what I'm unsure about. I'm not sure we did. We damaged them some, took out what looked like one of their lieutenants, but that didn't deter them. They kept coming at us. We even pushed them out to the mines. It didn't do much. We thought they'd breach us, so I gave the order to evacuate. We've rebuilt before, and I'd prefer to have my people alive among ruins than dead in ashes."

"But the town is standing?"

"Hardly touched. As if they decided once they had it, they didn't want it anymore. They took out the Apaches sent from McChord. Maybe proving a point."

"Do you think they'll be back?" Stiles' concerned voice echoed from the other line.

"I've got no doubt," Keaton replied immediately, bitterness edging his voice.

"What are your casualties, sheriff?"

"Twenty confirmed dead. Eleven unaccounted for, though we're still waiting for some to return. We've had survivors trickling in since dawn so I'm not ready to give up on everyone quite yet. You know how resourceful Jose can be—we're already planning our next line of defense."

"How's Janine?"

Keaton didn't reply straightaway, and Sherman immediately regretted asking the question. "She's one of the eleven unaccounted." The sheriff answered somberly.

"We'll do whatever we can to help, Keaton. I need to know the situation in Omaha, so we can allocate the right resources. Stiles? What's your sitrep?"

"Nervous, sir. I've declared an election for mayor to mitigate the threat. The only runners are myself and Michael McCartney, our latest favorite person to hate."

"The man who brought the sprinter to the party," Sherman stated to the room.

"The very same. Apparently, we don't have any laws against that, so you probably want to get some legislative types over there thinking about updating the statutes. As we hoped though, hearing about the election calmed things down a little while. We're seeing some crowds in the streets, though they're not aggressive at the moment. The consensus is they're going to stage a demonstration. I can't imagine it's going to be peaceful."

"I'm inclined to agree with you. What else? I heard that Dr. Demilio was hurt."

"She's okay, sir. Becky found her just in time. She was attacked at her lab and shot, but she's stable. We think it was one of McCartney's followers, an infiltrator."

This McCartney was sounding worse by the second. "So, we're not sure what the Nomads want; they just sound like moving chaos, but this McCartney sounds like he wants power?"

"The good doctor was given the full speech by her attacker before he died. McCartney and his followers believe that Morningstar should be allowed to naturally run its course. Those who remain will be the ones strong enough and deserving of a place in the, I don't know…the aftermath."

"They were going to sabotage the vaccination program? Who attacked her?"

"Her assistant, Robbie."

Sherman recalled the name, immediately picturing a young, goateed face, skinny arms, and the fades of acne scars. "A student, right? He was working with Anna for months. If he'd wanted to sabotage her work, he could have just interfered with the production."

"And without someone we've vaccinated willing to be bitten to see just how well it's working, we're not sure if he has or not. Anna wants to produce new batches from scratch and revaccinate Omaha and New Abraham."

"That's going to set us back months, never mind the panic it's going to cause. That plays right into this McCartney's hands."

"I'm open to other suggestions. I can't see that we have an option, though. If they've brought sprinters into the town, we have to consider the entire population is at risk at this point."

"I can't say I'm disagreeing with you. But we've been pushed into a hard corner, and I can't believe none of us saw this coming."

"If I could speak freely, sir, we've been spread thin trying to do a lot. We've been so distracted by the expansion of Omaha and the vaccine delivery that this unrest has probably been brewing for a while. It's not something that happens overnight, and while we're keeping things together, I can't imagine it'll be for much longer."

"Comments noted, Stiles, thank you for your candor. Okay, what we need now is a cohesive plan. You think you have enough personnel there to deal with the threat McCartney poses?"

"His numbers are unknown, sir, but we have resources and firepower to put down most threats. I don't think you need to spare us anything."

"And, of course," Bentley interrupted "the mission to drop in DC is obviously going to be aborted."

It was a statement, not a question. This wasn't lost on Sherman. "No, we are not canceling the assault on DC. The Hunters go out almost as soon as this call ends." He responded bluntly. Bentley paled further and looked taken aback.

Spivey jumped in. "But with these many threats how can your team possibly hope to complete their mission? They'll have no support."

"They were going in without support anyway."

"I assumed that was a front—a power play. That they'd call someone in."

"That is not my understanding of the situation, Mr. Vice President, nor is it the understanding of the Hunters." Stiles clipped. There was a sarcastic undercurrent to his voice, which made a smile edge on Sherman's lips.

"Now we're clear on that, we just need to identify what Abraham needs."

Keaton cleared his throat. "As you might expect, for those of you that have been to Abraham before, our friend Jose Arctura has a trick or two prepped to greet these Nomads when they swing back our way. We know they have modified vehicles with unidentified anti-aircraft firepower, so I'm hesitant to ask for more air support from McChord…"

Sherman broke in, "You can have whatever you need, sheriff. Now we know what kind of hardware they carry we can be more reactive to their threat. These Nomads sound like they need eliminating and fast before they become more of a threat than the RSA ever were. They at least had a sense of purpose. These Nomads are unpredictably dangerous and the opposite of what we need with what we're trying to build. Get Arctura's plan to my command with the extra support personnel you'll need, and we will make it happen.

"Stiles, Omaha sounds like a boiling pot, but I trust you to keep this under control. You are authorized to use whatever force he needs against McCartney and his men. Do not let their momentum overtake what we've worked so hard to build.

"The rest of you, this base is on lockdown until we have a full review of what happened to my flight. Dismissed."

Phone lines went dead as they all shuffled out of the room. Jessica was the last to leave, and Sherman called her back to him. "Jessica, could you send in Sanderson, please?"

She nodded curtly and hurried out, all efficiency. Sherman ticked her name off his mental list of those under suspicion.

Sanderson slid into the office a couple of minutes later, a manila envelope tucked under his arm and a sheen of nervous sweat across his pink forehead.

"What have you got for me?"

"Just as you suspected, sir. I found some sophisticated code in our intranet. It appears the EC-135's electrical systems were digitally set to FADEC, sir, with a remote EMP trigger, which would explain why it wasn't picked up on preflight routines."

"FADEC?"

"Engine failure, basically. Fully...Automated, no...Authorized Digital Engine, uhm..." Sanderson noticed Sherman's impatient expression. "Well, basically something in the engine compartment was triggered to induce a total system-wide shut down, including manual controls for restart, throttle...I mean, no electricity, no engine, and on purpose, sir. Sabotage with a capital S. Well, maybe a little s. If I had access to the actual wreckage, I could give you way more precise information. You know, it's actually pretty amazing Campbell was able to land that bird without—"

Sherman knew he and his agents owed Rachel Campbell their lives, but right now he couldn't dwell on it. He had to keep sharp. He'd honor her later somehow. "Right," he interrupted Sanderson. "So, any way of finding out the source of this code you mentioned?"

"With the technology I have available, it won't be easy, but I'm working on it. They had an anonymous login, but what I do have for you, though, are transcripts of some intercepts." Sanderson passed Sherman the manila envelope. "Makes no sense to me—some kind of military cypher, but you may have some trusted people that can look at it for you, sir, I imagine."

Sherman opened the envelope, rifled through a few sheets of printed paper with brief, clipped exchanges in encoded jargon. "Where did these originate from?"

"Well, yeah. That's the cause for concern, sir. These exchanges originated within our own network. If there's a conspiracy to have you killed, whoever's doing these things is pulling the strings from inside."

Sherman grimaced. Sometimes, it would be nice to be wrong. Even just once.

CHAPTER 15

UNTO THE BREACH

"ARE WE READY, HUNTERS?"

"As ready as we'll ever be, sir!"

Brewster didn't think he'd ever get used to the feeling of being a ranking officer, even if that rank still remained somewhat ambiguous. Given where they were about to drop, though, he wasn't sure he'd have long to adjust to his new status anyway. Carried in an Osprey, they were about to drop on top of a skyscraper a few blocks northeast of the White House. Securing that building, they should have a straight run to the Capitol, their primary target. The ease of that, of course, depended on how many sprinters remained between their LZ and the objective. Intel suggested Washington was totally dead, and any infected they encountered should be a shambler. Hopefully, that meant no matter how many dead came their way, he and his team would get to the supplies the helo was dropping to take out any major threats that stumbled into their path.

First things first: they had to land without breaking their necks.

"Drop."

Without hesitation, Brewster stepped out, the string tightening quickly to release his chute. Cold air whipped around his body as he fumbled to guide himself down. He had chosen to be the first out, deciding early on it would be his responsibility to lead everyone to ground. None of them were paratroopers; still, if they were Sherman's elite, there wasn't anything now they wouldn't have to learn.

Dawn had just broken, and a murky fog hung around street level. This high up, Brewster clearly saw the gray concrete tower he needed. The highest in the area, the most practical to maneuver through, it made the most sense from a tactical approach. Trying not to focus on the shrouded ground he still couldn't quite see, instead checking the altitude on his watch, he pulled down at the chute to slow his approach, twisting to the left to begin an arc around. If he tried to come into the landing straight, he'd miss it and end up slammed against an anonymous piece of brick, his death an absolute certainty.

One crate would drop for them on the roof to supplement the gear they already carried. One single crate of support gear to clear the route. Only time would tell if it would be enough.

Circling and slowing, Brewster tugged hard on his parachute and lifted his legs to land in clean. His heels scraped concrete. He released, hitting the ground with a *thud*. It wasn't graceful, but it didn't need to be. He was down safely.

The rest of the team, Garibaldi in the lead, followed. Krueger was the last to land, sticking a perfect drop and shaking off his cords like a pro. Brewster unhooked his M4A1 carbine, attached its sound suppressor and bayonet, fed the magazine, and checked the safety.

Satisfied, he took stock of their position as the rest of the squad did the same. Krueger slid a huge tactical bag to the ground, carefully unpacking his multi-cal DesertTech HTI sniper rifle. He went to work, sliding the free-floating barrel into the chassis and inserting the bolt with a satisfying *click-chkk!* He then swiveled the recoil pad on, gave it a slap, and tightened the barrel retention screws in record time. "Bullpup's good to go," Krueger said, hefting the rifle in one muscled arm and fetching his bag with the other.

The rest of the team would head to ground level while Krueger completed a recon of the streets below. With any luck, they'd secure a route without disturbing any infected—with no noise to stimulate them, there shouldn't be a reason for the shamblers to attack.

Too much to hope for, Brewster thought, *though one could hope.*

Krueger made his way to the edge of the roof, dropped the pack and attached his rifle's scope. The rest of the team looked on while their lonely crate descended steadily to the rooftop. "Let's see what we're up against," Krueger hissed, extending his HTI's bipod and dropping to a knee at the roof's edge. He put an eye to the sight. "Then we'll know just how much we need from that crate."

Ground fog made seeing what they were up against practically impossible from so high up. Krueger needed to give the team something to go on and hoped that with the right tools, he'd be able to give them a basic sitrep. Leaning only slightly over, he squinted below. Everything swirled. Guessing that was because of the weather, he put his scope up. His breath stuck in his chest a second and he nearly dropped his rifle. His knuckles whitened as they tightened on the grip.

"Brewster? You need to come look at this."

The unit leader jogged over and Krueger let him peer through the scope at the ground below. A grim look overcame Brewster's stern face. How on earth were they expected to get through this?

Brewster uttered one word. "Fuck."

"Fuck indeed," Krueger said. "I think my tactical rooftop position has just become redundant, sir."

At his first check, Krueger's view hadn't been blocked by the weather at all. The rolling mist hadn't marred his vision. What he'd seen was a packed mob of undead, all standing together, congesting the streets. A literal river of the dead from sidewalk to sidewalk, there wasn't room to put a single finger between the shamblers in that tight-packed horde. None of them could survive down there. No one could.

Taking his rifle back, Krueger scanned from building to building, trying to find any signs of life.

"What?" Garibaldi said in his usual nervous tone of late. "What the fuck is it, Krueg? Brewster? Sir?"

"Just let me think a second," Brewster said.

"That bad?" Castillo asked.

"Krueger, might as well let them have a look." *Damn.* Every check they'd done said Washington was dead. The evidence below supported it. Still, anything indicating some survivors at any part would give them hope of a safe route. But no one could survive the volume of infected below without a strategy or plan.

"One sec, sir," Krueger said. "Just scanning around."

"This isn't good," Garibaldi said to Castillo. He looked at Kiley, who was checking his M4's safety for the fifth time. Kiley shrugged.

"It isn't good, is it?" Garibaldi turned to Brent.

"Pull it together, man," Brent told him, though he seemed to be fiddling uneasily with his black Ka-bar kukri-style machete.

Castillo gave Garibaldi a shove. "Eyes on the prize, okay?"

That seemed to shift something in Garibaldi. He nodded slowly but took a breath and seemed to calm down. "Eyes on the prize."

Krueger kept scanning, but each building yielded less hope. In one window he thought he saw someone desperately waving. Perhaps they'd seen the drop from the chopper and hoped for a rescue? Focusing in, though, Krueger was disgusted to see the malnourished torso of an infected old man, slapping at the window, scraping his flat palms down the glass in bloody streaks. Jogging to each side of their tower, he was met with more of the same. Washington DC was the deadest city Krueger had ever seen.

"It's no use," he muttered, shaking his head and looking over his shoulder to the rest of the Hunters. "Feel free to have a look. It ain't pretty."

Garibaldi stepped up first and took his turn with the scope. To his credit, he was silent as he looked at the nightmare below them. No whining, whimpering, or cursing. He finally handed it over to Castillo, muttering "Eyes on the prize…" as he stepped away. "…the prize."

"What do you mean not pretty? Castillo said as she swiveled Krueger's sniper rifle around, looking through the scope. "I see all kinds of pretty faces down there." She handed him the rifle back. "Prettier than yours, at least."

That got a grin from Krueger.

"We got a little work to do, eh, boss?" Castillo said, bringing her M4 up to her chest and giving it a pat.

"Yeah, a little," Brewster said.

Kiley was next to look. "Damn, you ain't kidding. I hope that crate's got some grenades. Might as well have some fun."

The team's stance gave Brewster heart. No one looked all that disturbed, even after seeing the sheer level of the task they faced. Castillo seemed to have a calming effect on all of them and he was glad for her as his second. He looked the crew over, and each Hunter looked grim and determined as ever. They had been sent here for a singular purpose, and Brewster got the sudden prideful feeling each one of them would see that through no matter the cost.

"Okay, let's take this building," he said. "We can see if there's a way to move across neighboring towers and circuit the infected that way. The population has a limit; the buildings are packed close enough together. There must be an alternative route we can take. We just need to find it, am I right?"

"Hooah, sir," Castillo said, and the others echoed her.

"All right then. Hunters, move out!"

Kiley kicked in the door to the roof as they fanned into the dim stairwell. Washington's power had been out for nearly the entire outbreak; even the emergency lighting was long gone, leaving the Hunters to carve their own path through the gloom. Aiming the tactical LED on his rifle, Krueger lit the way as they took the first corridor. Before the infection, this had been a generic office building. If they were lucky, people chose not to come into work before the world ended. The way society worked before, that might not be the case. They moved as one as if they were in a war zone. No matter where you went in the Morningstar US, there was always risk of attack.

Brent tried the first door they came to. It wouldn't open. Krueger flashed his light at the frosted windows. There wasn't any indication of life or death behind that glass.

"Should I force it?" Brent asked, unsure of their next move.

"No," Brewster swiftly responded, firm, confident. "They've been locked for a reason. Either that room was cleared, or there's a risk behind there. Leave it."

Room by room they found the entire floor to be the same. Even more encouraging, there was no sign of blood and no hint of a struggle. Whatever had happened in this building, the top floor had seemingly been not just evacuated but organized so that anyone coming next would know precisely what had happened.

"If it can stay like this, we might just get out of here alive," Garibaldi said.

"Don't tempt fate," Krueger hissed back at him.

Up ahead, Kiley threw up a fist. They stopped in their tracks.

Brewster made his way to the front. "What have you seen?"

"I thought I saw movement up ahead."

"Infected?"

"Hard to say. I can't imagine there's anyone alive up here though."

They'd all seen the same thing up on the roof; the dead streets of the city below. The chances of anyone else existing up here this long with those neighbors down below were non-existent. Brewster fingered his safety, trying to think what action to take next. He'd taken lead before back at Fort Hood, but this was different. They were isolated, and there was no chance of backup. If he made a mistake, they were all as good as dead.

"Krueger, can you get eyes on what's up that corridor without being seen?"

Krueger silently stepped to the front. Without lighting, the only visibility they had was through the dirty and often-covered office windows. Brewster hoped it would be enough for Krueger to make out shapes in the murk.

The sniper peered through his sights and gave a small grunt. Brewster reckoned from that reaction Kiley had been spot-on with his assessment.

And it likely wasn't good news.

⭐⭐⭐⭐⭐

"Try to keep shots to a minimum. We don't need to bring them all to our floor. Remember, these infected are slow. We can deal with this."

Brewster palmed his M4, standing back-to-back with Garibaldi. The shambler pulled itself into view. It had no legs and dragged itself along palm-by-palm. In the pools of light between windows, Brewster saw a woman of indeterminate age with an almost-bald scalp, her skin stretched over her bones. She hadn't fed for a long time. Brewster didn't even fear her. There was no way this woman could harm him, even if he hadn't been given a fresh vaccine before leaving Omaha. No, instead of fear or anger, he felt a surge of pity.

Stepping away briefly from the protection of Garibaldi's back, he thrust his M4's bayonet into the poor woman's skull. She stopped moving immediately, out of her misery at long last. There wasn't time to dwell on her fate, though. More shamblers were pulling themselves towards their location, their ghastly moans echoing through the empty corridors.

For a few heartbeats, Brewster wondered if he'd made a mistake during the drop. Had they accidentally drawn every infected in the area towards this building? Would they just keep coming, wave-after-wave? He glanced over his shoulder to see Brent taking out an infected with a downwards kick to the knee before chopping his kukri deep into the rotten side of its melon-soft skull. Behind him, the rest of the team were dealing with over a dozen infected pulling themselves into the ever-closing space.

"It's no good," Brewster called to the squad. "We're going to have to move before we're overrun."

"We can't do this hand-to-hand," Kiley yelled at him. "We have to clear a path out."

Brewster wanted to do anything but unleash live fire in those restricted hallways. If they didn't, though, it looked like they'd be as good as dead.

"Dammit, okay! Fire at will. Let's cut a path out of here."

★★★★★

Sherriff Keaton and his people sat on the rickety stools in Eileen's bar making their own survival plans. The conversation, however, wasn't as optimistic as their previous defense preparations.

"We just don't have the numbers." Marie waved exasperated at the makeshift plans scattered across the faded bar table. With her head bandaged the way it was, and swelling and bruises all over her face, she looked like some monstrous offspring. Keaton didn't want her up and about so soon after being injured, but Marie was a hard woman to keep down. She insisted on being there. He was reminded of Janine, and he smiled. Janine was wounded, but she was home.

"You're right, we don't," Keaton responded, leaning back and crossing his arms. "But we do have something the Nomads can't ever gain: local knowledge. Most of us grew up in the area, and we know it like the backs of our hands. They're just driving around in their convoy setting fire to whatever they can see. They're not paying attention to the geography, or our location. All they see is another set of walls to burn down. We can use this against them."

"But how?" Eileen asked, laying more warm beers down in front of them.

"That, I'm pleased to announce, is where Janine comes in."

Janine, more commonly known to the residents of New Abraham as 'The Dentist,' strode into the room from behind Eileen's bar. Keaton suppressed his grin at the few gasps around the table. She didn't exactly look the picture of health. A livid purple bruise colored her right cheek, and her right eye was swollen almost completely shut. Despite this, she still shone with confidence and purpose. Janine was a powerful woman and commanded the attention of any room she walked into. Even in times like these, Eileen's little bar was no exception.

"All we have to use is our common sense against their egos," she said.

Jose Arctura, already part of Janine's plans, grinned from ear to ear. "They think they can roam around the state tearing the place apart? Let's let them think that. We'll drive them into dead-ends. We'll split their groups, isolate their leadership, and rip them to shreds."

"Like divide and conquer?" Eileen remarked.

Keaton slammed his fist on the table. "Exactly! Divide and conquer. It's that simple. They won't expect us to fight back, not after that first attack."

"How can we be so sure they're even coming back?"

"Because we're not destroyed yet," Keaton answered, his voice quiet and his anger subdued. "From what Marie has told us, they don't just glance at a place like New Abraham and leave. We can be certain they'll want to return to finish what they started, and Jose has already arranged us a fleet of vehicles perfect to run rings around the Nomads through the wider state area.

"They're coming back for us. Rest assured, people. This time, we'll be ready."

★★★★★

They kept their shots contained. In small bursts, they'd pushed McCartney's supporters back to a small pocket holed up in a couple of stores near the center of town. It had been a long afternoon, becoming what promised to be a sleepless night.

"We need to get another update into McCoy; are we in control here?" Captain Denny's face was tight, his forehead covered in perspiration.

They were trying to keep losses on both sides to a minimum, but McCartney's people hadn't made it easy. The resources at their new hospital would be stretched over the next few days to cope with the influx. They had perhaps fifty armed men and women all taking sad advantage of the presidential authorization to use force.

The Town Hall had been temporarily repurposed as a shelter for those unable to reach their homes, and the wounded were taken there for triage. Pregnant or not, Rebecca Stiles was leading the organization and effort there, and her presence gave her husband Mark peace of mind that there was one little part of this recovery that he didn't need to worry about—so long as the dozen troops and couple of sharpshooters keeping an eye on the building kept the enemy at bay.

It seemed, however, that McCartney wasn't keen on an all-out takeover. The fighting had been street-by-street, but it had seemed absurdly easy to beat their assailants back. Systematically, they'd drive them out of buildings, a complete retreat until there wasn't anywhere else to go.

Mark figured maybe they had no more than a dozen people left to kill or capture; his preference was the latter. Omaha was their home now, and he hated spilling the blood of folks that, prior to the events of the last couple of days, he'd considered totally innocent.

Mark nodded at Captain Denny, confident the tide was turning in their favor. "Yeah, the closest spot to call through would be the armory," he told the police captain. A heavily-defended building, if only for the sake of the firepower it held, it also had a secure line to Sherman. "I'll go and get back quick. You got this?"

"We'll keep them pinned here. Don't worry."

Stiles was about to turn and start the jog to the armory when a rumbling held him fast. The unmistakable noise of transports rumbled their way from a cross street, but no one was insane enough to drive around here with all the chaos going on. Still, it was to their utter disbelief when two military transports peeled into the center of the crossroads that marked the edge of the ground held by McCartney and his people.

"Hold fire!" Mark called over the rattle of gunfire. In short order, silence reigned over the streets; the only sound the idling of the trucks sitting ominously a hundred yards away or less.

A voice called out across the divide; it belonged unmistakably to McCartney. "I didn't want it to come to this! You're bringing this on yourselves."

"We're defending our people, Michael!" Mark called back at him. "You started attacking us! This isn't a peaceful protest."

"There isn't going to be an election though, is there? It's a ploy. Someone has to act. Someone has to do what's right, to make sure Omaha has the leadership it needs. Because you've been lying to us. And I have the proof!"

"Lying about what? What proof? What the hell are you talking about?"

"That this regime isn't curing a damn thing. The vaccine is a lie! We're all in danger, and we need to eradicate the sleeping leadership making us believe we're safe at night. Why else do we have the fences? The border patrol?"

"Good lord," Mark muttered, looking at Denny a second. He raised his voice at McCartney again. "You know the good that serves—"

"I've had enough talking! And so has everyone else. Actions speak louder than words, Stiles!"

At that, the trucks' engines stopped. The rear doors for the transports dropped. And out, coming straight for the exposed line of defenders, leapt dozens of sprinters.

CHAPTER 16

DISSENT

"Jose makes it sound so simple, but it can't be that easy," a resident of New Abraham protested.

Another added, "We've seen what they can do. We don't stand a chance against their firepower!"

Sheriff Keaton shook his head as the residents broke into a cacophony, all voicing their concerns about the plan to retaliate against the Nomads.

Brenda stood by him, hands on hips and intense as ever in her delivery of the borderline insane plan she and Jose had cooked up together in his workshop. She wasn't relenting now, even facing the cynical protests.

"The way I see it," Brenda yelled, raising her hands for quiet, "we have two options. We can wait here and let them attack us again and have no better counter than we had last time they ripped us a new one, or we can do what they probably never expect."

Dissenting mutters followed, and Keaton thumped his hand on the table top. "Brenda's right! Now, listen, you all. These Nomads are used to tearing through frightened small communities, they're not used to defending themselves. They don't know what they're dealing with now, no clue what we've gone through before and how we've come through it all. We have help on the way from Omaha, and by Christ, we're going to take the fight out into the fields and roads."

"But how?" came the general chorus of replies.

"The answer to that is simple enough," Keaton responded. "We know this area; they don't. We have the advantage of knowing the terrain. They think they can just drive at a town and scare people out of their homes. They think we're just going to be like everyone else, but they're wrong. We can take them to places where their high-powered cars mean nothing. We'll drive them into the forests and the mud and when they're unable to move any further, we'll pick them off like sitting ducks."

"How are we meant to do that with just the few of us?"

"Listen to me carefully: we are not fighting this alone. At the start of the outbreak, we wanted to keep outsiders away, and we knew what trouble that got us into in the end. Groups like the RSA and the Nomads, they're abusing people's fear of each other. We don't have that. We have the most powerful people and resources in the US today, driving here to defend us."

"Why aren't they here already?" someone asked.

Keaton sighed, pulling his fingers through his thinning hair. Tough crowd; they were usually a lot more receptive than this. He caught Janine looking at him and something flashed behind her eyes.

Janine stepped up in front of him, putting her hand up. "Alright, let's cut the bullshit here, people. Good God, who are you all? Now look here, the last two days have been hard for all of us. Nobody's had it easy. If Marie hadn't brought warning, I don't want to think about how much more we could have lost. But she *did* warn us, and here we are. Now, we all went to ground after the Nomads attack…" She put her hand on Keaton's shoulder before focusing back on the room; everyone hung on her every word. "…And I think I saw more of the Nomads than most. So, I'll tell you why *we* are going to take the fight to them. Because Brenda and our sheriff are right. We can't just hide behind our walls and hope they'll give up and go away. It's not going to happen. The Nomads want to destroy us and when they take the town—because if we don't fight it's only a matter of time—they're not going to show us any mercy."

"Janine, honey, how do you know that?" Eileen echoed the thoughts of everyone else in the room.

Janine didn't want to recall the horrific scenes from last night. She didn't think she'd ever get a good full night's sleep again. "We know some of us are still missing; it's why I took so long to come back. I didn't want to risk the chance of them tracking or finding me.

"Everyone here has to know and understand what I saw. When they capture you, they torture you. And they're not doing it for information, either. I heard…" Her voice cracked, and she paused, tears wetting her eyes. The uncharacteristic show of emotion caused a ripple of ill-ease in the room. "…I heard the screams. And I saw the fire. They were just burning people. And not just adults, either. Children. I don't think from here. I don't know where, but I don't know about any of ours that are missing."

Her pleading eyes sought out Keaton's, and although he'd reassured her that the cries could not have been from one of their own young ones, it didn't soften the hurt, that she couldn't help whatever poor souls were tortured for the Nomads' entertainment. "Only adults are missing. It can't be one of our own."

"But that really isn't the point," Janine continued, taking a deep breath and composing herself. "It just proves they only want one thing: to destroy us, and everything we care about. None of us will join their group; none of us will be left alive. And they won't give us a merciful death. Now I don't know about you, but I think I'd rather turn than be burnt to death tied to a stake."

"We get the idea, sweetheart." Eileen smiled, though there was little warmth behind the gesture. "But 'charge at the enemy because we know where we're going' doesn't sound like much of a plan."

"You know us better than that, Eileen," Keaton said. "Of course it's not the whole plan. During last night's attack, we identified several vehicles which appear to belong to those in the Nomad command. I thought it was a hunch before speaking to Marie, and even with her injuries she's gone above and beyond yet again and confirmed what we suspected. We will isolate those vehicles and take out as many of their leaders as we can. Like any mobile force, we can assume without clear orders, their forces are liable to scatter. They're the weak ones here. Think about it. They have limited resources on the road."

"Our resources aren't exactly extensive, sheriff," a resident countered.

Keaton, Janine, and Brenda all shared a look, and Eileen chose to keep her mouth closed. Keaton needed a united front; not for residents to keep questioning every decision he made, and Eileen must have finally understood that, for good or for worse. At least they had a plan, which was more than they could have hoped for after last night.

"You're right, they're not," he said to the crowd, "but we do have enough to take the assault to them. We still have a few tricks up our sleeves."

Keaton met Janine's worried gaze. He could see her unspoken words: *If this all goes to plan.*

CHAPTER 17

PINNED

"INFECTED! EVERYONE WITHOUT WEAPONS, get indoors, now!"

Mark Stiles' yell seemed to snap anyone nearby out of a daze. Seeing sprinters up this close and personal again was a shock. The years of training and the hard-fought campaign with Sherman, however, wasn't forgotten. Captain Alex Denny brought his sidearm up at the same time as Mark; the two soldiers, along with a couple Mark recognized from the gate patrols, began to calmly take shots at the oncoming sprinters. Not all of the infected headed for the small cluster shooting at them, which is what probably saved their lives.

Mark tried not to think about how the vaccine in everyone's bodies might be ineffective and focused on taking the sprinters down any way possible. He wasn't aiming for the head; he wanted to immobilize the threat, so his people could take them out once they were down.

From rooftops, in between the reports of gunfire, he heard McCartney's supporters jeering. "We can take these out, but what if there's more?"

The police captain had a point, although Mark couldn't see any other transports heading to the area. They were in the middle of a serious firefight, and they'd have to trust their instincts. However, it was a targeted attack, which McCartney would surely know any of the Omaha veterans would be capable of dealing with efficiently.

"He's not going to send anything else. He's not trying to kill me. He wants to win power off me; if he does it with murder he's not going to get the support he needs to keep control."

Mark put a 9mm round from his M9 into the knee of a man probably no older than his late twenties. The sprinter buckled and tumbled forward under its own momentum, skidding and rolling a couple feet away.

"I got it." Captain Denny pulled his knife, twisted it in his palm, and dispatched the threat with a thrust to the temple.

The Omaha veterans were effective. Most of the sprinters had been felled not long after exiting the transport. Denny, still in a crouch, took down the last one with a placed shot to the forehead.

Mark checked his magazine, heaving a sigh of relief. One round left. Talk about cutting it fine.

"We need to put down these infected and find out how McCartney managed to acquire two of our own transports to move them in," Mark said to Denny. "More important, I want to know how he found that many sprinters in the first place."

One of the guards, a no-nonsense woman Mark remembered as Helen, sounded in shock at seeing so many of them. "They all look so...fresh. Where did they all come from?" They'd all become used to shamblers, the faster threats of the living infected were now just a bad memory for most.

"I don't know. I intend to find out, once we show these bastards who's really in charge."

As if on cue, a shot rattled down from a rooftop, popping through the head of one of the prone zombies. Mark glanced up to see where the attack came from. Was it part of McCartney's crew, maybe completing what it would looked like Omaha's people could not? To answer that, a rattle of gunfire slammed into the bodies on the ground, their limbs twitching as they were riddled with bullets. Mark had no way of knowing how many of those shots destroyed the brain, because within seconds the assault moved up the road, towards him and the rest of the shooters standing like idiots out in the open.

"Run! Take cover!"

He would have to think later about finding and recovering shamblers from their streets. For now, he had to stay alive and ensure McCartney's people couldn't do any more damage than they already had, either to people, or his own reputation. Holstering his near-empty M9, he yelled to Denny he needed to re-arm.

Mark headed straight for the main police lock-up. It was only a block away, and he'd be able to re-arm and figure out a way out of this mess.

"How did things escalate so quickly?" Captain Denny was following on his heels.

"I don't know," Mark answered as he kept moving toward the armory. "But we need to shut this down before it gets out of hand."

"*Gets?* This looks beyond help already, Stiles."

Mark ignored the captain's words. With panic running through the streets, he needed to keep a clear head. He had to take control of his people and get McCartney's men put down and out of harm's way. A suppressed shot thumped out, chipping the tarmac behind them.

"They're the worst shots I've ever seen."

Mark knew different. "They're not professionals, but if they wanted us to be dead, I'm sure we would be."

"Why would they leave us alive?"

"Because they're taunting us."

"Why would they—"

Denny didn't finish his sentence as another close shot sent them diving to the ground, keeping to what cover they could. From behind an old postal service mailbox, Mark spied Helen and a compatriot retreating down a side street; he was glad they were safe. He went to move and swore as he stumbled and hit the ground, jarring his knee. Out of sheer instinct he rolled to the relative cover of a nearby dumpster. No one took a shot at him while he was prone, but despite his theory, Mark wasn't willing to take any chances. Even though the street around them was now deserted, he heard panicked cries from nearby blocks as McCartney's men caused havoc.

He had to get to the armory; he needed to put out a call and start coordinating a fight back. Sherman was going to have his head for this already, even if things didn't get any worse from here on out. Mark didn't want to contemplate the storm that would descend on him if he didn't put out this uprising.

"I'm going to make a run for it," he yelled across to Denny, who had his back pressed tight against a brick wall. The building he wanted was only a short sprint down the road. "Head across to your ten; there's a pharmacy. Secure it."

"Secure it? How?"

Mark glanced over and bit down a sarcastic response. The building didn't look touched. Structures like that were key in Omaha and gave even further weight to his burgeoning theory that they didn't want to destroy the infrastructure or wound too many people. McCartney didn't want to obliterate the city. Why would he want to rule over rubble? He wanted to discredit Mark's ability to govern.

"Does it look like there's a threat to you? I'm going to call in support as soon as I get in the armory. Get in the building, lock the doors, bring down the shutters. Check inventory for anything obvious, in case we have any heavy casualties—gauze, antiseptic, use common sense. Ready? Move!"

With only the briefest of looks to make sure Denny was following orders, Mark made a dash for it, ignoring the flashing pain lancing up his thigh from his knee. He'd been through worse in Hyattsburg. A scrape across the tarmac was nothing compared to the pain that followed a zombie bite.

Shouldering his way through the double doors of the police station, he dashed for the back office, fumbling for the keys that would get him through to the locked doors at the back of the building. *Why had he been wandering around with just a sidearm and one spare magazine?*

Getting through the door without a problem, Mark kept looking over his shoulder, expecting McCartney or his followers to be in close pursuit, especially with some of the hardware the military had access to. His fears were unfounded, and Mark quickly scanned the lockers looking for his best options. If their attackers were deliberately avoiding kill shots, then he'd have to do the same. It would be hard to bring a riot like this to a close without using any form of aggression, though people taking pot-shots from the top of buildings could hardly still be classed as peaceful protestors.

Peaceful. There had to be a way…

Grabbing an M4 for himself and shoving a couple of boxes of 5.56 into a vest, Mark locked up behind him—no need to give the enemy even more firepower—and rushed back out into the office. He needed something loud—anything he could use to broadcast to as many people in Omaha as possible. Grabbing a radio, he clicked it on and flipped to the general channel. *Where in the city was it?*

"Anderson, this is Stiles. Do you copy, over?"

He rubbed his sore knee in agitation as he waited for someone to cut into the static. It might be possible they weren't online; in this din, he wouldn't blame the general staff for bunkering down. After a tense thirty seconds, though, a quiet voice came in reply.

"Stiles, I'm here. Can you hear me? Over."

Mark exhaled in sheer relief. "I can. Listen, I need to know quickly. There was a truck. It had a PA system installed. We used it for herding infected around while we constructed some of the outer fences. Is it in storage? Over."

Static again. At least this time there was a sliver of hope. He didn't want to run out into the street with a gun and no plan. There was a way to end this madness without his people firing a single return shot. Mark held his breath, hoping beyond hope the truck hadn't been left at the perimeter near the fencing. That was a long trip, and there was no telling what damage McCartney's people could do in the time it took to retrieve it.

"I remember the one you need. Last I recall it's behind the hospital with the medical transports, but that was a week ago. We were going to use it at the grand opening. I don't know anyone else on base that might know if it's been moved, over."

The hospital was a hard ten-minute run from his position, maybe a little more on his aching knee. It was worth the chance. He doubted anyone would have had the need to move a vehicle like that since. Public announcements used to be few and far between.

"Thanks, you might just be the hero of the day. Stiles over and out."

Making sure one last time that the cage and door separating the office from the armory were locked tight, Mark dashed out into the street. In his haste, he forgot the rooftop shooters and darted back into the relative shelter of the doorway as the concrete dinged again in front of him. Taking a deep breath, he took a calculated risk and ran for it, trusting that no one would dare take him down out in the street for all to see.

Heart pounding, wondering every second if this was one risk too far, he sprinted towards the hospital complex, his adrenaline taking care of any pain in his leg. He passed a couple of confused faces; one man leaned out of a window to shout at him, asking why he was running away from the trouble.

Mark reddened, and not because of exertion. *They couldn't start thinking that.* The further away from the center of town, though, the quieter the streets became. No more infected appeared. The protestors were concentrating around where they could make the most noise— where they'd be most likely to be heard. The shots had stopped. He kept the radio at his hip, waiting for a report of the first person killed. Thankfully, nothing came through.

Wheezing hard by the time he got to the yard—he needed to get back drilling with their recruits—he scanned around desperately looking for the truck. It was an old thing, big wheels designed more for show than off-roading, and a sturdy dull grey chassis supporting three huge megaphones sitting in a triangular pattern on the roof. Mark imagined it had been used in parades back in the day. He pictured someone yelling to cheering crowds as a trail of floats drifted down a road packed with partygoers. Bright colors swam in his brain, at complete odds with the chaos he'd just left behind.

The keys were in the ignition; there wasn't much worry about car thieves these days. Tapping nervously at the wheel, Stiles muttered under his breath as he tried the ignition. The engine ticked over and spluttered. Nothing. "Shit!" he slammed his fist, jumping as the vehicle's horn blared. "Come on, you've just been idle, girl. Give me a break." He twisted again, and this time the engine responded, if lethargically. It ticked into life, though even idling it sounded like it could cut out again at any minute.

"No time like the present. Let's get this thing moving."

Mark shifted into gear and drove it slowly out of the yard, back down the main road and towards the bulk of the trouble. The roads were clear. Crawling at a snail's pace, he thumbed around the dashboard looking for the controls. The roof had a couple of round white speakers on, like something from a classic sci-fi movie; it couldn't be rocket science to get it all fired up. He twisted a few dials and was greeted by an ear-splitting screech from above. It was slightly muffled in the cab; he'd certainly have gotten the attention of anyone in the vicinity outside. As the whine settled, he saw curious faces peeking out of windows.

"McCartney, this is Mark Stiles. I know you're out there. Stop hiding behind your people."

He slowed even more, the truck barely rolling along now. His heart pounded as he fumbled for the right words. The whole situation seemed absurd. If only Sherman was here, he'd have known what to do. It would never have gotten this far out of hand. "McCartney, you know that neither of us wants this. I don't want to fight your people, and I know your men aren't hurting anyone. Come out and face me! I'm here, looking for you. I'm not hiding. I'm not running."

He repeated his callout every couple blocks, and the same old man who had jeered at him for retreating stood, mouth agape as the PA vehicle drifted past. He reached the pharmacy and then the center of town where they'd first released the sprinters. Mark hoped that those corpses were still there—the alternative didn't bear thinking about.

A glance in his rearview mirror showed him a curious group of people following his slow progress. Mark couldn't tell if they were friend or foe, but it was apparent that the shooting and the chaos had stopped. *If it took something this absurd to get them to see sense and put down their weapons, then so be it.*

"McCartney, I want to talk. Or are you too scared to face me, man-to-man?"

That seemed to settle it. A large figure strode out into the middle of the road twenty yards away.

Mark stopped the car, turning off the speakers and killing the engine—which seemed grateful for the rest. Opening the door, he was stunned by the deathly silence. The air buzzed with anticipation. Walking towards his opponent, Mark prayed to any deity listening that he wasn't making yet another mistake. Eventually, he'd run out of alternative plans.

"You guys been having fun?" he asked, trying to sound casual.

McCartney shrugged, a small grin turning up the corners of his mouth, his lips still scored with scabs from Mark's fists. "More entertainment than we've had around here in months. About time we had some fun in the streets. What do you want, Stiles?" McCartney used his last name like a slur; he might as well have spat on the ground afterward.

"I want you. We both know what this is about. You want us out. You want Omaha for yourself."

"I never said I wanted it—but you're right about one thing. And what of it? Calling off your precious election? Showing your true colors because you're too scared to stand against me?"

"Quite the opposite in fact. Bringing it forward. It's between me and you. Tomorrow, at sunset. Outside the Town Hall. You call off your people, and we bring this to an end. Deal?"

McCartney grinned openly then, a shit-eating grin that made Mark want to lay the big man flat out right there in the street. "I reckon we have a deal. But we're a bit spread out—going to be hard to get the word around."

Mark pointed flatly at the truck. "I think it's going to be easy."

★★★★★

"Mark, what are you going to do? None of us are ready for this!"

He paced their small living space, furiously raking his hands through his hair as he tried to process the day's events. His head pounded. He was tired, thirsty, and he needed to rest. But for Becky, and for the sake of all of them, he had to think. "I know, I know. If only I could speak to Sherman, to find out what *he'd* do."

"Then call him. He's back and—"

"He has enough problems of his own. They tried to kill him. The last thing he wants is a phone call from the man he left in charge, pleading for advice like a helpless child."

Rebecca sighed, lines of frustration etched across her forehead. "What about Anna? You know she's every bit as knowledgeable and sensible as Frank."

"Is she even awake? I feel alone in this, Becky, and I'm just a soldier. I'm not cut out for this."

She rushed to his side, grabbing his hand. "You're not alone, Mark. We'll get through this—we always do. We just have to think—what do we know about McCartney? What can we use against him, to bring people back on our side? We already know most people wanted us out, and someone like him in…well, we'd be out, wouldn't we? The population is huge now, far more than we'd ever hoped for. It would be easy to stage a coup. It's already happening, really, but you're still the man in charge. So, we trust people *know* we're in the right. We just have to show them how much they'd risk bringing a man like Michael McCartney to power."

Mark threw himself down into a chair, its old springs sagging in protest at the sudden weight. He put the ice pack Rebecca had given him to his knee. "And how am I meant to do that?"

She gave him a sly grin. "There are a few things you've told me about today, and you haven't realized just how significant they are. I think I already know what we need to do."

CHAPTER 18

SPY

SPIVEY LOOKED ALL BUT comfortable as Frank glared at him across the makeshift Presidential office. The VP pulled at his starched collar. The room wasn't hot, but Sherman imagined the man's body temp was through the roof.

Files littered the expanse of the mahogany desk; Sherman had requested the backgrounds of all of his team, even down to the juniors, trying to weed out the rot at the core of his government. A man that had made it to admiral should bear scrutiny and pressure with ease, but Admiral Morris Spivey, now Vice President of the United States, looked like he'd rather take a one-way ticket to hell than sit down and have a conversation with the only man in the country that could give him orders.

"I've done a lot of reading," Sherman began. Spivey shifted his weight, trying to find a way to look composed and comfortable. His leg started to shake. "And do you know how many people in this administration I trust right now?"

"Zero, sir?" Spivey offered, likely assessing there was no longer any point in false platitudes. The president was on the warpath, and it would have been obvious to anyone watching that the vice president was directly in his line of sight.

"Not true, actually, though it would be remiss of me to divulge any information like that to you."

"And what's that supposed to mean exactly, sir? You don't think that *I'm*—"

"In fact, that's precisely what I believe. With me gone you have the power, and so far, you're the only person regularly opposing any decision I try to make for the good of this country. Even if you haven't got a problem with me personally, it's not like it used to be. There's no Congress to stop me from making the decisions I feel are right to protect our people. And because you don't agree with my vision, you need me removed so you can become the man in charge. Am I right?"

Sweat sheened on Spivey's forehead, all formalities forgotten as the two former military men turned politicians went toe-to-toe. Behind the terror clearly in his eyes, Sherman could see a spark of anger. Was it because Spivey's ruse had been uncovered, or was it in dismay at the false accusation of plotting to assassinate his Commander-in-Chief?

"Frank, I don't know what you've been reading in those files, and I'm not going to ask you. It's none of my business and I know you're a level-headed and experienced soldier. You can make up your own mind on people's intentions without reading about their background from a bit of office paper. But you *know* me. We've served together. Do you think for one second that I'd be capable of plotting to, what, *assassinate* you? You think I could arrange the technology to bring down your transport or convince enough people to follow me, against you?

"I know my limitations, Frank. I might be a leader, but I've seen the way people react to you. Sure, maybe I disagree with your decisions, and God knows I think you're insane with what those Hunters are doing, but that doesn't mean I want you *dead*. I wouldn't trust any of these white collars in that seat. America needs a man who's seen it all these days and has the balls to make the hard choices. I've seen the way soldiers and staff look at you. That person isn't ever going to be me, Frank."

Sherman grunted, a bit stunned by Spivey's assessment.

The man himself even looked surprised he'd been so bold, his shaking hand rising with a handkerchief to dab sweat off his forehead and out of his eyes. Standing a bit straighter now, a man that finally looked befitting of his former rank, he laid his heart bare. "If you really don't trust me, then we both know I must resign. For the good of our country, if that's what you want from me, Frank, that's what I'll do."

"Do you *want* to step down?" Sherman asked, his voice sharp with suspicion.

"No, of course not. Frank, with everything going on you need every single supporter you can muster. Whether you want to believe me or not, I'm on your side in this. I will help you find the people trying to undermine you, or if you think that it's me, I will offer to walk away, and I'll do it today. Right now."

"I'll be honest, Morris, this isn't the response I expected from you at all, and you've warmed an old general's heart. Of course," he grinned, trying to climb down from the tower he'd built up for this confrontation. "This could all just be an elaborate ploy on your part."

Spivey opened his mouth to protest and was waved into silence with a chuckle. "No, I've known you long enough to be able to tell when I'm being spun a line. I believe you."

Palpably relieved, Spivey sank to the edge of a chair. "I understand why you feel the way you do. If I were in your position—Christ, if I thought someone in my own administration had tried to kill me, I'd have them all out in a line too. But that's not what you've done, is it?"

"Divide and conquer, admiral. When you're not sure where the threat is coming from, it's sometimes the best way. Now you've left me with quite the conundrum."

Sherman took his own seat. He began to rearrange the papers he'd had Jessica acquire and gave it up as a lost cause. He'd been *certain* the corruption began high up in the administration. If he'd been asked to stake a life on it, he'd have told anyone Morris Spivey would be at the center of any plot.

There were no photos or pictures of any of his predecessors hanging on the walls. It was just as well; Frank didn't think he was quite living up to their standards at that point in time. The American flag, its stars and stripes hanging proudly on the wall, was enough pressure. He looked down; he was dressed in combat slacks still, boots buffed to a shine. He wore a plain white tee which was clean enough, though at a glance no one would be able to tell that he was even an officer, let alone the president. By contrast, Spivey looked every inch the military man turned professional politician. If it were a matter of simply picking the man who looked the part, Spivey would have become president over Sherman in a heartbeat.

But Francis Sherman was the one they were trying to kill.

"I don't know what to do next, honestly, Morris. Any advice you give me, I promise you I will listen. I hope my suspicions haven't offended you; there are very few people in this building I can count as an ally right now."

"After everything that's happened in the last forty-eight hours, I can't blame you. I don't think I'd be doing any different in your position. If I can do anything for you at all...."

Sherman nodded, and it was as much a dismissal as it was an acknowledgment.

"I'll call. Thank you, vice president. Your candor is appreciated."

Spivey smiled and, without a further word, left the office.

★★★★★

Morris Spivey shook his head, closing the door to the president's office behind him. Jessica glanced up from her desk and spared a thin smile, which he barely returned. Everyone knew that *she* was loyal to Sherman, no matter how the grizzled veteran acted towards everyone else. For his own part, he felt lucky to have gotten out of that room not only with his head, but with his office, and barely a cross word. In fact, the shoe seemed far more firmly on the other foot.

Walking a little bit taller, Spivey decided if President Sherman did now count him as a trusted member of the staff, at least he could act like it. Those things he'd said hadn't been for show. He thought the Hunters had been sent on a reckless suicide mission, but there were few other men left alive that could have coordinated the recovery of Omaha, and fewer still that had the foresight to try and stage a vaccination program that was actually giving people hope for a once-bleak future.

Back in his office, he started by checking his own staff and make doubly sure that he wasn't being played. The last thing he wanted now was to gain trust only to have it snatched away through no fault of his own.

His hands shook as he went through the small bundle of files he had on his juniors. He leaned back in his chair, scratching absent-mindedly at a wound on his forearm that he didn't remember getting. *Where'd that come from*, he wondered, and made a mental note to get checked over by his doctor.

The room lurched. His vision swam. Something wasn't right.

"Wha...? What's going..."

His office door opened without being knocked. Spivey squinted up, but the room lurched again. He felt himself slide out of his chair. Groaning, groping for a handhold on the corner of his desk, he tried to call for help. His throat was suddenly parched, and only a pitiful croak came out.

"Dear, what do we have here?" the voice was taunting.

Spivey recognized it; if only he could put his thoughts together.

"Puh—poison?" he moaned, batting helplessly as a hand closed around his throat.

"No, vice president. Something much worse."

The pressure increased.

Already weak, Spivey could do nothing to defend himself, despite how much he wanted to try. Desperate for air, head pounding from the fever already raging through his body, he could only think of one thing as he slipped into darkness.

What could be worse?

CHAPTER 19

SOLDIER

Shouting into the chaos felt ridiculous. Under the circumstances, though, Brewster didn't know what else he could or should be doing to direct his Hunters. Using short, controlled bursts they'd managed to stabilize the situation, moving gradually down to the fourth floor without being overwhelmed. For whatever reason, the majority of the dead had congregated on one level in this building. They'd even allowed themselves to relax a little. Stupid mistake.

Brent had been the first to sound a warning as Kiley tested a set of double doors. There hadn't been any noise, but the tiniest opening released a stench that could only be described as decrepit decay. One thing on earth reeked like that. Death lived behind those doors.

The warning didn't come in time. Kiley had already released a chain holding the doors closed; was already pushing down the bar to swing those doors open.

A tide of dead came unleashed.

Shamblers of all shapes and sizes surged forward, forcing Kiley backward as he scrambled to close the doors again. Too late. The infected had seen their prey, and nothing would hold them back. A dozen? Maybe they'd have stood a chance. It had been a canteen once. The infection had to have hit here around lunchtime, or a gathering of some sort. So the squad glanced at scores of them, and every dead head in that room swiveled to gaze on the Hunters, their hungry maws opening to sound the alert in their shuddering moans.

Corporal Chris Kiley hadn't stood a chance. He'd stumbled backward in the opening as he fumbled to bring his rifle to bear. He unleashed a spray of a few rounds. Some of the bullets struck the infected, but it was like throwing a match at an avalanche hoping it would melt.

They were on top of him.

Seasoned as they were, none of the Hunters moved forward to pull Kiley away. Castillo delivered a merciful round to the man's head as decayed bodies, some more skeleton than skin, pulled the soldier in every direction. Kiley's body popped, limbs coming from sockets.

The sounds of biting and chewing was then masked by gunfire as the squad rained metal on the wall of hands and teeth shuffling towards them.

"Keep calm," Brewster yelled. "Place your shots! We can get through this."

"Just how fucking calm do you want us to stay, boss?" Krueger yelled through gritted teeth as his HTI punched .412-caliber rounds through a group of suited skirts that probably looked professional before they were torn, dirty, and caked in blood.

"You know what I'm saying, fucker. Let's not lose our heads! There's still a way out of this if we keep it together."

"If you say so," Castillo chimed in as she deftly swiveled on her left heel, burying a knife in the skull of a shambler that had crawled too close before re-shouldering her M16A4 and resuming controlled shots into the never-ending horde. "Got any more words of wisdom before we're overrun?"

Brent, Krueger, and Castillo were fanned out shooting at the lines.

Garibaldi tapped Brewster, indicating the empty passage behind them. "Let's just get the fuck out of here, man!"

A quick scan of the corridor; it remained blessedly empty. Any infected able to reach their position would have surely made an appearance by now, given the racket.

"You wanna flip a fucking coin, boss?" Garibaldi asked. "I'd rather go that way than try to finish cutting our way through *that*."

Brewster grunted. "We have no idea how many more are coming, but this must have been one hell of a gathering before the infection hit. Okay, let's not waste the ammo if we can leave this shit behind!"

"Oorah!" came a quick agreement from Brent.

"Castillo, turn with me," Brewster hollered over the din. "Krueger, Brent, keep up cover fire. Don't waste shots. Kill them if they're getting too close, but we should be able to move quicker than they can," and a final muttering under his breath, "*if we don't run into anymore*."

Brewster checked his magazine, moving into a shooting stance and shuffling forward, Castillo moving to match him. Her face was set, her focus on the task at hand. Brewster knew that losing Kiley would hurt, but there'd be time to grieve if they managed to get out of this alive.

Step by agonizing step, they built up a lead. The moans of the dead echoed against the walls, seeming to rattle the very fabric of the building. None of them had time to think about losses, lack of ammo, or dwell on the knowledge that they had no support. The immediate objective was to survive, and with the odds they faced in those hallways, even that seemed unlikely.

The further they moved from the canteen, the worse the lighting became. Their small squad was heading into the rear of the building, where the elevators and the emergency stairwells would allow them to traverse all floors. Brewster had wanted to take each floor as it came, completing a steady and methodical sweep so they knew they had at least one clear building in a city congested with the dead. The most likely way to survive now, though, might well be to chance the street.

He remembered the mass of infected huddled together through Krueger's scope and shuddered. *Talk about being caught between the Devil and the Deep.* Was running into *that* really their best chance of getting through this with anyone alive?

"Movement," Castillo reported.

Brewster snapped his attention back to the present. The corridor ended in a junction ahead. Without emergency lighting to show the stairwell or even the direction of the exits, they were moving with guesswork. Whatever approached them now, though, didn't care about basics like 'adequate lighting.' These things hadn't cared about anything for a long time.

"Krueger! What's the sitrep on our six?"

"Thirty feet and rising. Orders?"

"Unknown movement ahead. Might just be one target. I think we all agree there's no chance of a sprinter coming out of that pack?"

"Agreed," snapped Krueger.

"Then all eyes up front. Garibaldi, got some light for us?"

Garibaldi obliged, lifting his tactical flashlight to illuminate the end of the hall. What had somehow managed to catch Castillo's eye was an arm flapping helplessly on the floor. It was only visible past the elbow, the rest of it hidden behind the wall. The hand smacked at the gray carpet tiles, a slapping liquid sound audible between the moans of its shuffling compatriots still making their way glacially down the corridor.

"Brent, take point and check it out. We'll provide cover."

The squad kept close, wanting to maintain the distance between them and the following pack, as Brent shuffled forward.

Garibaldi held the light high, and Brent pulled his trademark kukri from its sheath as the pool of light highlighted the arm; pale skin with prominent veins, no sleeve covering it, to reveal the emaciated body of a blonde-haired woman in a nice dress trapped underneath a photocopier, which could only have been pulled down onto her. There had to have been a struggle, at least.

"Hand me that, Garibaldi," Brent said, reaching out for the flashlight. He took it and crouched down, shining the torch directly on her face and shaking his head slowly. "Too bad. She must have been a looker before all this. How long do you think they can stay alive? There's no way she's managed to grab a snack since this all went down."

The infected woman moaned pitifully, her arm stretching out at him, trying to reach the hot meal in front of her.

"Poor chic—" Brent tailed off midsentence as something caught the corner of his eye. Flicking up the light, he aimed it at the end of the corridor.

A sign declared emergency stairs at the end of the short space. The set of double doors weren't secured; there was no window to the outside, suggesting these acted as fire blocks, too.

"Orders?" Brent looked over his shoulder at the rest of the team, who'd bunched up behind him. There were no other shamblers down here; just the same crowd following them from before. With the small delay they had gained, there wasn't much time to make a decision.

"Let's get out that stairwell," Brewster decided. "I want to go all the way down."

Castillo lifted an eyebrow. "We're going to ground? Without completing the sweep?"

Brewster shrugged, trying to sound confident. Given that Castillo had already led squads of her own—she was an experienced officer— if she wanted to counter him, he wasn't sure he'd argue with her. "We're wasting ammo we'll need out in the street," he said. "I'd rather get our bearings out there and make a decision instead of pumping bullets into bodies that are never leaving this building."

She seemed to consider it for the smallest of moments, then looked at the shamblers less than twenty feet away and ceded to his decision with a small nod of her head. "Makes sense. Lower floors might be worse than this. You're right about wasting resources. We don't know when the next crate will be coming."

Brewster felt a cold shiver at that. Their isolation in this was constantly at the back of his mind. What he *was* avoiding thinking about, was what they'd do if they ran dry. There must be sporting goods stores—places they could restock. Chances were, though, that those places had been looted early on, and pickings would be few and far between. Police stations would be a better call, but he had no idea where the nearest of those were.

"Brent?" with the unspoken question the man tore himself away from the prone woman, turning his light to flood the end of the hall. It was plain; the offices left behind, there was no embellishment beyond dull gray walls, darker gray carpet tiles, and the occasional fake potted tree to break the monotony.

"Damn, some of the people here probably prayed for an apocalypse to happen," Brent said. The group was moving for the doors and Brent looked down at the moaning, grasping woman. "Here's a little mercy, sweetheart," he said, and he took her head off with a downward swipe of his machete.

The doors were weighted. Looking at the hinges, they'd pull open, and swing back shut. "Let's go out one at a time," Brewster said. "Brent, drop the flashlight and get this door. We should get some daylight once we get out there, and we need to be alert."

Brent nodded, placing the beam so it shone at the door. Brewster counted down and Brent yanked the door back.

Mottled daylight filtered in through the opened door—and more shamblers. A stairwell full of them, surging forward.

Brent screamed as hands grabbed for him.

"Jesus Christ!" Krueger brought his HTI to bear, but it was too long, and he couldn't get a shot.

Behind them, the hallway filled with the relentless dead, while shamblers clustered in the emergency exit ahead, filling the stairs and platform, groaning as one and piling on top of the screaming Brent. Their mass and weight kept him from even raising his kukri, and kept the door open too.

There was no chance to give Brent a merciful death as he was lost under the weight of the living dead and their grabbing hands and gnashing teeth.

"Push by while they're..." Brewster yelled, stabbing down at an exposed face with his bayonet. "Just go, go!"

"Down the stairwell?" Garibaldi said, gawping at the scene in front of them. There was hardly room to squeeze by, despite all the attention on the fresh butchery of what was seconds ago former Marine Sergeant Johnathan Lee Brent.

Castillo popped off a couple shots behind them. "Better that way than this!"

The metal stairwell groaned, creaked, and let out a metallic wrenching noise. The sudden movement and mass of bodies had evidently caused the metal to come tearing away from the fabric of the building. The stairwell suddenly collapsed, coming apart in pieces. The dead tumbled away as well.

The noise of the tearing metal crashing to the tarmac below echoed deafeningly, and as one, the nearby hordes of Washington DC turned, seeking the source of the noise. Scores if not hundreds of them against the building pressed against the lower floors.

Glass burst.

And the dead filed into every space in search of the living.

The Hunters were trapped.

CHAPTER 20

TAILOR

"You've been upgrading since I visited last, Jose."

The mechanic—perhaps considered now to be more the 'Mad Scientist of New Abraham'—grinned enthusiastically. "The town isn't really expanding, sheriff. Remember you said I could use the warehouse?"

Keaton arched an eyebrow. "I thought you meant to store equipment."

Jose waved an arm, nearly catching Brenda, who stepped back, a similar grin plastered over her own face. Keaton didn't doubt the woman was playing a significant part in Jose's apparent expansions. She'd helped mastermind for them before; it seemed she was doing it again, and maybe, just maybe, they'd keep the hopes of New Abraham alive.

"This *is* equipment. It's just slightly more…volatile compared to what we're used to keeping."

Janine whistled, impressed. She wasn't fooled by the pair of them downplaying what they'd achieved in such a short time. "Have you two even been sleeping?"

"We've had a surprising amount of help. Haven't we, Jose?" Brenda said.

"Oh, yeah." Jose nodded, still smiling.

"You know the way the town works," she continued. "We all come together. Besides, these are pretty easy to build. Eileen's going to be disappointed, though."

"Oh?" Keaton stretched out a hand to the first set of racking, stroking his hand down what resembled an adapted leaf blower. "How so?"

"Some of these," Jose gestured at the racking, "run on ethanol. Eileen wants to keep a hold of as much of that stuff as she can. But needs must, and we've come up with some impressive firepower, sheriff."

"What's this? A flamethrower?"

Jose laughed. "No, though that would be amazing to see. No, it'd melt, maybe even explode in your hands. It's been adapted so it's... well for want of a better phrase, a cannon."

Janine laughed, grabbing it and twisting it around for a better look. It still looked like a normal garden tool. None of the mechanisms she could see had changed. Turning it upside down to make sure there was nothing in the funnel, she even glimpsed inside.

Keaton rolled his eyes.

"You're the model of health and safety," Brenda drawled with a sarcastic slant. "You're not even wearing goggles."

Janine went to put it back down, more than a little embarrassed until she saw the grins around her. "It's not loaded, is it? It doesn't weigh enough. What are you planning to fire out of it?"

"We were thinking ball bearings, that sort of thing," Jose told her. "Doesn't sound much, but if you can hit a moving car with it, from one of our watchtowers, say, I don't think the driver is going to care whether it was a leaf blower or a grenade launcher."

"A grenade launcher would be *quite* the find, though." Keaton knew his friend well and saw the mischief dancing in the tinkerer's eyes. "I don't suppose that was a leading statement, Jose?"

"As you come to mention it...."

Janine put the 'leaf blower' back on the table. "What can we actually make, weapon-wise, just with ethanol? Aren't we getting the support from Omaha in a couple of days, too?"

"We are," Keaton said, "although I'm still not sure exactly what they're sending us. So, we're going to do the best with what we have—and it seems thanks to our miracle-workers here, we've got quite a lot."

"Ethanol is terrifyingly useful." Brenda beckoned Janine to follow her. The women walked through the rows of racking. It wasn't all weaponry, though Janine's eyes got wider as she saw just how much the pair of them had managed to construct or hoard. "When you work from a basic Molotov, then figure out how many ways you can set fire to things, then point them at other things...and *boom*. Well, that's the basics we worked on. It expanded from there."

"*Boom?*"

Brenda grinned. "Big ones. After what we saw, and what I heard about Marie. Well, you know the phrase. *Fight fire with fire.* It was just a matter of figuring out how we could do it." Brenda sounded like she was talking about a papier-mache volcano she'd made for a science fair.

"I really can't believe what you two have managed," Keaton said, clapping Jose on the shoulder. "Now I hate to ask but...can any of this be mounted? Just how much of this fuel do we have?"

"Sheriff, we're way ahead of you. Keep walking this way, and I'll do my best to explain the situation."

Keaton followed as Jose kept talking. "Firstly, we need to be careful about who we give these to. If any of these go off in the town...

well, water will be no good to us. That's where I really hope we catch those bastards out."

"That's right—foam, isn't it? Water will just...."

"Make the fire worse. You got it, sheriff. You wanted those lead vehicles targeted? I'm hoping that we just get a few decent shots in with some of our more...specialized adaptations, they try to put the fire out, and bam! Their entire leadership is blown up before they even know what's happened to them."

"I've got the people in mind for these. What's this surprise you've got for me?"

At the end of the warehouse, a huge blue tarpaulin was tied down at each corner. Keaton had seen reveals like this before, when they'd sent Sherman's men out of town to help rescue their people from Herman Lutz. His anticipation cranked up a notch. "Is this going to be what I think it is?"

Jose grinned. "I'm not sure what you've got in mind, sheriff, but you know how I get when I have a new project. It was Brenda's doing, really..."

"Nonsense," Brenda said as she and Janine joined them. "This is all you. I just provided the science."

Keaton hadn't taken his eyes off the tarp. He knew their town was beyond lucky to have found and kept a creative brain like Brenda's and skilled hands like Jose's. "I hope this dynamic duo stays on our side, that's all I can say. Come on then, Jose, let's see what you've masterminded for us this time."

"Without further delay, sheriff, may I present to you..." Jose unlashed one of the ropes, tugging the tarpaulin back.

Janine whooped with delight as Keaton's jaw dropped.

CHAPTER 21

FALLOUT

"How are you feeling, doc?"

Stiles sat in a utilitarian chair as Rebecca stood at the side of the bed, checking over Anna's vitals. She was healing well despite how dire the gunshot wound had seemed. Their new facilities, combined with Rebecca's fast actions, had prevented her bleeding out, and infection from setting in. It would still take a lot of bedrest though before the good doctor would be up and about and able to get back to producing the vaccine.

"Under the circumstances, I think I have to say I'm okay," Anna said with a smile. "I'm worried about you though, Mark, and everything that's going on outside. What's the situation? How's Frank? And Brewster? And Abraham...."

Rebecca all but shushed the older woman. "I think you have enough to deal with right here, Anna. We need you as part of this recovery, and don't you dare think about getting out of this bed early.

I don't want to see you anywhere near BL1, let alone BL4 until you're signed off by a professional."

"I'm a professional," Anna responded. "Can I sign myself back on duty?"

"If I let you do that I'm positive you'll be back to work in a heartbeat, and President Sherman would never forgive us if we let any more harm come to you."

Anna dropped her head, color tainting her cheeks. "You've done enough already. I'd be dead if you hadn't found me, Becky. Thank you. I shouldn't have been so stupid."

"It's not your fault, doc." Mark tried to sound consoling. "Robbie was a good assistant, you always said so. This radical movement has caught us all off guard, me more than most. If anything, I should be apologizing to you for letting it get this far."

"Don't be ridiculous," she said dismissively. "We've all been in this together for too long to start point scoring. We just need to be certain of what we're doing next. Is that why you're here?"

Mark nodded, sitting upright.

Rebecca helped Anna to do the same, holding out a tissue as the doctor was caught by a coughing fit. Anna then looked at the tissue. "Not bloody this time; that's progress." She then looked seriously at Mark. "I know about the sprinter attack. Was anyone hurt?"

"No, thank God. There were enough of us around with guns to take them down. It was strange enough being shot at without being injured. They were leading us. The sprinters—it was a clear trap, and I was a fool for walking straight into it."

"No one could have guessed they'd be that foolhardy, Mark," Anna told him.

"The important thing is that no one was badly hurt," Rebecca added. "I've seen a few people with minor wounds. I've spoken to them, though, and they were mostly from panicking and rushing. McCartney's people didn't actually directly engage with anyone."

"If those sprinters had made it any further into the town then that would have been a very different story," he said.

"But people would assume the vaccine would keep them safe," Rebecca countered.

"And yet we shot the sprinters anyway." Mark sighed. "Are people going to think we don't trust the cure we've given them?"

"It's not a cure, per se," Anna said. "And no. I think they'll see we did the sensible thing. Sprinters might not be able to infect us now—if Robbie didn't contaminate the batches he did," she added quietly, "but they can still do incredible damage in their rage. Even kill, and we don't want those kinds of losses on our hands."

"It doesn't make this any easier to stomach." Rebecca moved, perching on the side of his chair and wrapping a comforting arm around the back of his neck. She placed a hand on his shoulder, squeezing it gently.

"You did well. And…well, we wanted to speak to you, Anna, because we have a plan. And I told Mark to call Frank, but…"

"But I think our president has enough to deal with right now. The last thing he needs is to be worrying about a settlement he thinks is in trusted hands."

"With you, Mark, it *is* in good hands, no matter what you might think right now. I can't imagine anyone else except perhaps Frank himself dealing with this any better. What exactly do you need to ask him? Maybe I can help."

Mark nodded. "Thanks. We think…well, we know McCartney is using the infected against us, and we think it's to try to prove the vaccine isn't working. When you told us what Robbie said, it sounds like they want Morningstar to just run its course, right?"

"Yes." Anna's memory drifted back to her last moments with her former assistant. He'd always seemed so keen. Now her main thoughts of him would be those last dying screams as his body dissolved from the inside out. "It's evangelical, to a point. They believe that it's a heavenly act, and only the worthy should be left alive once the infection is done."

"But if we don't try to stop it, it'll end up killing everyone."

"We know that. I think that Robbie knew that. The terrifying thing was that it seemed like he just didn't care."

"I think," Mark began, trying to pick his words carefully. "I think their views are ultimately how we're going to win this. We don't know everyone in our community personally, not anymore. But the majority of them definitely have something in common. Any sane person fears Morningstar. We've seen what it's done to our families, and to the world. The fact that he has the balls...."

"More like the lack of sense," Rebecca muttered.

"Or that. To just bring one into town? To *release* them? Normal people aren't going to want someone like that in charge. It would be terrifying."

"So, you're going to meet with him tomorrow and explain this to people?" Anna asked. "A straight-up bad versus good scenario?"

"Not even that simple. We've recovered the bodies of a couple of the sprinters. Do we still interview people when they arrive in the city? Give them a basic medical?"

"Yes—that just makes sense. Why?"

"Even if Robbie managed to damage some of the vaccine batches, I don't understand how McCartney's people collected as many infected as they already have. I have my suspicions. Do we vaccinate people as soon as they come in?"

"No, we hold them in quarantine for twenty-four hours in case they're harboring infection. Then they're vaccinated and sent for work assessments."

"Who oversaw administering those vaccines? You? Nurses? Did Robbie ever take a shift there?"

"No, we were always too busy in the labs, but he had friends who...oh shit. You think they just gave a placebo to people?"

Mark nodded. "It would make more sense than sabotage. You run such a tight ship in the labs that I couldn't believe he'd be able to get anything past you. You check things, after all, and he could never be sure when a poor batch might be noticed. But, if they were claiming to vaccinate people, then simply *didn't*, those people could be targeted later and turned, without question."

"That's so callous!" Rebecca had stiffened, her hand settling unconsciously on her stomach. Already protecting.

"It's worse than that," Mark said, looking at his wife. "It's premeditated murder."

"There's no way people would support him if we proved he's been murdering refugees," said Anna. "How, though?"

"Simple. We check the records against those sprinters that came in. Hopefully, we've got notes of who applied the vaccines? Then it's some simple calculations. And we have him right where we want him."

"Now *that* could be perceived as callous," Anna said darkly.

Mark flinched a little, surprised.

Anna shook her head, realizing what she'd said, and who she was speaking to. "Sorry, Mark. I know you're doing what needs to be done. I just didn't expect this much subterfuge happening right under our noses."

"We can stop this early, though. We're talking murder here. I thought their little rebellion was quite far gone. The more I work out, the less I think that's true, and McCartney is panicking in case his plan falls apart. Talking of plans, did they disrupt anything in the labs? Was BL4 okay?"

Anna shifted. She was uncomfortable talking to almost anyone about her research. Even as much as she trusted Mark, and how instrumental he'd been so far in their recovery efforts, few people knew just how far her research efforts stretched now. Not even Rebecca.

"It's fine, Mark. Robbie wasn't able to damage anything. Once I got him talking, he could barely stop."

"Did he already know what was happening down there?"

"He knew that I had some research," Anna answered slowly. *You don't even know what I'm doing down there.* Mark picked up on this; the dangers of working closely with those that got to know you.

"Doc, what aren't you telling us? What happened down there?"

Her mind flitted back to Robbie's corpse and shuddered. "The way Robbie died, that's all. I—it's difficult for me to remember. Those test vaccines were never meant to be used on a live human being. It was terrible to watch."

"He was going to shoot you and potentially destroy everything we've been working towards," Rebecca cut in. "I'd say he had it coming."

Anna was shocked at the embittered tone in Rebecca's voice. Everyone knew the young woman had come through more hardships than most.

"Look. Anna…" Mark said, putting his hand on her bed rail, a gentle gesture at odds with the powder-burnt fingers and scraped-up knuckles. "If there's something you're not telling us, now is the time we need to hear it."

Anna bit her lip. She wasn't sure, friends as they all were, they'd appreciate quite the extent to which she'd been manipulating both the vaccine and the virus itself. In the early days of her research she'd questioned her own motives, but as she and Frank had discussed it, she'd put her morals aside. If this research came off, then they could save a hell of a lot more people. If it didn't, then she'd need to make sure her notes and samples never saw the light of day, and for that, she needed as few people aware of the scope of BL4 as possible.

"There's nothing else," she finally said. "I'm just worried about cleaning up the mess down there as soon as possible. You both know I don't want anyone else moving Robbie's body. The risks are too high."

"Do you believe her, Mark?"

They were lying in bed together. It was rare, throughout the growth of Omaha, never mind the turmoil of recent days, that they had such luxuries. There was no heating or air conditioning in their home. One window was slightly open, a gentle breeze rustling their curtain and sweeping over their light blankets.

Rebecca nestled in the crook of his armpit, and Mark couldn't have been happier. On nights like this, he liked to pretend they were just any other couple: young, in love, awaiting their future and their family, with nothing to worry about but jobs and bills and schools. No civil unrest threatening their doorstep, while rebels attempted to attenuate the existence of a world-ending virus.

Her question, important though it was, was an unwanted interruption to his daydream. Back in reality, he remembered the way the doctor had tensed up when BL4 came into the conversation. Mark knew she was still completing research alongside the vaccination production. Beyond the little he comprehended past his own contribution to the vaccine, Mark left her and Becky to it. He was a fighter; they were the brains providing the cure they had fought so hard for.

"I'm not sure what she's hiding. Definitely something. She wasn't acting like the Anna we know."

"Could it just be her injury? Maybe she's worried about Frank?"

"Clamming up when we mention the lab and her research? No. Something else is going on. It's making me nervous. Not that we need anything else to worry about now, right?"

He saw Becky put her hand on her stomach. "Right," she said low.

CHAPTER 22

SHERMAN CLUTCHED TWO MANILA envelopes in one white-knuck-led fist and strode determinedly down the hallway towards Spivey's offices. After his VP had left, Sherman had returned to the aftermath of documents with renewed vigor. He thought that perhaps he'd been going about this all the wrong way. That it needn't necessarily be a senior member of his staff causing so much disruption; not when it had only taken one persuadable techie before, to take down a heli-copter and the Command-in-Chief, along with one of Sherman's closest friends.

Sherman didn't think for one second that Sanderson, trusted for such a long time, would be responsible for such a transgression. That being so, after hearing about Robbie's exploits in the lab and how close he came to destroying all their progress and killing Anna, Sherman had decided to look much closer to ground level.

There were two new hires associated with the JCS who had access to the technology capable of distributing encrypted messages or even injecting new programs into their existing infrastructure. Both unheard of before their arrival in McChord, it had been Spivey that ultimately signed off on their contracts and positions. Sherman wanted to know just how closely his second-in-command had questioned these people.

The door to Spivey's office was closed; no oddity, the man liked and enjoyed his privacy, as did anyone who could get it these days. Sherman knocked, more out of politeness than as a request. Waiting for a few seconds, he raised an eyebrow to Spivey's assistant, Alastair. An awkward, lanky man in his early twenties, Alastair had been born to desk jobs and had embraced his role in the new White House with enthusiasm.

"Is the Vice President here?"

Alastair nodded, reddening slightly at being addressed directly. "Yes, Mr. President. He went in around half an hour ago. I left for ten minutes after he requested some documents, but he hasn't been out since."

"How do you know? Have you checked?"

Alastair shook his head, dandruff dancing to his blazered shoulders. "No, Mr. President. He hasn't been out to get the additional documents, yet. I wouldn't dare disturb him, not if he's studying."

I bet you wouldn't, you poor sap. "Thanks, son. I'll step in if you don't think he'd mind?"

"Oh, I don't think he'd mind at all, it being you, Mr. President."

It had been a rhetorical question. Such subtleties were probably beyond Alastair, whose worldview from what little Sherman knew of it, was very black-and-white. Smiling amiably, Sherman twisted the handle, pushing the door open and hearing little more in response than a forlorn squeak.

"Spivey?"

The chair behind the desk was empty, the desk itself resembling Sherman's. It seemed like Spivey had taken to some research of his own. Sherman wondered if that had been before their little talk, or a result of it. Edging forward into the room, his instincts suddenly screamed something was wrong. He caught sight of a limp hand sticking out from behind the only couch in the room.

Bodies were on the floor for a reason, and admirals were rarely predisposed to nap on the job. Sherman instinctively went for his holstered M-9, checking the magazine and taking off the safety. Side-stepping quietly so that he had a full view behind the couch, he saw Spivey prone on his back. One arm sprawled, the hand palm up and locked in a frozen grasp—what he'd seen when he came into the office.

Putting away his gun, there being no other obvious threat in the room, Sherman dashed to the man's side. Spivey's eyes and mouth were open, the former looking beyond terrified. He was obviously dead.

"Morris?" Futile though it was, he checked for a pulse, revealing fresh purple bruises along the man's neck. It wouldn't take a coroner to diagnose a cause of death here.

"Sorry, old comrade. Sleep well."

Sherman pulled the lids down, resting his hands on the man's forehead in a moment of thought. Sherman bent his head, thinking of a prayer.

Spivey's eyes snapped back open.

Sherman had been squatting; he jumped back now, falling to a sitting position and scooting back as the VP's reanimated body moved. The eyes rapidly became bloodshot, and Sherman cursed himself that he'd missed the small telltale signs of infection.

Hadn't the vice president been vaccinated?

Reaching for his sidearm, Sherman yelled for Alastair, who came hurtling through the office door. On seeing his former boss sitting up and hissing at the current President of the United States, Alastair turned heel, shouting for help.

Better than just running, Sherman supposed.

Unbuckling the M-9 again, Sherman composed himself, crouching as Spivey struggled to his feet. "I'm sorry that I have to do this, Morris. I would have chosen any other way for you to leave this world."

Spivey swiveled at hearing Sherman speak. His eyes shone with red malice and hatred. The tall, skinny man, formerly quite nervous of most people and quiet-mannered with the rest, opened his mouth and howled in bloody fury.

Sherman released one shot. It slammed into Morris Spivey's forehead. Blood splatter coated the back of his cream couch, and the body slumped to the floor, this time permanently dead.

Holstering the sidearm, Sherman looked up as his detail sprinted into the room. He cocked an eyebrow at Adams, who at least had the courtesy to look embarrassed. "Better late than never isn't always an accurate philosophy."

"Mr. President, we weren't aware you were at risk."

"Isn't it meant to be the case that you're constantly at my side *for that reason*? I want all of you," Sherman pointed at his detail, "to gather the junior chiefs, Major Bentley, and get as many of my remote command on the phone as you can. I want everyone in or on the line to my office in twenty minutes."

The men paled, parting as Sherman passed. Adams moved to follow, and Sherman whirled on him.

"It's a bit late for that now, isn't it? You've got your orders."

Eighteen minutes later, as many of the junior chiefs as could be assembled were gathered in the room, along with Major Bentley and Jessica Chastain. The Hunters were out on a mission so there was no way they could raise Brewster. Stiles wasn't answering. Neither was Keaton. None of this boded well, and Sherman couldn't help but wonder if these attacks were being coordinated to cause maximum disruption.

"Is this everyone?"

Adams clicked the door closed, clasping his hands behind his back and nodding firmly. Now looking all-business, Sherman couldn't help but hold them all under suspicion, even though the men were the reason why he was alive right now.

"You are probably unaware why I've gathered you here. What I fear is that there is a small minority who knows exactly what's going on."

Jessica coughed, clearly wishing to speak. Sherman nodded his head slightly, opening the opportunity for her. "Mr. President, we know that there is trouble in Omaha and Abraham, and I thought perhaps you were going to communicate something to us, about how we could support our allies?"

Sherman was impressed. That would have been a decent enough excuse if done under pretense. "Sadly, no. It is true, yes, that both New Abraham and Omaha are under attack by apparently different enemies. We have our own enemies to deal with though, right here in our own facility...

"...Vice President Morris Spivey is dead."

Jessica gasped. Alastair looked like he'd faint any moment. Several of the juniors' hands went to their faces, covering gasps that could only be genuine. Major Bentley looked deathly pale; no wonder. If someone was attempting assassinations of senior politicians, starting at the top and working down, he'd be soon in line.

"We all know that an attempt was recently made on my life and that it failed. This killing is clearly a warning—there is a power in the White House that none of us have control of. They have murdered, in cold blood, one of the few people trusted to me here. And as time goes on that number is rapidly dwindling.

"People are trying to derail what we've all worked so hard to achieve. We can't let this happen. You all know that Vice President Spivey was fundamentally opposed to some of my military decisions, but in wanting the best for the people of the United States to rebuild a future for us all we shared the same vision. If you believed in him, then believe in me. If you know *anything* about his movements before his death; any conversations you had, or any suspicions you might have about something within this complex, I want to know first. Don't speak to your friends or colleagues—I don't even want you to speak to your mother if you're lucky enough for her to be alive.

"We have a rat to find, ladies and gentlemen. And it starts and ends in this room."

Sherman needed Sanderson's help. He'd spent time looking over the documents Spivey had, and a few of them were in code that he couldn't work out. Adams, stiff to attention behind his left shoulder for the majority of the day, couldn't help either despite his time in the service. Neither men could find the cipher, either, so assumed that despite Sanderson's comprehension of the suspected military encryptions from earlier, he still may be of use as the tech had a strong curiosity and was an unraveller of the raveled.

He'd usually find the man in his office, where he seemed to live and breathe amongst his towering labyrinth of devices, tech both old and not-so-much. Surrounded by monitors and food cartons from their supply canteen, Sanderson threw himself into his work and was notorious with his predictability of rarely retiring to his quarters but opting to sleep and eat in his office.

The first thing Sherman smelled was the iron tang of blood. It permeated the air. The hall and room beyond were silent. After what had happened in Spivey's office, Sherman went on immediate alert.

He needn't have worried though. Sanderson was at his desk.

Well…most of Sanderson—his seated torso, blood splattered and drying over the keyboards, food cartons, and monitors surrounding him. On his desk, Sanderson's head, the mouth open in a permanent scream.

CHAPTER 23

THE HUNTERS STOOD OR leaned against blood-splattered walls. Brewster took a few deep breaths and checked his M4's magazine. Following the stairwell collapse, they'd had no choice but to fight through the shamblers in the wide hall behind them, pounding them with gunfire, cutting them down with blades, whatever it took. Now they needed somewhere to bunker down and take stock of what they had left. They needed a new plan. For now, they had dropped their packs to suck wind after one hell of a terrifying close-quarters brouhaha.

"I think..." a bloody-faced Garibaldi said from his place standing amidst a heap of bodies. He was pointing and counting. "Yeah, thirty-nine. Or maybe forty."

"What?" Castillo said across from where she leaned with her hands on her knees. She was covered in splashes of gore as well—they all were.

Garibaldi looked up. "It's hard to tell from all the…parts, but…I think we took out thirty-nine of them."

"Whoop-dee-fucking-doo," Krueger growled while wiping blood off the barrel of his sniper rifle. He pulled what looked like an ear from one of the barrel vents and flung it on a dead infected. "They got two of us, and Kiley and Brent were worth more than thirty-nine already-dead assholes."

"Maybe forty."

Brewster cursed; this was all going wrong. He kicked an overturned water cooler. "Fuck!" His second mission—his first proper—and he was going to get them all killed. Every goddamn Hunter. Sherman had put faith in him, even knowing the enormity of what they faced. How more misplaced could his confidence have been?

They weren't sweeping the other floors now. Brewster knew they'd only encounter more undead. "Okay, grab your gear, tight formation on me."

"Where we headed?" Castillo asked, picking up her pack and shouldering it with a grunt. "Damn, this feels heavier now."

"Mine too," Brewster said, pulling the straps back on. "We're gonna stay tight and hit the stairs by the elevators, proceed floor to floor, no sweep, just get the fuck to ground."

"Then what, boss?" Garibaldi asked.

"I don't know yet. I'm making this up as I go. You with me?"

"I'm not staying here."

They dashed down the first set of steps, encountered nothing, then hit the next flight to the third floor and so on, going from the fourth floor to the lobby in quick time. That's when Brewster held up a fist. "Jesus," he hissed.

The lobby was filled with what looked like at least two-hundred shamblers. Luckily, potted plants by the stairway here hid him from view, and none of thme had come up about five steps to the raised receiving area that encircle the lobby. Not yet.

Brewster made hand signals for them to follow low and quiet.

He made his way behind a wide curved reception desk, its computer long dead, along with the person that manned it. Blackened blood decorated the chair and floor. The four of them stayed low.

"They'd better sing songs about this," Krueger muttered angrily.

"What? 'The Idiots Who Got Themselves Killed?'" Garibaldi whispered. "It hasn't really got a fireside ring to it."

"We're not dead yet," Castillo said.

"Shh," Brewster hushed them, then risked a glance around the corner of the desk. They'd all faced steep odds before and come out to tell the tale—hell, they just did—but this time looked particularly steep. The entire lobby beyond was, as expected, pressed in hard by infected. There wasn't a single gap anywhere. Several windows were shattered, where'd they'd come in. Blood and plasma smeared every pane in the front. The infected moved gently now, their initial desperate fury as the stairwell fell tempered again by a lack of noise and movement. But there was no way they'd get out the front. He turned back and faced the remainder of his squad. "There has to be more than two-hundred of them on the other side, and another three-hundred outside."

"Four against five hundred?" Krueger scowled. "Yeah, they better sing some goddamn songs."

"Where next, then?" Castillo cut in.

"We need to know what we've got left. They said they might be able to do another drop for us. If we can get to a decent waypoint—the top of another building—we can call in more support."

They removed their heavy packs. With unspoken consent, they agreed that they wouldn't be trying to recover the gear from their fallen comrades. They all wore the same AR and could pool ammo if they needed. No one had been suicidal enough to use the six grenades they each had. Scopes, goggles, canteens, magazines, rappelling gear. They had rounds enough still, thank goodness. Brewster refilled his tac vest with mags. They had enough to survive in short bursts, but not enough to get through an entire city of the dead.

"Looking at this we definitely need to get to a clear area," he said. "We haven't moved from the drop zone. It should be easy enough to work out from the map and our reccy up top."

"To do that," Krueger whispered, "we need to get out of the building."

They all glanced at their rappelling gear.

Castillo gave voice to what they were all hesitant to say. "Which floor did we clear again?"

"Five," Garibaldi said. "Maybe it was four."

"I hate this shit."

"Stop whining, Brewster. You jumped out of a plane not long ago. You're meant to be in charge." Brewster was channeling his inner PFC, and Krueger was happy to play foil to that. "Now go, man."

The airdrop into the city had been insane enough, as far as he was concerned. Now they found themselves in gear ready to drop down five floors of an office building into the one area clear of infected they had managed to spy from above. And it was a tiny window of opportunity. The office complex, attempting to give their overworked staff some respite, had a small garden area with a few benches and an area for smoking. It was fenced off from the rest of the street and, by some small miracle, free of infected.

Shamblers trudged over the sidewalks at all angles, though, so they had to be fast and as silent as possible. Once down, they were going to cut a channel into a similar garden area, then into a nearby under-construction building. Their solid theory was that they'd only encounter construction workers there, if anything.

Seated in his straps, Brewster felt neither safe nor secure. He dropped the rope down anyway, passing it through his hands to start a slow, controlled descent. His hands were shaking more through nerves than for the bitter cold wind that shook past, rattling his gear and biting him to the bone.

His boots rested against the thick, tempered panes of each floor. He dropped past the fourth-floor windows; it was blessedly empty inside. He looked up to see the others right above him and getting a nice shot of Garibaldi's bony ass.

In their rush downstairs inside the building, they'd consciously avoided the third floor, assuming there were more infected to clear. That assumption was correct. As the team descended past, a whole office contained shamblers, many still seated at their desks as if eagerly waiting for their shift to end.

"Rush this one! We can't risk them bursting out!" Brewster hissed as one shambler looked out and noticed him. Its mouth opened in a silent warning as they all zipped by. The others at their desks turned to look as the Hunters dropped from their view.

They found themselves looking in the second-floor window. This office, too, was packed to the brim, the infected already pressed up against the windows. On seeing live humans dangling tantalizingly like carrots just within reach, they smacked and pawed frantically at the glass, the ones in the rear pushing the others forward. It only took seconds for the glass to start cracking under the strain of their weight. Splinters appeared on the panes.

"Fuck…" Brewster said to himself, then, "Move!"

All caution now gone, they slid the rest of the way, thirty-five or so feet, boots touching ground as glass shattered above their heads. Bodies and glass rained down on them. The first few landed with a sickening thud, heads landing on benches, picnic tables, and the cold, frosty ground. Most smashed like melons; bone, brains, and viscera flew everywhere.

The team struggled out of their harnesses, Krueger swearing as he stumbled and tripped. Castillo had her weapon to bear, ready for any of the near-decomposed shamblers that survived the fall. None of them had, much to their relief, though it riled the infected standing just beyond the wire fencing.

Brewster threw Krueger a hand, helping him to his feet. "Okay?"

Krueger nodded, shouldering his pack. "Yep, but my bullpup's fucked," he said, picking up the sniper rifle and pouting at a slight bend in the chassis.

"Route still straight ahead, chief?" Garibaldi asked.

Brewster nodded. "Now or never. Let's do it."

Darting between falling bodies, the fence they needed to climb was a mere eight feet—simple for soldiers with their fitness and training, even with a full pack. Made of simple planks, it was a solid enough construction for them to scramble over. Brewster went first, pack and all, glancing around to make sure the coast was clear before whistling the others over.

They landed without a problem, glancing over their shoulders to see the relentless tide of undead still pouring out of the second and third floors of the building they narrowly escaped. The tumult had caught the attention of the passive onlookers, too, and they could hear the fence groan and break under the weight of pressure.

Was this the design of their mission? Brewster wondered. To be pressed, almost literally, from place to place, until they couldn't find anywhere else to run?

They jogged toward a gate and into an enclosed courtyard designed to one day be parking. The entire complex was enclosed by metal fencing, so they weren't too fearful of being spotted or pressed just yet. They kept to perimeters as closely as they could, not wanting to catch the attention of onlookers higher-up and causing another waterfall of blood.

A skittering of feet caught them cold. Brewster threw up a fist, bringing them to a halt.

HUNTERS

A pack of dogs rounded the corner, their jaws damp with blood. Their canine eyes were normal; their thin bellies and pronounced ribcages were not. They weren't infected, but there was no doubt they were hungry—and no longer tame.

The leader, a vicious cross-breed, lower its haunches, growling. The others followed suit.

Brewster dropped his pack, sighing. "You've got to be fucking kidding me."

CHAPTER 24

"I HAVE A PROPOSITION for you," he'd said.

Keaton had small cells at his office, but they never expected so many dissidents in their close-knit community, and so when Tanner Whitehead and his small crew had banded together to form a revolt in New Abraham, Keaton had to make do with what they had to hold the remainder in custody.

The barn smelled of moldy hay, rotting vegetables, and manure. It hadn't been a pleasant place to work before the outbreak, and now it had been a makeshift prison for half a dozen prisoners. Every single one of them was remorseful for their actions. It didn't mean, however, that they'd gained any leverage with or trust from the people of New Abraham, after everything they'd done.

Keaton had spoken with Janine about this. As far as plans went, this was tickling the edge of what he considered 'comfortable.' With the Nomads poised to attack at any moment though, they were lean on options, and New Abraham needed every able body it could muster.

They all looked alert, hungry even, to be involved. They'd been stuck in the barn when the Nomads had attacked the town, and Jerry Pulver had been the first to express his terror, and the folly of leaving them inside the barn to burn when they were fully capable of supporting the defense of their town.

"We were proud to live here once," Jerry stuttered, his skin flushing underneath brown-stubbled cheeks. "I suppose Tanner told us some lies, made us believe that we were more than what we thought we were. That you were less. He was wrong." Jerry looked up, meeting Keaton's eyes. The young man seemed beyond determined to show his honesty now. "We were wrong. And if we can help, then we have to."

Keaton slapped the man on the shoulder in thanks, though Jerry's slight flinch at that touch didn't go unnoticed. "And what about the rest of you? Do you stand with Jerry?"

Chick and Charmain Harrison shared a glance with each other before letting their eyes rest on Adelina. Jose's daughter; he'd been so proud of her once upon a time, assisting him in his workshop and coming up with almost as many fantastic inventions as her father. Her long black hair was twisted tight in a braid, and she played with that now, wrapping it around her fist.

"What we did was wrong," she said. "We all know that. We've had enough time to sit in here and to think. We could have tried to escape, you know?"

Keaton knew it. The barn was hardly the most secure building in town. It was an old steel and wood prefab and some of the slats could easily be kicked out from the inside, especially around the hastily-sealed windows. Knowing that, the barn was under constant surveillance. They wouldn't have gotten far.

"But I wouldn't leave," Adelina said. "Not without showing my father how I really feel about here. About him." Adelina's fist tightened around the braid, her knuckles stretching over skin and turning a pale white.

"Tanner wanted power for himself," Keaton said. "He wasn't the only one. He was a passionate man. I'm not surprised he managed to sway some of you."

"It wasn't just that. You were being *fair*. There were elections, you told us all that. Tanner led us on the lie that we were selling out. That'd we'd be Omaha's puppet." Her deep green eyes held his for a long heartbeat. "That's not true, is it, sheriff? But we don't know, because we're stuck in here." She gestured around, to their makeshift cots which served as beds, their threadbare blankets, and the scraps of the meager breakfast they'd eaten that morning.

"You knew we were attacked. And you were told about the group."

Adelina nodded. "Nomads. What of them? Why do you want us to help, after all this time? After we were already left to die in the first attack?"

Keaton tried not to show his sorrow at how that had happened. In all the chaos, their barn full of young prisoners had been at the back of everybody's minds. What they weren't saying, was that Adelina and her group had been left to die. So, what was going to stop Keaton from sacrificing them again?

"New Abraham is no one's puppet. Omaha is our ally; Frank Sherman is the president, and one of the biggest supporters of our town. They're sending us men and resources to fight back this threat, even fighting one of their own."

"So why do you need us?"

"Because nothing much beats local knowledge. We plan on using your father's ingenuity to run rings around the Nomads and bring the fire back to their door. Do you want in on that?"

Adelina grinned, life coming back to her olive complexion at the mention of her father. "*Cristo, sí, ha sido demasiado tiempo.* I told you before that I wanted to prove my worth again, and I think I speak for everyone here when I say we'd gladly lay down our lives to protect our town against anyone."

Adelina stood, the rest joining her. Every inch her father's daughter at that point, full of fight and fire, and Keaton knew he'd made the right choice.

"Our plan is simple," he told them. "We have an idea that the Nomads are gathered in clusters a few miles outside city limits. We sent out a scouting party to confirm that. They haven't returned yet. That just confirms what I first thought—that they're out there, and they're not going to leave us alone until the town is burning and we're all dead."

"So, we're going to take the fight to them?"

Keaton nodded, drawing lines in the dirt. "Let's say this is us. We're sitting at the base of a valley. There are forests nearby and sheer enough drops that we could use bikes to run them off the road. We're going to send people out as bait and run them in rings. We'll split them up as much as possible. We have some special hardware—courtesy of your father, of course—which we're saving back for their big guns. Anything else you need to know?"

"When can we get those *cabrones*?"

CHAPTER 25

WEAPONIZED

MARK'S RELAXED NIGHT DIDN'T last long. The first call came in on the radio, waking him at just gone two in the morning. Blinking in the darkness, he'd fumbled for the handset he kept at his bedside as Rebecca struggled to stir.

"Stiles here, over."

"Sir, we need backup…attacks all over the city." Static interrupted the rest of the transmission, although Stiles had heard more than enough to jolt him into wakefulness.

"Mark?" Rebecca's voice was muffled, thick with fatigue. He didn't want her in this.

"Stay here, Becky. Lock yourself in this room. Don't open it for anyone except me."

"What's happening?"

"I don't know yet. Whatever it is, it's not good. I have to go." Dashing to his closet, he pulled out his BDUs, stepping into them and hauling out his boots. Rebecca had just managed to heave herself upright as he left. "Remember, don't open the door for *anybody* else."

At the bottom of the stairs, propped up like an umbrella, was his beloved Winchester. "We've been through a lot together. No better time for you, old girl."

Mark Stiles ran into the night. They didn't have street lights.

A burning ball streaked towards him through the darkness.

"Holy shit." Mark levered a round into the Winchester, holding it out in front and looking down the sight. The fireball kept coming. Mark thought for a shocking second that New Abraham had been a fade, and the Nomads had been coming for Omaha all along. He shook that off. Their scouts and lookouts would have hailed any approach long before now. It wasn't human. Nothing could withstand fire like that and keep running at full pelt.

That left one possibility.

Holding the Winchester steady, Mark calmed his breathing. The sprinter, entire body engulfed in flames, burned his vision. Stars danced. "Closer. Come on you bastard, just a little bit closer." Mark could barely make out a silhouette when he squeezed the trigger. The infected dropped like a stone, the charred corpse skidding a small ways. Mark's nose curled at the stench of burning flesh. He couldn't do anything for whoever that poor soul had been; it wasn't worth another bullet to finish it off. Even if it came back as a shambler, the flames would destroy enough of it to make it useless.

"Tac comms, this is Mark Stiles. I need a sitrep, over."

Captain Denny's voice responded: "It's hell, sir. There are infected all over the city. Fast and slow. We're broadcasting on any radio channel we can for people to stay indoors."

Mark waited for more on the transmission before realizing Denny had broken protocol. "For Christ's sake, Denny remember to say over when you're done. Are people being bitten? Over."

"Sorry, sir, we're not in a good way here. We've had a couple of reports of bites. The vaccine is holding. Uh, over."

"That's good news at least, about the vaccine. What's your position? Over."

"I'm back at the pharmacy in South Central. We have wounded. I'm sending them to the hospital. They're leaving us to recover the wounded, sir. They're not trying to kill. Do you have orders? Over."

Mark sprinted towards the hospital. He had to see for himself that their population wouldn't turn and that McCartney was leaving the wounded alone. "Hold your position, Denny. What support do you have? Who have you seen? Over."

"They've got us pinned down tight. I'm here in case they need extra supplies at the hospital, over."

"Good call. I'm heading to the hospital now. Stiles, over and out."

★★★★★

Captain Alex Denny sat on the floor in the corner of the room hugging his knees. The radio kept buzzing with updates from across the settlement and throughout the night. He tried to shut his ears to them. They just kept coming.

A sprinter broke into one house. The family had all been sleeping in the same room. It had bitten chunks out of their seven-year-old daughter and ripped the mother's arm clear of its socket before the father had woken enough to fight back. He hadn't been injured. His wife was in critical condition, a suspected heart attack through shock. His daughter would probably never walk again.

Another couple had come home from an evening on guard shift to find a shambler somehow in their closet upstairs. It had fallen on them both, getting two deep bites in before they put it down. They were both in the hospital.

McCartney's people were setting sprinters on fire and releasing them into the streets. Living Molotov cocktails, Denny saw five or six run past his position leaving an orange burn on his tearful vision.

He knew he should take his weapon and fight back. The hospital didn't need him; there were others who could just sit and wait for a call on a supply run.

Denny hadn't been a fighter before Morningstar. Coming to Omaha by chance rather than skill, he thought that working with soldiers would make a man out of him.

Shivering through the night, snot and salty tears staining his cheeks, Captain Denny knew he was a coward, and that's all he would ever be.

★★★★★

The doors to the hospital were propped open. There was no one in the waiting area. Triage as they once knew it was a thing of the past. White medical coats were all that distinguished staff from victims; everyone Mark looked at was covered in blackened blood.

He made a beeline for Anna's private recovery room, hoping she'd taken the sensible option and stayed in bed. The sheets were unkempt, pulled to one side like she'd left them in a hurry. Bedmaking wasn't priority number one tonight.

Mark grabbed an orderly by the arm. The woman circled around him carrying a tray of syringes.

"Woah there, you trying to get yourself stabbed? Oh sorry, I didn't recognize you, sir."

Stiles didn't recognize the woman either, though she clearly knew who he was. That wasn't surprising, given his involvement in the development of the hospital. "Do you know where Doctor Demilio is? It's urgent."

"Yes, sir. She's treating a couple on the third floor. Room 303. They were attacked by an infected in their house."

The woman rushed on with Mark's thanks as he followed her down the hallway. Outside room 303, the once sterile white walls were streaked with splashes of blood. As he approached, Anna exited. She was pale, her hands shaking as they held onto a clipboard.

"What's happening in there, doc?"

"Too much, Mark. She probably won't survive the night. We still don't have the facilities to treat major cardiac trauma."

"I'm sorry."

"Not as much as I am. This is McCartney's doing, isn't it?"

"Who else?" Mark kept step with her as she marched down the corridor, flipping over a page to examine another set of notes. "How many have you got in?"

"We've had four deaths, perhaps fifty injured. Most of those before the news got out to stay indoors. They're controlling it now, I think. There's less coming in. We can cope with the staff we have, though it's a close call. Is Becky available to help?"

Mark thought of her, asleep in their bed, heavily pregnant. She'd help in a heartbeat. "I don't think that's a good idea."

"No, of course. I forgot. Sorry, Mark, this situation is making everyone lose their heads."

"Not you, it seems."

She quirked an eyebrow at him. "You mean you're not going to tell me I should be in bed resting right now?"

"I think I know what you'd say to that. Where are we heading?"

"Another patient. It's a little girl. The daughter of the woman I just saw. The Archers. Laura is the little girl. Alison had a cardiac arrest after having an arm torn out by a sprinter. She hasn't been bitten. She's fighting, but there's nothing else I can do for her. Laura's wounds are more severe. She's lost a lot of blood. I think we're going to have to amputate."

"Can I see her?"

Anna shot him a look. "I don't think that's appropriate, Mark. What are you going to do? She's only a little girl."

"How recently did the Archers come to Omaha?"

"I don't know," she glanced down at her paperwork, flipping over another sheet. "It says Laura had her first check three months ago."

Mark nodded. "So, they're new. I don't think these attacks are random, Anna. McCartney's too clever for that. I think he's targeting people who haven't been vaccinated properly."

She yanked him through a door into an empty office, shoving him bodily up against a wall. The sudden movement and her strength took him by surprise. Mark froze. Anna put her head close to his, her voice dropping to a hiss. Gray hair flecked across her forehead. This close, he could feel the fever pouring off her.

"Do *not* say anything like that out there again. Christ knows we're all trying to hold this together, but these people need to believe they're safe from what's being thrown at them. That maniac is trying to tear this city apart from the top, and right now it's working. The last thing you want is rumor spreading that the vaccine doesn't work.... It does. We *know* it does. Veteran residents have been bitten, and they haven't turned. I'm not stupid. They're all in isolation."

"And Laura?"

Anna grimaced. "I don't know. She's showing signs."

"I need to see her, Anna. It's our proof."

They walked the remainder in silence. Orderlies pulled Anna to one side now and again, asking brief questions she gave terse answers to—mostly about patient positioning; they knew they needed to keep anyone bitten away from the general population. A haunted atmosphere had settled over most of the medical staff. Mark was glad, knowing what they faced, that Becky was safe at home. McCartney wouldn't target her: she had received one of the first vaccines before Robbie even joined the Fac.

Laura's room was at the end of a corridor of closed doors. Mark could hear groans of pain behind some of them, but none of the anguished cries he'd long since associated with those succumbing to the virus. Laura was sitting up on the bed. She looked exhausted. Her skinny legs were bound tightly with medical dressing. Even with the layers of gauze, black blood still oozed through.

"Hello, Laura. Do you remember me?" Anna's voice rose a few octaves, almost chirruping as she addressed the little girl.

Laura frowned, looking as if she didn't understand the question. "Are you going to take me to my mommy now?"

"I'm sorry, darling. Your mommy is quite sick, and we need to keep a close eye on her right now."

"I feel hot," Laura mumbled, leaning back on her pillows and closing her eyes.

Anna scooted to her side. "I need to take your temperature, okay?"

Laura nodded as Anna unpacked a sterile tip, placing it on the end of the thermometer and clicking. Anna frowned at first, quickly changing that to a smile as Laura glanced around.

"Am I okay?"

"You'll be fine, sweetheart. It's just your legs. They're making your body feel hot. Would you like some water?"

"I have some, thank you."

Laura closed her eyes again, collapsing back. Anna lifted an eyelid. "She's out. Her temperature is 110, Mark. I think she's infected. Help me."

Anna reached under the bed and pulled out a set of restraints. Mark's eyes bulged. "You've *planned* for this?"

"Of course, we have," the doctor answered. "Even after the vaccine, we knew that we might get refugees in who were infected. We can't just leave them behind closed doors. Any sprinter is a threat, whether you're vaccinated or not."

"But…she's just a little girl."

"A little girl who could become a sprinter. I know you're about to become a father, but think with your head, not your heart. Come on. I don't think we've got long, the way her condition has deteriorated."

All Mark could think as he worked, was if this had been his own little girl, how he'd be reacting. The child's mother, Alison, lay dying at the other end of this corridor. What if she wanted to see her little girl one last time before she passed? How could Mark explain to a dying woman that her daughter was gone, too, because their security procedures had failed?

Was he really the leader they wanted? That Frank wanted?

He dropped the cuff twice before securing it around the girl's tiny ankle. Her limbs were so small that he could easily get his hand around her leg and wrist. They had to stuff cloth in the cuffs to make sure her hands wouldn't just slide straight out the second she started to resist.

Tugging at each one to make sure she was happy they'd stay put, Anna placed a hand on Mark's cheek, squeezing gently. "This isn't easy for any of us, Mark, but it's necessary. Can you wait here with her and let me know what happens if you need to see it for yourself? I have…other patients to see."

"Sure." Mark nodded dumbly. "I can wait. If she turns?"

"I think it's a case of when, unfortunately. Don't let her out of those restraints." Anna eyeballed him as she left. "And if she *is* a sprinter, don't put her down. I…we need her."

Mark's hackles rose as the doctor left. His mind drifted back to her comments about BL4.

What are you hiding, doctor?

CHAPTER 26

JESSICA SIPPED AT A cup of sweet tea. Her thin fingers wrapped around the mug. She held it with both hands, the liquid still sloshing as she raised it to her lips. She slurped, the noise over-loud in the large room.

"Did we miss anyone out of the calls, Jessica?" Frank kept his voice soft and low. He didn't think his young assistant would be able to cope with much more today. She certainly wouldn't be in the room for his last conversation.

"No, sir. Hunters, Omaha, and New Abraham, all either out of range of comms or checked in."

"Thank you. Take the rest of the evening off. I insist. You've done more than enough today."

"Sir, if there's anything else you need?"

"Not today, Jessica. Thank you."

He waited until she'd gone, dwelling on the damning reports coming through; hopeful that the people he'd left in charge were still fighting back against seemingly insurmountable odds.

The Hunters were still offline. That much, he expected. Brewster would keep their radios dark until they needed to call something in. The last thing they would want is radio static while trying to creep through a city of undead. Sherman hoped they were still alive. That was one call he'd leave the line open for, any time of day.

He'd finally spoken with Mark Stiles. On face value, Omaha was an utter clusterfuck. Infected in the streets, in people's homes, civilian deaths, civil uprising, an unscheduled election. Sherman wanted to unleash hell on the man at first, but with Jessica in the room he'd kept his cool. Besides, without being on the ground, he couldn't tell just how well Stiles was doing, and against what odds. Keeping a neutral tone, he was able to see things from Stiles' perspective. If this election was what the man needed for people to see this McCartney for who he was, so be it. At least there was a plan.

Too, with New Abraham. Keaton reported he had rallied his people, and Jose—bless that tinkering mechanic—had come up with the goods once again for their fight back. Sherman didn't even question the sheriff's move to recruit Adelina and her rebel friends. The experience with Tanner Whitehead had been long enough ago. They were good kids, Keaton told him, and not beyond redemption. The man had a gruff exterior, no doubt, but a heart of gold.

In his own backyard, things were totally different. The bodies of Spivey and Sanderson were laid out in the makeshift morgue. Their deaths, and especially the shockingly violent murder of the always-amiable Sanderson, cast a gray pall over everyone.

He'd interviewed every junior chief, every newcomer to the staff, every single person that he could even feasibly think to be a part of this scheme. He'd taken Jessica into his confidence, sure that she was beyond reproach. He'd managed to keep quiet, the fact that Spivey had turned at the last. No matter how he'd gotten infected, the man—all of the staff—were meant to be immune, Sherman first amongst them. He'd seen the small wound on the man's arm, clear signs of a local injection. Someone had deliberately infected Spivey, knowing that the Veep would turn. Someone like that couldn't be allowed to run riot for much longer. Stiles was worried about keeping control of Omaha: Sherman was worried about keeping control of the country.

He picked up the phone, dialing. It didn't ring long before someone picked up the receiver at the other end.

"Anna?"

"Frank. It's so good to hear your voice."

"You have no idea what it means to hear yours. Mark informed me a few minutes ago about your situation. Do you think he can suppress this, Anna? Can we win?"

"I honestly like his plan. These people aren't military, and they aren't RSA. They're organized, sure, but they don't seem to know what to do with it. They're following McCartney, and he's a lunatic with too much power."

"Hmm. Maybe you're right. I have to trust you both. I can't risk leaving here again, not with everything else that's going on."

"Aside from the fact that if you ever suggest getting in a helicopter again I'm going to have you strapped to your chair until you see sense!"

Despite himself, Frank chuckled. Anna always seemed to bring out the humor in a situation. Having her now, at the end of this, was one of the few things keeping him going. "I hope it doesn't come to that. How are you?"

"I'm fine, Frank, don't worry about me."

"The fact that you're saying it means I'm just going to worry more. I know you. You've had patients in, and the first thing you did was leap out of that bed. Am I right?"

"You got me. We aren't exactly replete with medical knowledge here. I thought the profession had a skills shortage before most of the population was killed. The team has pulled together well. I'm surprised we've had as few losses as we have."

"Any bad?"

"The worst was a family. Their home was broken into by a sprinter. The mother, Alison, had her arm ripped off. It gave her a heart attack, literally. The daughter, Laura, was bitten on the leg. I thought she'd lose it, but it doesn't matter now. She turned, Frank."

"Wasn't she vaccinated?"

"Mark has a theory that Robbie wasn't sabotaging the batches—he thinks that would have been too risky with my close involvement in production. Robbie was involved in setting up the vaccination stations, though, and with the ingestion of new refugees, Mark believes Robbie arranged for McCartney's people to get involved, and they administered placebos instead of the vaccine to the general population."

"How long do we think this was going on?"

"Hard to say. We can't even assume if Mark's theory is correct, that it was just Robbie behind it. We had to recruit volunteers to get people injected. I'd say we still need to go back to square one and revaccinate the entire population, just to be sure."

"Except you?"

"There are a few I trust. I didn't administer your vaccine."

"No..." Frank sighed heavily. "You didn't."

CHAPTER 27

"What the fuck do we use to fight *dogs*?"

"They're not Old Yeller," Brewster shouted. "Just shoot them!"

"Are they infected?" Castillo shouted as she hit a smart shot through the forehead of German Shepherd that leaped too close. The crack of gunfire sent the remaining four dogs yelping, skittering away, but not far.

"I don't think so," grumbled Krueger. "From the looks of things, they're so hungry they've gone feral. I think I'd rather be taken out by one of the infected."

"You might get your wish if we don't get out of here," Castillo said, aiming at another canine. "Let's get these pups put down and get somewhere inside."

It still tugged at Brewster to kill the guard dogs. He was a dog person. Even if it was another clear survival scenario, the animals hadn't asked to be left alone to starve in a dead city. They were all off their chains, which hinted at the worst of the infection—or the attempted evacuation—happened at night. During the day, he'd expect the animals to be chained up to prevent them from harassing construction workers passing through the site.

"Everyone inside. Let's hustle, come on." Brewster stood point as the other three followed him in. The ground floor was open on all sides, and it took them mere minutes to confirm the building site was clear.

Sitting in the center of the concrete floor, Brewster laid out the map again, pointing at their location. "By my reckoning, we're around here, northwest. It's a straight run about half a mile down to the Department of Justice. It should be a secure building with little staff, and we can clear it with the ammo we have. There's huge potential for an LZ on the road out front. From there we can cut west to the White House lawns, and then the president has his beachhead to try and take back the city."

"What's between us and our waypoint?"

"Much of what we've seen. This area is all office buildings primarily, and coffee shops, I guess. Best case scenario, most of the workaholics here didn't want to call in sick on the day the world ended, so they're all still stuck at their desks."

"And worst case, boss?" Garibaldi asked.

Brewster shrugged, grinning. "They're all packed in the streets having one huge-ass party."

"Not funny," Castillo said, her face turned sour. "Have we got any other options if our way is blocked?"

"Sorry. I guess we can't use Franklin Square as an LZ; it's too overgrown. There's a park at the end of Pennsylvania. That'll just attract even more infected though, if the area's already packed."

"So, we're saying it's this way or this way?" Castillo didn't look impressed with their options. "I take it the third choice is death?"

"I'd rather not think of option three. We've caused a hell of a shitstorm behind us, though. I say we open tac comms and call in for help. We give them our coords and the plan, and we get our drop ahead of time. That way if it all goes to shit we've at least got a chance of picking up more goodies."

"Die in a blaze of glory!" Krueger said.

"Rather not." Garibaldi looked offended.

Brewster thumbed the map. "Do any of you have a better idea? Because right now I'm open to any fucking opinion."

"You both know agreeing with Brewster isn't my favored state of being," Krueger said. "But looking at what little choices we have, this plan seems solid enough. We're definitely going to need to call it in, though. We haven't got the resources to cut our way through a crowd."

Brewster looked at Garibaldi and Castillo, but they were tight-lipped. "We're all agreed then? I'm not calling rank on this, whatever my rank is meant to be. We've lost Kiley and Brent. I won't be responsible for another fucking loss."

"Their deaths aren't your fault." Krueger shook his head. "It could have been any one of us. We all know that. It's the risk we all signed up for. I'd rather book my ticket doing something big out here than kicking my heels at home."

"We lost two good men today," Castillo said, her face dry with blood. Brewster thought some wetness was welling in her eyes. "They were my friends before they were soldiers. I still agree with Krueger. Sherman is trying to build something, and he wanted us out here to get it started. If we go down fighting, then so be it."

She and Krueger bumped fists.

"Hooah."

"Oorah."

It didn't feel like the start of an ending. Heroes had their stories. They were the Hunters, and their best tale was yet to come.

The radio felt like the weight of the world in Brewster's hands, though. He hefted it a few times before turning it on. "Base this is Hunter One, do you copy, over?"

"Hunter One! This is base, reading you loud and clear."

"We are situated at H Street, Central DC. We are locating to the Department of Justice and request a resource drop in four hours. Can you comply? Over."

"Hunter One, request acknowledged. Not to sound too blunt, sir, but things here are going south of shit, rapidly. Stand by for ETA on your resources, over."

"Base, are you telling us that you cannot supply? Over."

"Please stay online for further instruction. Base, over and out."

"Well, shit." Brewster felt like throwing the walkie on the ground. Gritting his teeth, he knew better.

"That sounds fucked up," Krueger muttered. "I thought we were top priority. I don't even want to know what's happening on the ground if we've been shunted. Actually, yeah. Yeah, I do."

"We know that McCartney fucker paraded a zombie around Omaha like a party clown before we left," Brewster said, leaning back against the wall. "Can't be a coincidence. I feel like hailing Stiles directly."

"Do it, boss. Let's see what the fuck's happening, man." Garibaldi was biting his nails in nervous fashion.

"Except we need to stay free for their update to come through," Castillo said. "They won't take long. They knew we'd be sitting ducks out here when we needed it."

"As long as they haven't totally forgotten about us." Garibaldi began pacing.

"Command wouldn't let that happen," Brewster said. "Sherman's got our backs."

As things stood, it was a tense ten minutes before the radio sounded again, the same operator on the line. "Hunter One, do you copy? Over."

"I copy, base, what's the sitrep?"

"We will have a supply drop for you in twenty-four hours. Bunker down and set watches. Acknowledge? Over."

Brewster couldn't mask the disappointment in his voice. "Twenty-four hours confirmed. Hunter One, over and out."

"They want us to sit here for a *day*?" Garibaldi sounded incredulous, and Brewster couldn't blame him, though he tried to shrug it off.

"We're safe enough here." Castillo walked over and punched Garibaldi lightly on the shoulder. "The dead fucks didn't see us come in, and the dogs are all gone."

"Well, except that one." Krueger pointed.

Brewster followed his finger to see a Doberman limping towards them.

"Aww, shit," Brewster stood, moving towards it, hand outstretched in greeting.

"Woah there, we already shot it, and most of his buddies. I don't think he's going to want to suddenly be making friends with you." Krueger brought his pistol to bear.

"So, you're just going to shoot it?" Brewster said.

"Damn right, I am. We already did it—and his buddies. Just because he's injured doesn't mean he's going to want to kill you any less."

As Krueger shot, the dog skittered away. Its back legs failed; the dog fell to one side, the unexpected movement causing the usually faultless sharpshooter to miss. The shot pinged through the fencing. Outside, the clamor of undead rose, their strangled voices rising as one at the new stimulus.

The Doberman huddled down by the fence, rose its head, its own high-pitched howl rising to join the cries of the infected. The fence started shaking.

"Here we go again! Goddammit," Garibaldi grabbed his M4. "Man, I thought we'd at least be able to get some grub in our bellies before we had to start running again. This sucks."

"Where are we heading?" Castillo looked at Brewster.

"We stick to the plan—and hope all these distractions are clearing us a path."

"If not?"

"Then it was nice working with you!"

The four remaining Hunters grabbed their packs, running south, out the opposite end of the site with teeming hordes once again trying to run them down.

CHAPTER 28

"YOUR LEADER MUST THINK he's so clever. You know we left you alone on purpose, right?" Johnny kicked out at the prone scout. The boy hadn't divulged his name yet, and sadly Johnny didn't think he ever would. He'd have been barely out of high school, pre-pandemic. Now here he was, all alone, the last of a group of three they'd found scouting their position.

"You can think what you want, you sick fuck," the boy spat blood, some of it landing on Johnny's boot. "Attack again. We know you will. We're waiting for you. We're ready."

"If you're so ready, why have they sent boys and girls to do the jobs of men? We've killed your people before. Is your town running out of real soldiers?"

"I'm one of the best scouts we have." Billy was lying. He was new. Janine hadn't wanted him to go. Billy had insisted. In the end, Billy's father had given permission.

"They're not going directly to camp," his father had said to the woman, who stood by the sheriff like they were both in charge. "It's remote recon, right? He'll be with two excellent senior scouts. If you have anyone else to nominate, go ahead. I'll support my boy's decision. Our grandparents went to war younger than him."

Billy turned eighteen three weeks ago, and his dad had taken him for his first drink at Eileen's. William had assured his son beer tasted much better out of chilled barrels, in cool, clean glasses. He didn't know Billy had gotten drunk at a party for his sixteenth birthday; he knew perfectly well what cold beer tasted like. The stale, lukewarm fluid the barwoman poured had reminded Billy of soggy cardboard. His first one had been on the house from Eileen herself; the next from Sheriff Keaton, who'd come to wish him well. His father had stood him the third, as Billy didn't have much to barter with. After that, well, he'd been tipsy, and it seemed every regular in the bar wanted to get in on the act of getting Abraham's newest eighteen-year-old drunk.

He remembered slurring at some point that he still wasn't twenty-one. The Sheriff had laughed, mentioning something about parental consent, and him being the last letter of the law anyway. The drinks kept coming, and Billy spent the next morning vomiting in an empty barrel in his father's back garden.

"What lesson have you learned?" his dad has asked.

Billy had answered that he didn't.

"It's better to make decisions on your own terms than keep taking on someone else's. You could have stopped those drinks coming, but you didn't. If you'd had something to barter, and bought your own drinks, do you think you'd have stopped sooner?"

"Much." Billy had admitted through dry heaves.

And so, he'd volunteered. He didn't want to wait for someone to tell him how to serve his town, knowing that serving might mean his death. Billy felt like a man, and he'd decided to choose how to live. And how to die.

"We're all men in Abraham, all of us better than you."

"Is that so? Well, little *man*, you can start by telling me what little Abraham has left to offer by way of resistance. Remember, I've seen inside your pathetic little town. There's no point hiding anything from me. I like your spirit. If you tell me what you know, I might even let you join us."

"That's quite the offer, boy." A fat man, tall, fading tattoos smothering his neck and cheeks, offered encouragement. "Not many new joiners these days. No need for them. The Nomads only want the reckless and the brave."

"I don't think you quite understand what you're going up against. No, thanks. I'll be keeping my information to myself."

Billy didn't want to admit that even if he wanted to answer their questions, he couldn't. He knew that Keaton was planning an attack and had been working with the Mexican mechanic named Jose. Apart from that, most folks were in the dark about their next steps. Billy hoped they wouldn't wait for the Nomads to come. They were in a forest clearing. Four cars and one people-transport idling nearby. The standout car was a burnt orange Mustang; the sort of car Billy had coveted when he was learning to drive. Being a Nomad would mean getting one of those for himself, one day.

But, not at the cost of the lives of everyone he cared about.

Johnny crouched down, grabbing him by the jaw, which was sore from being punched a few times already. The man shook Billy viciously, like a dog he was bringing to heel. "I don't think you quite understand the nature of this offer. You tell me what you know, and seeing as you're being a little shit, *maybe* I let you join. Or I try to smoke the information out of you."

The tattooed man grinned, revealing rows of gold and silver-capped teeth. He held up a thin curved metal pipe. A tube ran from it, down to a cylinder on the back of a truck. "You curious, son? This is what they call in the industry, an oxygen-acetylene torch. To you and me though it's called a welding torch. We use it to adapt our trucks as we see fit. Sometimes though, we use it for other more pressing things." He held something in front of the torch and clicked it once. An orange flame spurted out. He twisted a nozzle on the pipe. The flame hissed, streamlining and turning a brilliant blue. Billy felt a warm trickle down one side of his pants.

"Now, I'm going to ask you again, just the once, and I'm going to ask nicely. Are you going to tell me about your little town and its absurd plans to put up a fight?"

Billy clamped his mouth shut, not trusting his voice now, and shook his head. Tears came into his eyes.

"I'm not sure if you're brave or stupid. Eric?"

"I'd say he's stupid, boss. Let's burn it out of him."

Billy's first mistake was looking directly at the flame. Spots sprang in his vision. He closed his eyes, turning his face, but it was too late. He could already feel them burning. "Oh dear. Getting cold feet are we, little man? Don't worry. We can warm them up."

The man who'd been called Eric grabbed Billy's leg at the shin, holding the limb easily in his meaty grasp. Billy struggled; Johnny stepped around, standing on his shoulders and keeping him still. He crouched, slapping Billy across the cheeks. "I promise you, this is going to hurt. A lot."

Billy spat blood and phlegm in the man's face.

Eric held the torch to his knee. Scorched flesh mingled with burning denim, and Billy's world went white.

★★★★★

The screams made him hoarse. He couldn't really talk now, just pant. He'd lost control of his bowels, he knew that much. But he hadn't told them a single thing. Now, they'd gone too far. He probably wouldn't even live long enough to recover his voice. Eric had laughed too much. Billy hoped that his dad got to that one in the end and punched every single gleaming tooth out of the sadistic bastard's smiling face.

"I think we'll leave you here. Unless you want a merciful end now? We can do that much for you. Just write us down some things. You know what we want to know."

Billy glanced at the paper with teary, blotchy vision. He wasn't sure what looking at that light had done to them. It felt like he was going blind.

Eric held the torch loosely in one hand. Billy coughed, trying to produce some phlegm to coat his throat, to try and get out some final words. Eric leaned in closer. The Nomad put his ear close to Billy's mouth.

Billy coughed again, pitifully, clearing enough to make himself heard. "My own choosing. Fucker."

Billy twisted, his unexpected movement catching Johnny off guard.

Eric dropped the welding torch. Billy picked it up, shoving it in his own mouth, pointing up towards his brain. He wasn't conscious long enough to scream again.

CHAPTER 29

"No, YOU DIDN'T." FRANK sighed down the phone. "I crossed that bridge already though, Anna."

"Frank, please promise me something. We both know they're trying to kill you. Stay safe. Please. I love you."

Anna held her breath for the longest time. "I love you, too, good doctor."

The line went dead. Anna placed the receiver down gently, not willing to try and swallow past the lump in her throat. Tears streamed unbidden down her cheeks. It didn't feel like a gesture of love. It felt like a goodbye.

Frank was beyond her help. Tomorrow, everything they'd worked for could be lost. Years of struggle to get this far. Anna knew she wasn't feeling sorrow just for her, or for Frank. The sacrifices of friends flashed through her mind unbidden. Julie Ortiz's contagious desire to find the truth; Mbutu's steadfastness; Mason's stubborn selflessness, right to the end. They'd fought government agencies and born-again movements. They'd battled against a virus that Satan himself couldn't have conjured any better if he'd tried. All of it, together, they'd pulled together and conquered.

And now, in one night, an arrogant upstart with a sociopathic agenda could bring it all to an end.

Still, they weren't defeated. Not yet. And while they had a chance, Anna had a job to do. She'd distract herself from her inner demons by doing what she did best. She'd throw herself into her work and let the result speak for itself. Refocused, Anna headed straight for BL1. Phyllis would be on shift. The pleasant old woman was just the company she needed. Some absent chatter while formulating vaccines.

Phyllis wasn't in the lab, though. She was in the corridor. Phyllis didn't walk, or stride. She barely ambled. The deep lines across her forehead seemed deeper. Her body was stiff.

"Phyllis, are you okay?"

"No, doctor, I really think I'm not. Can we talk? In private?"

Anna gestured around the empty corridors. "The Fac is secure Phyllis. We're alone here. What's wrong?"

"I don't think this is quite what I meant, doctor."

"But I'm telling you that we're alone and this conversation is confidential. What's wrong?"

Phyllis turned. Anna thought she'd walk away. Whirling back, Phyllis cried, almost screeching. "What's happened to Robbie?"

"Robbie?"

"Yes, Robbie. The young man we've worked with for months? Someone in the street, they told me he's dead. That you'd killed him. That you're working on a new virus. Is it true?"

"God, Phyllis, no, it's not! None of it."

"No? Then, where is he? Why hasn't he come to shift? Or gone home? I've checked. None of his friends have seen him. More than one person has told me he's dead. What have I gotten myself involved in here, Anna?"

Anna thought for a crazy second that Phyllis would turn a gun on her too—her second assistant to go rogue. The woman's hands were empty. "Phyllis, I'm not going to lie to you. Robbie is dead. I don't know what you've heard, but you need to listen to me."

"So, you can kill me, too?"

"I have no reason to kill you, Phyllis. Robbie...Robbie was a member of a group that wants to try to stop vaccine production. They think what we're doing is unnatural, and they think it's better to see Morningstar run its course."

"If good boys like him end up dead because of it, I can see why they think they're right!"

"Phyllis please, think about what you're saying. We've all worked so hard to get to this point. We can't throw it all away now because of one radical upstart."

"What *are* we working on now though? You didn't answer me about the new virus. Is that what you're doing? Did Robbie find that out, and you had to murder him to keep him quiet? I know the vaccine didn't work, Anna. I heard. People in the hospital, last night. They got infected after they were bitten."

Phyllis was an old woman, a gentle reminder for Anna of her own mother. She could have been a member of a knitting or reading group. Anna could imagine the woman volunteering at soup kitchens, or just sitting in a park, retired, happy, watching the world go by.

Phyllis had just put herself on the list of people putting their entire program at risk. Anna was so close to a breakthrough. If McCartney won out, Anna could lock herself in BL4. Perhaps she'd even be able to get a working sample before they broke through.

"Phyllis, I can explain all of this if you'd just let me. People turned, yes, that's true, only because Robbie helped McCartney and his people sabotage the vaccination program."

"Robbie didn't do anything to what we produced! I'd have known. You would have, too."

"I know that. That doesn't mean that what they were giving people when they came here was the actual vaccine. At best, they were injecting people with sugar water. Don't you understand? McCartney made sure that people came in without vaccines. He's been planning all of this, for longer than we all thought."

"And why should I believe you above anyone else? You're one person. All I hear out there is that we've been doing bad things. I'm not a bad woman. I'd never forgive myself if I knew I'd contributed to *anyone* being hurt."

"Phyllis, I promise you, and I swear it by God himself, that you've done nothing but help since the moment you arrived with us. I couldn't have done any of this without you. Please, just let me show you."

Phyllis' demeanor cooled a little, her posture relaxing as Anna's words sank in. *No one wanted to be the bad guy.* "Well, since you put it like that, I do get thanked a lot. And all the new people we've had recently, I suppose it's possible that we got some bad eggs in the batch."

"Michael McCartney is definitely one of those."

"And there's been no other research?"

"I've been doing more work, Phyllis. But it's not what you think. I can show you if you'll just come with me."

Phyllis came to Omaha in the early days of the vaccination program. The old woman's arrival had kickstarted Anna's efforts. The doctor hadn't been lying when she said that Phyllis had done nothing but good; that the program wouldn't be as far along as it was without her. Phyllis was literally instrumental. But sentiment couldn't get in the way. This far along, nothing was going to stop her work.

"How can I trust you? I'm so confused."

"That's how they want you to feel. We're just going to a ward. There's something I want to show you. It's not in a lab, so how bad could it be?"

Phyllis chewed her inner lip, hesitating. "I've worked with you for so long. Show me, then. I want to see for myself what you've been doing versus what those people on the street are saying."

The wards Anna referred to were locked rooms, more isolation chambers with rudimentary medical equipment than specialized areas. In days gone by, they'd house voluntary test subjects enrolled in controlled drug trials, at the worst. They'd stood empty for the majority of her tenure here in the Fac. A couple of new residents had been enrolled and were already acclimatized to their new surroundings.

Room 1.07 was the most obvious candidate. Grabbing her keychain, she opened the simple lock. "What's in there?" Phyllis sounded understandably nervous.

"Like I said, it's harmless at the moment. It's a demonstration of my research."

"Then why is the door locked?"

Anna glanced in and waved with a smile, beckoning Phyllis forward. "Oh, precautions. You know the way I can be. No one minds."

Phyllis peeked around the door. Before she could register the child strapped to the gurney, Anna pushed the unresisting woman all the way into the room. Phyllis staggered with a moan.

"I'm sorry, Phyllis. You won't be in any danger. But I can't risk you endangering this any more than you already have."

Anna shut the door, twisting the lock. Turning her back, she slid against the door to the floor, openly weeping now. She tried to ignore the pathetic slaps of Phyllis' palms against the door. They weren't quite as traumatizing as the juvenile's howls of hunger.

CHAPTER 30

"I DON'T UNDERSTAND, MR. President. I've been nothing but loyal to you. Why are you dismissing me?"

"I've made it perfectly clear on my memo, Jessica. My investigation into the heli crash, the murders of Sanderson and Spivey, they can only have been coordinated by one person. Until I can prove that, you are dismissed from my service and under formal arrest. If you're as innocent as you claim, then you have nothing to fear."

Jessica's hands clutched the arms of the chair, her face red, veins popping out against her pale skin. "Without proof even? Sir, this is absurd. Please, just ask any of your staff, they'll all vouch for me."

"And they'll all get their chance in an interview. Up until now, I've thought of you as nothing but exemplary. After an investigation, if that proves to be true, I'll welcome you back, fully reinstated without question. If you're as loyal as you claim to be, you'll understand why I'm doing this. I don't want to cause a scene unnecessarily. You'll be escorted back to your rooms, and one of my detail will accompany you at all times. Your access to restricted areas is revoked. Have I made myself clear?"

Jessica bowed her head. "Yes, Mr. President."

"Good. Please close your door on the way out."

"I'm sorry?"

"Close the door, Jessica."

The poor girl had every right to slam it, but she didn't. The paperwork didn't stack up. Still, decisions had to be made. Frank poured himself a neat scotch, turning off all but his desk lamp. Taking a sip, he relished in the burn as the peaty alcohol seared down his throat. When was the last time he'd allowed himself such a luxury? A drink, some peace and quiet? The only thing missing was a cigar.

Business remained business, though. His respite was brief. He dialed the familiar number.

"Anna?" Frank twisted in the swivel chair, his back to the door, his military boots propped up on the window ledge. He leaned back, trying to make himself comfortable. "It's done. Have you contained everything there? Good. And the last batch? When are you going to try that? Okay. I understand. Is there anything else you need from me? Have you spoken to Mark? That makes sense. Let me know how it goes if you can. I still love you."

A shaft of light slashed down the wall and across the window as his door opened. Sherman placed the receiver down on the desk, the phone call still open. Anna was silent on the other end.

"Jessica, I'm sorry but I've made myself as clear as I can be."

"Luckily, Mr. President, Jessica isn't here."

"Major, I wasn't expecting you. Take a seat. Scotch?"

"I don't think so, Francis."

Major Trevor Bentley lifted his right arm, revealing a small pistol. Without fanfare, he pulled the trigger. Sherman shot a hand to his neck, straight away pulling out the tiny dart.

"Sorry about this, Francis, but business is business. There's no need to call your detail. They're indisposed at the moment, I suppose, making sure your precious assistant is holed up in her quarters. I can't believe you thought that dumb blonde would be capable of orchestrating all this. I mean, technological sabotage? Extracting live strain samples to use on the unvaccinated? Making sure there'd be humans left in this hellhole to infect with the virus?"

"You? But why?" Frank's hand was steady as he dropped the hot dart to the desk. It shook as he lifted the scotch to his lips. He downed it all now, wanting the quick numbing effect of the alcohol. He hadn't poured himself a big enough shot.

"I think you'll need more of this, though it doesn't matter how drunk you get now, Frank. We all know how little infected liquid it takes to turn someone, and the neck has some pretty major veins in it. I don't need a medical degree these days to calculate that you'll turn in, what, an hour? Two at the most? A mortifyingly undistinguished end to such an illustrious career."

Frank felt his heart rate accelerating. His skin was hot. He thought of the scotch, and his rising anger, not the Morningstar virus trying to pump its way through his immune system. "You still haven't told me why."

"No. I'm going to enjoy this bit, though. I've had to listen to you bleating on for so long. *Recovery* this and *cure* that. Have you ever stopped and listened to yourself for one second? You're a broken record from an outdated era."

"McCartney? He's one of yours?"

"No, actually, though it was easy enough to convince him that we had some similar aims. His ideals were somewhat more…radical than what I'm aiming for. I at least want some of the human race alive after all this is said and done, which is more than can be said for your precious Hunters."

"We've had comms from them. They're almost at the Department of Justice. They're doing exactly what I asked."

"I know. I've been tapping your comms for months. You've barely been able to take a shit without me knowing about it. It's a shame you made it out of that chopper mess alive. I'd been hoping to manipulate Spivey; a much easier subject than you. But no, the great Francis Sherman, General-turned-President, had to come riding back into town somehow unscathed."

"What did you want from us? Command?"

"Not directly. Enough to manipulate proceedings. Perhaps, eventually, when the world realized that *my* vision was the right one, then I'd remove Spivey and take the seat for myself. You see, Francis, what you want from the world just isn't right. The United States as we knew it is dead. The RSA saw that, these Nomads outside New Abraham see it. You refuse to, and you have everyone dancing to your tune like the Pied Piper of the Apocalypse.

"The dead infected are hardly a threat to us. They'd be easy enough to handle, in small numbers. New Abraham was perfect. Small communities like that, easy to sustain, easy to rule, from a new central government in another small, highly-militarized colony. Wall off the cities; firebomb them even. Not *save* them. Not try to clear them. How feckless, how self-righteous can one man be, to think he can save everything?"

"We have been, Bentley, haven't you seen that? Omaha is a massive coup for us. And when the Hunters…"

Bentley slammed his fist down, the scotch decanter dancing along at the force of his blow. "They're going to die, dammit. Your precious elite squad hasn't got the manpower or the resources to keep going for much longer, and the support they've asked for won't reach them in time to save them. Abraham is probably attacking the Nomads as we speak. With what little support Omaha could spare, and a little band of farmers with flamethrowers? There goes another one of your little pet projects.

"Your rule is a clusterfuck, Mr. President. All it's going to take now is for people to see that not even our Commander-in-Chief could be saved by a vaccine, and it'll be easy for me to convince them to start towing my line. Because you never took it, did you? I heard your calls to your beloved doctor. Why on earth didn't you even use a secure channel? I *know*, Frank, that you left Omaha without getting vaccinated. Hell, that's probably why you wanted to fly back in the first place, wasn't it? To get your shot before it all went to hell?" Bentley gestured at Sherman's neck. "Look how well that worked out for you."

"Those cities could still have survivors," Frank said, glaring at the man. "Leaving them to rot is tantamount to murder."

"It's mindful negligence at worst. And who's going to know any different? You think the people out there really care how much of the country you get back? Piece by bloody rotten piece, this country didn't function as a whole before it fell to shit, and it certainly isn't going to start because someone who used to wear stars tells them it can."

Bentley pulled out a pistol, holding it limply in his wrist. "You're going to turn, I'm going to kill you and save the lives of everyone in this complex in the process, and I'm going to put a stop to your lunatic recovery program before it goes much further. The vaccinations? I can keep on board with that. On my own terms."

Frank grinned, pouring himself another scotch. He'd regained control of himself now. His skin cooled; his heart thudded steadily in his chest. He glanced at the phone. He couldn't hear a dial tone. He still had his audience.

"My door was always open, Major."

Bentley leaned over in the chair, elbows on the desk, gun still held loose, safety on. "What's that supposed to mean?"

Jessica burst out of his filing closet. Screaming, she threw herself bodily into the chair. Bentley, the chair and all, tilted to the ground with a yelp.

Sherman vaulted the desk and was straddling the prone traitor before he could even raise his head. "Just what I said. The problem with wiretapping, Major, is sometimes you only hear one side of the conversation, and sometimes you hear just what you want to hear."

Bentley tensed against him, torso straining against the weight. It was no use. Lighter by twenty pounds, Sherman still had the idiot pinned, unable to pivot and gain an advantage. "You're still going to die, you blithering old fool."

"No, he's not," Jessica replied coolly, kicking the gun further out of reach.

"I might have left Omaha without being vaccinated, that bit was true. And as I saw my friends and close colleagues murdered; rumors of a spy in the program, that's exactly what I'd want someone who was after my blood to believe. I brought my own personal supply. For safety's sake. You couldn't assassinate me the traditional way, so you'd try more modern methods, especially if you believed I'd be vulnerable. We've seen it with Spivey; not so beyond imagining that I could succumb, too."

"And now what? Do you kill me? You won't let me live, I know you well enough for that. You and your assistant try to explain all of this to an office of junior chiefs that have seen their leadership decimated? Whether you live or die, your leadership here and abroad is discredited forever. They won't let you stay in office. I still win."

Jessica drifted over to the desk, picking up the receiver. "Did you get all that recorded, doctor?"

Jessica held the phone out so that Anna's voice could clearly be heard in the quiet of the office. "Hearing you loud and clear. There won't be any doubt as to what the Major's intentions were."

"You…you bastard."

Frank grimaced. "If that's the only insult you can come up with, I think I'll keep you alive. For trial. See if you can improve on it next time you see me."

"Are you okay, Frank?"

He had never felt so relieved. "The vaccine works like a charm, doc. There's not a damn thing wrong with your wonderful work!"

CHAPTER 31

"Shit, we've actually got some luck for once."

Krueger wasn't wrong. They'd jogged south to Pennsylvania Avenue and found themselves staring straight at the Department of Justice building. Two ionic columns stood proudly between the once-cream stone, now streaked with dust, dirt, and moss after years of neglect.

"'Justice is founded in the rights bestowed by nature upon man. Liberty is maintained in security of justice.'" Castillo quoted from memory.

"How apt," Brewster said to her. "Its relevance to our current situation?"

She rolled one shoulder. "It's going to give us somewhere safe to stay for the night for once?"

Garibaldi tapped her with the butt end of his rifle, pointing up. "Would you look at that."

Willow oaks still lined the streets, growing wild and proud with-out the vigilance of park maintenance keeping them trimmed back. Castillo wasn't sure what he was showing her until she spotted a flicking tail. She'd thought it was a small branch.

"Well, I'll be damned." A set of amber eyes met hers, their owner licking its lips. "These don't seem as hostile. I knew I was a cat person for a reason. And people thought dogs were the intelligent house pet."

Now she knew what to look for, Castillo could see them every-where. All sorts of breeds just sitting there, waiting and watching as the Hunters walked past their perches.

"Zombies can't climb. Makes sense to stay there and just scavenge for food when they can." Castillo smiled. "Clever little moggies. I wish I could pet one."

"I'd wait to see what kind of meat they've been scavenging first." Garibaldi said with a sniff. "At least we won't have a shortage of pets in this place, huh?"

"Time to stop dawdling, fellas," Krueger interrupted them. "Looks like we have company at last."

A handful of shamblers crested the hill, their slow gait aimless, for now. The four Hunters dashed for cover against the DOJ building. The longer they kept out of sight, the less likely the shamblers would sound the alarm and bring others to their location. If they had to wait a day for their drop, and they were already at the LZ, they didn't want to bring another city's worth of trouble onto their doorstep.

"Where's our route in?" Garibaldi asked.

"The front door looks like a pretty decent candidate right now, if you ask me," Krueger answered with a jerk of his head.

"He's got a point." Brewster agreed. "The lobby should be empty enough. We can take the rest of the building from there."

The doors were open. No one thought to close it behind them as the world fell apart. Their boots left footprints in the dust as they stepped over white marble, the smallest noises echoing in that cavernous space. Two wide sweeping desks sat in front of security gates. The lobby was devoid of both life and death. They wouldn't be lucky enough for the building to be totally deserted. If they could just secure the first floor and keep the infected away, that would be good enough. Even without water and MREs, they'd be able to last the night.

"We stick together," Brewster whispered, his voice still carrying into the corners of the hall. "I don't want to lose anyone else. We'll sweep this floor, see if there's any hardware we can use, then set a watch rotation and get some rest. We'll need it for tomorrow."

With fast efficiency, they confirmed that the ground floor in its immediacy was free of infected. The power was out. Most of the department's offices lay beyond security doors, which none of them had a desire to force open; the potential reward didn't warrant the risk. A store cupboard yielded nothing but angry mice and cleaning supplies. A security booth had 9mm rounds for their sidearms, which they gratefully took, but nothing else of use. There were no signs of struggle here, as if they'd managed to somehow gracefully check out.

"This all seems too clean," Castillo noted. "Do you think they got advance warning here somehow?"

"It'd make sense," Krueger said. "If any departments were going to get wind of this, you'd think it'd be around here."

"A shame they didn't communicate that to the rest of the fucking city," Brewster said. "It would've made our jobs a damn sight easier."

"Now, Brewster, since when have we liked things easy?"

"I heard that's the *only* way you liked 'em, Krueger."

Finally sensing a window of safety, they sat in a circle sharing a canteen of water and a few bites of oat bars. They all felt like they should be properly hungry, though the adrenalin buzz from the last few hours no doubt masked the worst of any injuries or symptoms. They all carried bruises on their arms and legs. Brewster gingerly patted at a lump growing on the side of his head. He couldn't remember where he'd hit it.

"Maybe it's your brain finally growing in," Krueger growled.

"Fuck you. You can take the last watch." Brewster smiled.

Outside, the streets were bathed in silence. It was unnerving, in a city that used to be home to millions, to listen to nothing but the occasional howl of now-feral animals. That deep silence was much preferred though to the alternative. Every now and again, though, a shambler took up a call, and that high-pitched scream reverberated through the night, sending shivers down the Hunters' spines.

CHAPTER 32

AT BEST, THEY WERE a motley crew of enthusiastic residents. It was all New Abraham had to offer now. Despite all their shortcomings, Keaton was grateful, and he was proud. Even if he didn't see out the end of the day, his people were standing tall. It was an honor to be their sheriff.

"Are we all ready?" Keaton was in the lead car, armed with ethanol grenades, which they hoped to use against the lead vehicles so prominent in the Nomadic convoys.

Three other SUVs had their more experienced defenders, with assault rifles and what ammunition they could spare from their dwindling stockpiles. Adelina took point in one of these, along with Chick and Jerry. Charmain was in the lead with Keaton, with Marie now well enough to take shotgun. Between the three of them, they pooled an unrivaled knowledge of the backroads in the area. Keeping radio intel live throughout, Keaton hoped to track down and take out as many lieutenants as possible before his people started taking losses.

Help was on the way from Omaha. Keaton's plans, though, almost relied on them *not* arriving. There was no way the Nomads would miss a military convoy rolling into town. Keaton wanted to maintain the element of surprise. They sure as hell wouldn't get that with MPVs packed with armed troops, along with whatever else Sherman sent their way.

He'd checked in with the president the night before, making sure that his old friend knew just what was happening out in his favorite backwater community. Sherman had sounded weary, not just through fatigue either. Just when they thought eliminating the RSA would see the back of it all, problems had escalated, one after another. Fighting on all fronts, in all of their strongholds, it was hard to see an end in sight.

Sherman had approved of their plan, though he'd declined to withdraw the troops. In case the Abraham offensive went wrong; in case the Nomads split and needed rounding up; to ensure there weren't more of the enemy waiting behind, their numbers not properly scouted. They weren't being left to fend for themselves, not this time.

"Fighters of New Abraham, this is Sheriff Keaton in Advance One. Please report, over."

"Advance One, this is Arctura in Advance Two, over."

"Garcia in Advance Three, over."

"Johnson, Advance Four, over."

The advance vehicles were the SUVs. They had eight quads, all to be used like shepherds, herding the Nomads as they directed each other. They'd keep on separate channels, moving to open chatter for general updates. They had enough fuel to harry the Nomads for most of the morning. If those attempts failed, then they'd line up at a ridge five miles outside of town where the Nomads would have to drive past to get to Abraham. If their scouts were accurate, most of the Nomads were gathered past this marker, to the north and west of town.

It won't get that far. Keaton had promised them.

Janine sat in Advance Four. Keaton had wanted her to hold back. It was a futile conversation, even if it did result in something positive.

He'd asked her to marry him. He didn't even know where the words had come from. They'd just dropped out of his mouth almost of their own volition. He hadn't expected her brilliant smile or smothering hug, or....

Keaton shook his head, grinning despite himself. Time to focus. "New Abraham, let's roll out." Their cars churned up dust. Marie grinned, holding the steering wheel tight in both hands as they mounted the road, kicking up gravel as they gained speed. "Are you ready to get some revenge young lady?"

"Am I ever!"

Johnny couldn't believe what he was hearing when his driver told him the gates of Abraham had opened, and their people were pouring out.

"They're retreating?"

"No, boss," his driver sounded hesitant. "It looks like they're coming this way."

The Nomads were parked up, split along a line of around half a click. Johnny couldn't understand it when the Abraham people headed straight for him.

Towns weren't meant to fight back. They were supposed to tremble in fear, fail, and die.

He thumbed his repaired CB. "All drivers in! Looks like the fight is on!"

The lead bikes did just as Keaton had hoped. Between the 50cc and 125cc along with several quads, they split the Nomads. Engines started venting steam as wheels ground up dirt and dust, and they revved out into the mid-morning air. Seeing the enemy respond, Keaton gave the order to split. Three different groups headed west, north, and south, with the Nomads' cars splitting into groups to pursue the smaller vehicles.

The Mustang headed away as their group split, along with a red Charger. Keaton recognized both vehicles.

"Advance Four, this is Advance One. We are going for their lead. Follow me. Advance Two and Three, I want you on the Dodge Charger. I've seen those tailing each other. If we don't take out someone in charge between us, I've got no idea who's running this show.

"And I want the Mustang," he added. "Over."

Keaton had listened stone-faced to Janine's tearful retelling of Billy's torture. The young driver of that damned car was to blame for all of this. Keaton wanted the satisfaction of taking him out himself.

Speeding across tarmac, then onto a single-track road, Keaton allowed himself a smile. They were driving to nowhere. This track was disused. Long ago wagons hauling dirt had used it to dump their load off the edge of a ravine; literal dirt tips. Now it was used by kids on dirtbikes looking to practice climbs and race their friends.

The Nomads were driving themselves into a trap.

Their SUV climbed steadily, Keaton calling for them to slow. Up ahead he could see the clip drop-off. Both cars skidded to a halt.

"Drive up on 'em!"

"Fuck! How did these country fuckers pull this stunt!"

The driver didn't answer, clinging with both hands to the steering wheel and waiting for more orders. He'd only done what he was told. They hadn't been this far out, this side of the township. The terrain wasn't friendly. The car couldn't take much more debris being kicked through the hood, and he'd told his boss as much.

"That's it. They want to fight me? They'll fucking learn."

Johnny wound down his window. Eric had done the same and leaned out.

"My car's fucked! It's two on two."

"What you wanna do, boss?"

"Ram 'em!"

Eric arched his eyebrows. "Your car?"

"The car's screwed. Might as well finish the job properly."

"What in God's name are they doing?" Adelina had either arm on the back of the front seats, leaning forward to look through the windscreen.

"They're turning," droned Keaton, stating the obvious.

"But why? There's no way out past us."

The cars accelerated, heading straight for them. Their own cars idled; the gap wouldn't last long looking at the acceleration of the pair. "Fuck. Strap in ladies! They're not going past us. They're coming straight for us!"

Dark eyes, gleaming with insanity, kept staring at Keaton. The bonnets crunched; the SUV thrown backwards down the ridge. The sheriff rocked in his seat, hoping beyond hope the others had all seen the danger and made themselves safe. Adelina screamed. His vision went black as his neck pistoned, his body jarred against the belt. The back of his seat was thrown violently forward. Marie was silent.

Ears ringing, Keaton fumbled to unbuckle himself. Swallowing down bile, he leaned against the door, opening it more through luck than intention. Rolling out, he glanced up to see blood splattered on the rear passenger mirror. Smoke billowed out of the crumpled hood. Fifty yards away, the other SUV looked no better, though doors were already opening. Janine tumbled out, followed by Chick. He didn't catch sight of anyone else before a boot connected with his ribcage, sending the rest of the wind out of his body.

"Thought you'd be the big ones, eh? I'm guessing you're the one in charge." The boot lashed again, against his side this time. Keaton felt bones crack. He curled into a ball, yelping at the agonizing lances of pain. Another heavy blow connected with his spine. "I'm going to fuck you up like we did all your little scouts," he kept kicking as he spoke, Keaton staying as still as he could to limit the damage. In his line of vision, he saw the red Charger crumpled and on fire.

"Let's see how much you like the smell of scorched flesh." The man laughed and gave him another kick. Keaton covered his head, curling in as far as he could, taking the blows.

A woman suddenly screamed, and he more felt than saw the man fall.

Keaton was aghast to see Janine rolling on the ground now, her fists pounding at the prone Nomad. The man roared, pushing up and throwing her aside as if she weighed nothing. She rolled away to get back up, but as she scrambled onto her hands and knees, the man kicked her in the temple. Janine crumpled, her cry of pain broken off as she slumped, unmoving.

Keaton Wallis saw red.

He tackled the Nomad at the waist, hauling him to the ground and straddling his hips. Keaton, weak as he was from the crash and the beating he'd just taken, felt no pain. A savage rage overtook him as his fists pummeled the Nomad's face, cracking his cheek and jaw. The man—no, boy, really—laughed as his lip split and teeth flew out to the side. He started coughing, choking on blood.

Keaton was dimly aware of Chick and another man—a Nomad, maybe, standing over him. Neither dared approach. Keaton didn't care if this man had family or friends. He didn't know his name. He'd never speak it again.

Keaton kept punching until his fists bled. The Nomad was unrecognizable when the rage left him; a carcass of meat discarded on the bloody ground.

He looked up at Chick, tears, snot, and blood all over his face. She stepped back a couple of paces. His body went rigid as he realized what he'd just done. Shock taking hold, Keaton went numb, convulsing with shivers. Crawling off the Nomad's corpse, he tried to vomit. All that came up was bile. When was the last time he'd eaten? Or rested?

"Ja…Janine?" He looked up through tears.

The other Nomad had run. No one wanted to be next in line to that rage.

Keaton crawled over to Janine, desperately pawing at her body.

Chick took his shoulders, tried to drag him away. "Sheriff, the cars…we're in danger here. We've got to go."

"I can't leave her. The others. We need to save them."

"Everyone else is dead, sheriff. Come on."

"Janine isn't. She's not…."

Chick pushed his hand away, feeling impatiently for a pulse.

"I can't leave her, Chick. I can't…"

The Charger suddenly exploded, and they hunkered for a second, then Chick glanced at Keaton and squeezed his arm.

"Let's get her up. She's alive."

CHAPTER 33

REBECCA DIDN'T LOOK AMUSED as she surveyed the crowds gathered outside the town hall. At the moment, the atmosphere was one of curious ambivalence, although it seemed like half the city had appeared for the occasion.

Sitting on an uncomfortable foldout chair next to Mark, she leaned over and muttered out of the side of her mouth. "I don't remember local rallies being this popular when I was younger."

He smirked. "I don't remember them at all. I think I was either already deployed or in a bar."

"*Eurgh.* You were probably a Democrat, weren't you? You didn't tell me that."

"Rethinking your life choices, my love?"

"Considering it." Her smile said anything but.

"I wish McCartney would turn up, so we could get this over and done with."

"He'll be as late as possible, Mark. If we've learned anything about that idiot, it's that he likes to show off."

"Well, he's taken it one step too far this time. His games are over."

Rebecca folded her arms, resting them on her small baby bump. "I hope so. I don't know how much more of this I can take."

Anna hadn't left the labs since leaving the hospital. Rebecca had gone to BL1, prizing the doc out of BL4 only briefly to give her a quick medical and ensure she was eating and drinking. Mark had calmed down noticeably when Sherman called to confirm they'd captured the dissident in the New White House.

Major Bentley.

Mark had been shocked. Bentley was one of the last people he'd guess to buckle against Sherman's plans. He and Sherman needed a long overdue sit-down and chat.

Even more heartening was the knowledge that McCartney wasn't working with a more powerful authority. He and Bentley had allied, to a point, so that Bentley could get the virus and information out of Omaha. Beyond that, McCartney had no support. This rally would be the beginning and the end of it. If New Abraham won through with their assault against the Nomads, then they could all fling their full support to the Hunters—if they were still alive.

Mark hated giving the order to delay air support for his friends. The greater good had been at stake. If Abraham or McChord had needed them more, it needed to be free.

A hush fell over the rear of the crowd.

"I think that's him," Rebecca whispered.

Mark nodded, getting to his feet and brushing imaginary dust off his immaculate uniform. He was in full military dress, looking every part the leader. His service medals shone; the Winchester held rested at his side, cleaned and oiled.

McCartney had tried, as much as a man his size could. His jeans were washed but creased, as was his patched-up lumberjack shirt. His baseball cap was new, as was the baseball bat he carried by his side, swinging it around like a junior softball player on the way to the plate. The crowd parted for him. Clearly relishing the attention, he waved, trying to look every inch the winner.

Taking the platform, he held out his hand to Mark. Mark took it, shaking it suspiciously. The handshake was fierce and hard. McCartney pulled him sharply, stepping forwards with a malicious grin. "Enjoy your last moments in the sun, Stiles."

"This isn't over yet."

McCartney's eyebrows arched. "Oh, you think so?" he dropped Mark's hand like it was poisonous, pushing him away and turning to the crowd. "Omaha! Good evening!" A good-humored chuckle rippled around the onlookers, with one or two up front shouting in response. "It's a bit quieter tonight don't you think?"

They stilled then, faces tensing as families hugged each other and friends moved closer together.

"And why do you think that is?" Mark began.

McCartney spoke over him, not letting him get a foothold in the conversation.

"It's because your supposed leader, who might I remind you *none* of you have asked for, can't control the perimeters, or the streets."

"Because you caused chaos inside the city?"

"Maybe I had some people take a few shots," McCartney waggled his hands, trying to look affable to the people he had cowering in their homes the night before. "I have to admit that. But we didn't hurt anyone. I was proving a point. Look at how our police reacted; quite poorly, wouldn't you say? They've had long enough to build a defense, and this is how well they react to a couple of kids with guns, *deliberately missing*? What happens if we get an *actual* attack?" This speech didn't seem to gain the sympathy of the crowd, though there were more than a couple querying murmurs at his point. "I'm sorry that I was the source of so much disruption these past few days, but you have to break some eggs to make a cake and I think we've shown, clearly and beyond doubt, that Mark Stiles is not a man capable of running Omaha, nor is he able to keep us safe."

"President Sherman never had to prove why he was keeping us safe," Rebecca suddenly interrupted. "We just always have been. It's *you* that's making the difference. These problems only started since you brought that sprinter in at the hospital ceremony!"

"Ah, I'm glad you mentioned that, madame. Because we don't get infected around here, do we? We don't get sprinters anymore. And why is that?" McCartney cupped his ear, leaning out and playing to the crowd, who eagerly responded.

"We have the vaccine," someone said.

"Ah yes, you do. So how did I get a sprinter in here?"

Someone sniggered. "You went outside the perimeter and got one?"

McCartney flushed, his momentum stopped. "Be that as it may, I *shouldn't* have been able to do that. Guards should have stopped me," he recovered well. "Even still, do you remember seeing how scared they were? How eager they were to shoot those sprinters down? Why does that matter if we're all vaccinated?"

"Sprinters can still kill people, you idiot," Rebecca snarled.

"But we have a fabulous hospital now, and all these resources. So, if we're not scared of them spreading the Morningstar virus anymore, why are they all so scared…? It's because their famous vaccine is a lie. All of it. You'll still get turned if you get bitten."

The crowd went into a buzz. "How do you know that?" a woman yelled out.

Mark panicked. McCartney was already stepping into the territory that they wanted to use against him. If he didn't interrupt soon and start swinging this back to the Omaha view, McCartney could steal the win.

"I've seen it! My own friends! You saw what happened last night. Sprinters and shamblers everywhere. All it took was just one bite."

McCartney started to sob, almost convincingly.

Mark had had enough. "You know full well where those sprinters came from. He's had his say on what he thinks of our administration, well let me tell you what I see. I see a man who is grieving the loss of his brother, but in the wrong way. You're trying to explain it, and all you can think is that Morningstar is the natural way of things. Believing that you would do or try *anything* to perpetuate, as you see it, the evolution of humanity through the release of the virus. Only the worthy survive, isn't that right?"

McCartney's mouth turned up in a sneer. "I wouldn't expect a soldier like you to understand the complexities of what I believe. But you're right. Morningstar was meant to cleanse humanity. You and your people are stopping it from doing its work."

Mark suppressed his glee at the shocked looks of the crowd. McCartney's supporters, those used to hearing his rhetoric, started whispering. Whether it was to each other, or to try to convince those around them to keep listening, he wasn't sure.

"So, what you're saying, Michael, is that you think the majority of the people within the Omaha safe zone should be dead?"

"No, you're putting words in my mouth."

"But you think that we should just let Morningstar loose again, and let the virus work out those who should survive and those who die?"

McCartney's mouth worked as he tried to think of a response.

Rebecca glared at the big man. "How do you like the complexities of a military mind, you ignorant fool?"

"Becky…" Mark put his hand on her shoulder. "Can you just wheel it in please?"

Rebecca motioned to someone off stage, and the crowd took a few paces back as a couple orderlies wheeled a gurney onto the stage. An infected, a sprinter from the way it thrashed around, was alive, awake, and very much in their midst. Unlike McCartney's, though, it didn't seem likely it would slip the leash and run anywhere.

"This unfortunate young man was named Josh Bennett," Mark said to the crowd. "He came to Omaha two weeks ago. He received the vaccine from a volunteer orderly. The orderly worked under the instruction of a known rogue lab assistant named Robbie Chastain. Robbie has been recorded admitting he wanted to disrupt the vaccination program. The orderly was one Michael McCartney."

All eyes moved to McCartney, who took a step back. A pair of soldiers stepped onto the stage, hands on their weapons. Mark, resting his hand on the butt of his Winchester, looked just as impassive. "We have reason to believe that last night, Michael McCartney and his people deliberately targeted the people they *knew* would be vulnerable to Morningstar…."

"Then what did I inject him with?" McCartney pointed at Mark. "The needles in that tent all looked the same to me."

"I'm sure Robbie helped with that. Our best guess is sugar water, but you're the only man that can really tell us the truth of that."

"How many people?" this cry went out from the front of the crowd, and its momentum carried. The sight of a sprinter—one of their own—had people rightly worried.

"We can't tell from our records who was vaccinated and who was not. McCartney is right. We couldn't take a risk last night, knowing there might be a chance some of you could be infected. But we're going to put it right."

"How? How can we know the vaccine works at all?"

Mark gulped. He'd been waiting for this. He hadn't told Becky this part of his plan. "I know the vaccine works. This is a new sprinter. We know how quickly the infection spreads."

Mark had already removed his coat and rolled up his sleeve while he'd been talking. Before anyone could figure out what he was doing, he shoved his bare forearm against Josh Bennett's gnashing mouth.

The infected man bit hard, and Mark yelled from the pain. He'd forgotten, in these long weeks since Hyattsburg, how much a human bite hurt. This reminder touched a nerve in every way possible. He yanked his arm back, dropping to a knee in pain. Blood gushed from his arm.

"Mark!" Rebecca threw herself at him and grabbed his shoulders.

"Get the gurney away. Take him to Doctor Demilio. She's dealing with him." The shocked orderlies did as they were bade as the two soldiers stepped forward.

McCartney laughed maniacally. "You idiot. You fool! You've just given it to me. You're infected. They've got to shoot you!"

Rebecca's face twisted in anger and hurt. "You made him do this! You selfish, arrogant prick of a man!"

"Get her back," Mark hissed at the soldiers, clutching the wound to try and stem the flow of blood oozing between his fingers. It dripped to the stage, splashing against the dry wood. "And keep her away from him."

"That's right, Stiles. Get your crazy bitch away from me before I show her how she should really behave in front of a man."

The soldiers tried to pry Rebecca from Mark, but she pushed them away from her, hunkering down next to her husband. "Someone get me some gauze, we need to stop the bleeding."

She looked around. "Why is no one listening to me?"

McCartney swung his arms up in pleading, moving in circles across the stage. "It's because the man is bitten! He's going to become a sprinter. Just another one of them. He's going to show you just how ineffective their magic medicine is."

Mark gritted his teeth, looking up at McCartney, then across to the crowd. He met the eyes of a young girl, her eyes wide in terror, sitting on the shoulders of her horrified father. "Trust me," he said, looking at the small girl. He smiled. "I won't turn."

"He should already be unconscious," a woman called out from the side of the stage. "A fresh bite like that, a new sprinter, I've seen people turn in seconds."

"Take my temperature, if you like," Mark muttered. His head was light; he'd lost quite a bit of blood. "Won't turn." Amazingly, he stood—with Rebecca's help. Wobbly, but standing. "Not turning…it works. The vaccine works."

"Sit down, Mark," Rebecca said. He felt hands on his shoulders, sitting him into a chair. Someone wiped something in his wound; it burned. He screamed, slumping forward. Soothing hands on his cheek cooled him as a sweet familiar voice muttered reassurance into his ear.

★★★★★

"See? He's not feverish. He's not infected. He's just a damn fool who cares about Omaha. Now do you believe him?" Rebecca shook her hand in McCartney's direction. "Do you think that man would take a zombie bite for you, just to prove how much he believes in what he's saying? Because *obviously* he's one of the chosen in this new world he's carved out for himself. This world needs men like Mark Stiles because when it comes down to it, he would sacrifice himself like this for any one of us. He's done it before. I've seen it.

"This isn't an election. It isn't even a contest. You've seen what this man wants to do to you, to your homes. He's killed people we love to prove a point! And, in doing so, put so many more at risk."

The calls went up then. For McCartney to be arrested; to be hung; to be shot right then and there.

Seeing the crowd becoming a mob, McCartney vaulted off the stage, knocked some citizens down, and went sprinting into the streets. The nearest perimeter fence was a couple of blocks away. Becky watched as he went straight for it. Without a backward look, he climbed up and over, running into the unclaimed streets of the dead city beyond.

Michael McCartney was gone.

"Did I win?"

Mark Stiles came to at home, his arm bandaged and a gallon jug of water by his bed.

Rebecca frowned, slapping him, then smiled. "You frightened me half to death in the process, but you won. You idiot."

Mark's head fell back on the pillows, a foolish grin spreading across his face. "I won."

"And what would the mayor like to do as his first order in charge of the city?" She leaned down and kissed him slowly, running her hand through his hair.

He looked at her apologetically. "I think I need to call Sherman."

Rebecca took a long breath through her nostrils and let it out, feigning indignation. She then smiled gently at him, her hand still in his hair. "You probably should. I'm pretty sure Brewster would like a little help in DC."

CHAPTER 34

"You have no idea how happy I am to see you alive, Mr. President."

"Please, Adan, we've known each other long enough now. Can't you just call me Frank? You've earned it."

"I'm not sure that I have, but if you're ordering me to, I'm not one to say no. And if we're being informal, how are you, Frank?"

Frank grimaced, clutching the tall glass of water. He wanted something stronger, but Anna was insistent that alcohol was not the answer. The vaccine protected him against the virus sure enough, but a fever had still set in and his head throbbed. The good doctor reassured him regularly that it wasn't symptomatic of full infection. The dart Bentley had used contained a dangerously virulent strain; if he was going to turn, he'd have done so by now. Sherman guessed Mark Stiles felt about the same after his stunt in Omaha. The two men weren't so dissimilar in the risks they'd take to keep the people around them safe.

"I feel like a vacation, truth be told. What's Cuba like this time of year?"

Adan chuckled. "I don't think I'd recommend it. The forecast is heavy infected with zero guarantees of sun. If I were you, I'd try to take a couple of days off."

"I didn't think those existed anymore. I'd try locking myself in my room if I didn't think Jessica would worry and call in the sappers. And besides, we have more pressing matters at hand."

"The Hunters?"

Sherman nodded, sipping at the warm tap water with a grimace. "Now that the situation in Omaha is stabilizing, they can send ground. We both know they'd just hit a wall of infected and be slaughtered. The whole point of sending in the Hunters was to clear a central area."

"Like you did for Omaha."

"Exactly. The population pull is the problem. There's a huge core of infected in the central DC area, like you'd expect. Everything Brewster's team has come back with works in our favor."

"What do you need from me?"

"Two things. We know the shamblers are drawn by sound, no matter what state they're in, so we need to start thinning the herd away from the beachhead. I want two runs. One with personnel to land in and support the people on the ground. The other to start drops in the outer city area to draw out as many infected as we can."

"Distraction techniques?"

"The same."

"Why didn't we just try that at the start?"

"Because even if we could draw them out, we have no way of knowing what we'd be left facing in the center. Our focal point is the White House, and we had to get as close as possible to that before we could take any other action."

Adan wasn't sure whether to be shocked or in total awe. "It was a huge gamble. Have they reported losses?"

"I don't know, to be honest. All I've heard is that they need reinforcements. I'll need you to co-ordinate McChord, and I'll join one of the front transports to drop in."

"Does your doctor know that?"

"No," Sherman kept Adan's stern gaze as he sipped the water again. "And she's not going to know, correct?"

"I can't allow you onboard, sir. President or not, there's no order you can give me that will let me risk your life out there."

"My people need to see me, Forrest."

"Yes, that's true. And you're right where they need you the most. I can't think of any other man that could have orchestrated what you have from here. To trap Bentley the way you did."

"Omaha and Abraham saved themselves; I put good people in the right places and they delivered. Bentley? He wasn't exactly subtle about his intentions. He wrote his own warrant, and I look forward to seeing him stand trial. I'll be on that transport."

Adan stood, folding his arms behind his back and standing to attention. "Sir, I'm sorry. I'll do as you ask and arrange the resources you need, but you've made sure your administration stays intact for another day, and to keep that going, you're going to have to stay right here. We all know you hate desk work, and you hate politicians even more. What say you start changing all our opinions on that?"

"You're not going to budge on this, are you?"

"No, sir."

Frank sighed, staring at the desk with its mountain of paperwork, which never seemed to subside. A discarded pen. A forgotten cigar. Then, he remembered Sanderson and Spivey. Dangers were everywhere. Perhaps office life wouldn't be as boring as he feared.

"Can I get a live feed on the action?"

"Audio? I can do that much."

"I suppose that'll have to do. I don't want them to think they've been abandoned out there."

"When they see what we bring in for them, I don't think that'll cross their minds."

CHAPTER 35

"IT WAS NICE WORKING with you."

The four of them had taken turns in shifts. Garibaldi woke them in the early hours as dawn broke across the city. Without street lights there'd been no visibility. The streets outside would be jackpot or ruin as sunrise broke the horizon.

In terms of luck, they were bankrupt.

Infected were pressed up against the windows. They weren't pawing at the building. There couldn't be any way they *knew* there were living people inside. Had it been that last dog? The cats? What the hell had led them here during the night?

"If any group had ever been more shit out of luck," Garibaldi remarked.

"Any plans to get out of this one, fearless leader?" Krueger was wiping his face with a dirty rag.

Brewster cursed in frustration, butting the back of his head against the desk. Against the hum of the infected, his noise was nothing. Still, it echoed in the corridor.

They'd waited what seemed like an age. Support was on the way, they'd been told. They just had to wait. As if they had any other plan. They had enough ammo left to punch a hole out into the street. Past that, they had a glorious death awaiting them and nothing more.

"They're on the way," Castillo said. "Wait and see."

Krueger growled in frustration. "And they'll do what, drop us another crate of goodies? We won't get to it in time before we're ripped apart."

"They said we'd get support," she persisted. "That's not a crate drop."

"We're fighting wars on three fronts. We don't even know if Sherman is alive. The rest of the administration didn't even want us here. Let's face facts. We're dead soldiers walking."

Brewster couldn't let himself believe that. Even if Sherman were gone—God, anything but that—Stiles still had Omaha, surely. Who else would have their back?

No one.

They'd been dropped into a dead zone with no promise of support. *But support was coming.*

"How long do you guys want to wait?" Brewster hated how bitter those words sounded in the echoing space of that room. There wasn't even any point clearing the building. What would they do? Just head upwards. Then what? Starve to death on the roof? Die of thirst? Watch as a single crate of munitions dropped in for them and hope that it exploded on impact and wiped out a block of the shambly bastards?

Krueger exhaled, shaking his arms and loosening his wrists. "I feel like I've waited long enough. We're well past the drop time, right?"

Brewster didn't need to glance at his watch. "If they're keeping military time, they should have landed nine hours ago."

They all glanced around expectantly, letting go of a miracle that wasn't coming.

"Well, that sells it. I'm ready to go now. Do we take a vote?"

They shuffled into a circle, pausing to share in the moment. An undead hand slapped at the plate windows. The echo reverberated around. More joined, like a rainstorm of flesh on glass. Somewhere along the lobby one of the panes split.

"I guess they don't want this to be a democracy," Garibaldi said.

Brewster smirked, holding back tears. "Then, let's go, Hunters. You wanted a song. Let's give them something impressive to find during recon."

The first thing they had to do was survive the wave that poured in through the broken windows. Shamblers tore themselves fighting their way past shards of tempered glass. Brewster stood on a desk. He wanted the high ground; to shower bullets on them as they came. His M4 had eight rounds left; his jacket held four magazines. For the final curtain, he'd left a grenade. He wanted to go out with a bang.

A toddler, dead from her wounds long ago, didn't cry out as an obese naked woman, her saggy breasts sitting over a stomach striped with stretchmarks stood on her back, driving her further down onto a jagged jut of blue glass. Brewster put a round through the creature's forehead. Her mass blocked others for only a heartbeat as others poured in afterwards, crushing her body like the child's before it.

Castillo took up a position between the two wide desks; Garibaldi and Krueger moved to match Brewster's spot on the opposing desk. Dozens of infected poured towards them. Krueger's voice snapped with staccato laughter as he opened fire.

This was it. After all they'd faced together.

A biker in full regalia pushed his way forward. He still wore a helmet, his gray beard flecked with blackened blood.

Garibaldi punched a round through his chest. It didn't stop him. Flanked all around with his undead allies, they lurched towards their prey.

Castillo began screaming before her gun ran dry.

Brewster saw it too late. The round he punched off penetrated the helmet but couldn't do enough damage to stop him. It didn't even put the man off stride as he threw himself onto Angela Castillo, his hungry mouth drawn straight to her neck. She kept firing into him, the shambler's body convulsing even as his teeth broke flesh. She screamed with the indignant rage of a Greek Fury, then her yells distorted as she gargled blood.

"Get back," she managed to utter wetly.

Brewster saw her pull a grenade off her belt.

Blaze of glory. Halle-fucking-luhah!

"Grenade!" Brewster yelled. Garibaldi and Krueger threw themselves off the desks, running as far as they could before the explosion punched through the lobby. The first wave of infected were thrown apart like confetti as the explosive went off.

It still didn't stop them. More of them kept coming.

"Ergh…" Brewster wiped an arm across his face, spitting away blood and bone. He didn't want to know where from and didn't care. He was vaccinated. The fuckers wouldn't take him that way.

A baseball player came at him from around the corner of the desk. He stood and put his bayonet through the roof of its mouth, kicked it away, and turned to keep firing rounds into the masses.

When the first explosion struck outside, he thought he was hallucinating.

When the second came, he realized the crowd of infected was thinning.

Garibaldi and Krueger stepped up next to him and the three of them in a line hammered their final rounds into anything infected that still moved. Outside, a fireball flooded through the street, blowing out any glass that remained in the ground floor of the building. Shards flew everywhere. Brewster turned, shielding his face, still feeling the sting as tiny fragments split his cheeks.

"I'm dead already," Brewster said it, and Garibaldi and Krueger believed it.

In the street beyond, following the flames, men and women in green BDUs were clearing a path. The infected that hadn't been eviscerated by explosions were wiped out in a hail of bullets.

"Is that...Stiles?"

Mark Stiles entered the building, picked his way over bodies, wielding a machete to take out any stragglers getting too close. Infantry flanked him, systematically working their way into the building.

"Brewster! I'm fucking glad to see you, man!"

"What...what happened?"

Stiles embraced him, slapping his back hard in a hug. "You wanted support. You got it."

"What about...what about everything?"

"We're okay, Brewster. It's all going to be okay. Air support from McChord is taking out Justice Park. You've got your beachhead. Well done, soldier."

Brewster dropped to his knees. They'd done it. All around them, infected dropped.

"Where's the rest of the squad?" he heard Stiles ask.

Brewster raised his eyes to the last place he'd seen Angela Castillo. So close.

He hoped the cost was worth it.

EPILOGUE

THE BLUE FELT WAS familiar now under his hands. They'd moved it to Omaha. He was just the announcer today; the undercard to the work others had continued to do as he brought the White House back under control.

What remained of the Hunters stayed in DC, for now. Brewster, his rank still not formalized, volunteered to stay and oversee the clearance of the buildings around the White House and the erection of fencing to create a safe zone.

Kiley, Brent, and Castillo—what they were able to find of them—had been flown back to Omaha and buried with full military honors.

Behind President Sherman, a baby cried.

"Friends…" A hush fell over the expectant crowd. They'd decided to have the announcement outside the hospital. It seemed poignant, for a number of reasons. This time, they all felt confident there wouldn't be any unexpected interruptions. "Not so long ago, many of us stood here to commemorate the next big step in Omaha's evolution. Behind me," Sherman presented an arm, necks craning to see what they already knew was there, "we all worked hard to secure a working hospital. We've lost people we know and love to ensure a safer and brighter future for all of us. Recently, a small percentage of the population used that as an excuse to rebel, bringing unnecessary conflict and fear into our streets.

"You all know who I mean. Some of you followed him; others, not here, will stand trial for their crimes. No matter how hard they tried, they could not break the community and spirit that we've built between us. Today is proof of that. I'd like you all to hear from a woman who has potentially, and somewhat deservedly, gained legendary status amongst you. Ladies and gentlemen, Dr. Anna Demilio."

A ripple of applause broke across those assembled, with a few hollers coming from the braver amongst them. Blushing and holding up a hand in respectful thanks, Anna limped towards the podium. She still hadn't fully recovered from her wounds, mainly because she didn't give herself the chance, but she was far enough out of the woods that Frank had stopped bothering her about it.

"Thank you everyone, and thank you, Mr. President." Anna smirked as Sherman colored; she never used his formal title and her playful tone wasn't missed by anyone that knew the couple. "A lot has happened since the last time I stood here. People have sought to discredit our mayor, Mark Stiles, and the vaccination program we've all worked so hard to get off the ground. Mayor Stiles led by example and showed you all to trust in us, not to listen to the lies of those with their own agendas."

It still wasn't common knowledge that Mark was the source of the immunity.

"We listened; we know that Michael McCartney's people disrupted our treatments in Omaha. You've all been retreated, personally, by me. Trust me—I didn't get this wrong." A trickle of laughter met this statement. Anna had insisted on being the one to administer every new inoculation and was no longer leaving hiring to chance. "Now we're going statewide. Settlements across Nebraska, Iowa, Kansas, and Missouri are in line to receive their first shipment of the Morningstar vaccine. Like us, they can start resting easier at night knowing they have a chance to fight back without fear of infection."

Cheering rose up and became raucous and full of enthusiasm. Anna waited for it to die down a bit before continuing. "This is just the start of the next chapter in our growth…"

The child's wailing behind them increased. Rebecca stood, shushing the bundle in her arms, making her way off the stage to settle the infant down, but Anna turned, beckoning the young lady forward. "Here we have a perfect symbol of that. You all know Rebecca, Mark's wife. Let me introduce you to their beautiful daughter, the first baby born in our own hospital. Angela Julie Stiles."

Whistles and cheers erupted as Anna embraced her friend and her Goddaughter. Little Angela, oblivious to the adulation she was receiving, continued bawling at volume. Rebecca laughed. "Thank you, Anna. I'd better give you back the spotlight though; this one isn't going to shush any time soon."

Anna led applause as Rebecca left the stage, raising her arms for silence when she felt the enthusiasm wane. "This isn't all. Part of McCartney's movement was convinced, and told many of you, that we were completing secret research in our labs here in the city. He wasn't wrong." She had their attention then, a nervous hush coursing through the crowd as they comprehended the meaning of her words. "And for good reason. Because I haven't been creating an alternative to Morningstar, like McCartney wanted you to believe.

"Up until now we've only been able to vaccinate; to enable those still alive to become resistant to the effects of the virus." Anna gulped, aware of the eyes shining on her, and the television cameras broadcasting to anywhere that could pick up signal. "I'd like to introduce you to a special little girl."

Anna twisted, ushering forward a small blond girl. She walked with the help of crutches, and though she found them cumbersome, she made her way slowly across to the doctor before hiding slightly behind Anna's hip.

Anna stroked her hair reassuringly. "This amazing young lady is named Laura Archer. When Michael McCartney decided unleashing sprinters into the safe zone was a good idea, one broke its way into Laura's family's home. Her mother was hurt, but will thankfully survive thanks to the hospital McCartney hated so much.

"Laura, on the other hand, is lucky in two ways. We managed to save her leg," a few in the crowd wiped at the corners of their eyes. "And we also *cured* Laura of Morningstar."

Line by line, people's jaws dropped.

"Laura was bitten by a sprinter. She turned. Her wounds, though grievous, weren't beyond repair. With her parents' permission, I administered my cure.

"And how do you feel now, Laura?"

Laura looked up at Anna, then out to the sea of expectant faces. "Nervous." Her tiny voice brought out smiles across the city.

"Anything else?" Anna nodded encouragingly.

"I want to play with my friends when my leg gets better."

Anna thought she'd melt with pride. Cheers erupted, for her, for Laura, and for Omaha.

President Frank Sherman stepped forward as the crowd roared. He placed a hand on Anna's hip. She stepped into him, the most forward they'd ever been in public. "As the doctor says," he said into the microphone, "this is just the beginning of a wonderful next chapter. It's time to bring the world back to life."

THE STORY CONTINUES
IN MORNINGSTAR BOOK SIX

HEROES

ABOUT THE AUTHOR

DAWN PEERS IS A UK-based author of post-apocalyptic horror and fantasy. She is also a full time IT consultant. When she's not wrestling with technology, or creating and destroying worlds, she enjoys reading, gaming, and mountain biking.

PERMUTED PRESS
needs *you* to help

SPREAD (THE) INFECTION

FOLLOW US!

f | Facebook.com/PermutedPress
🐦 | Twitter.com/PermutedPress

REVIEW US!

Wherever you buy our book, they can be reviewed! We want to know what you like!

GET INFECTED!

Sign up for our mailing list at PermutedPress.com

PERMUTED PRESS

KING ARTHUR AND THE KNIGHTS OF THE ROUND TABLE HAVE BEEN REBORN TO SAVE THE WORLD FROM THE CLUTCHES OF MORGANA WHILE SHE PROPELS OUR MODERN WORLD INTO THE MIDDLE AGES.

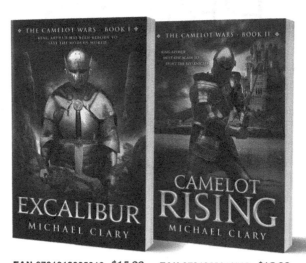

EAN 9781618685018 $15.99   EAN 9781682611562 $15.99

Morgana's first attack came in a red fog that wiped out all modern technology. The entire planet was pushed back into the middle ages. The world descended into chaos.

But hope is not yet lost— King Arthur, Merlin, and the Knights of the Round Table have been reborn.

PERMUTED
PRESS

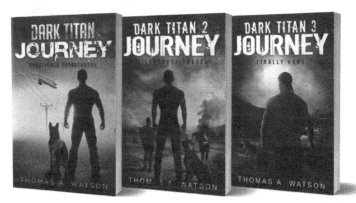

THE MORNINGSTAR STRAIN HAS BEEN LET LOOSE—IS THERE ANY WAY TO STOP IT?

EAN 9781618686497 $16.00

An industrial accident unleashes some of the Morningstar Strain. The doctor who discovered the strain and her assistant will have to fight their way through Sprinters and Shamblers to save themselves, the vaccine, and the base. Then they discover that it wasn't an accident at all—somebody inside the facility did it on purpose. The war with the RSA and the infected is far from over.

This is the fourth book in Z.A. Recht's The Morningstar Strain series, written by Brad Munson.

PERMUTED
PRESS

WE CAN'T GUARANTEE THIS GUIDE WILL SAVE YOUR LIFE. BUT WE CAN GUARANTEE IT WILL KEEP YOU SMILING WHILE THE LIVING DEAD ARE CHOWING DOWN ON YOU.

EAN 9781618686695 $9.99

This is the only tool you need to survive the zombie apocalypse.

OK, that's not really true. But when the SHTF, you're going to want a survival guide that's not just geared toward day-to-day survival. You'll need one that addresses the essential skills for true nourishment of the human spirit. Living through the end of the world isn't worth a damn unless you can enjoy yourself in any way you want. (Except, of course, for anything having to do with abuse. We could never condone such things. At least the publisher's lawyers say we can't.)

PERMUTED
PRESS